PRAISE FOR HELL AROUND THE HORN

"Rick Spilman brings alive the rough and tumble world of the windjammer with authentic and well-chosen detail, in a voice that is at once historically authentic, yet fresh as a salty gale. One hand for yourself and one for the ship on this fast-paced and gripping ride."

Linda Collison, author of the *Patricia MacPherson Nautical Adventures*

"Battling against endless contrary gales, constantly struck with disaster and tragedy, the crew of the Lady Rebecca encountered the same privations that hundreds of unsung sailors endured. As well as a story that grips with gathering tension, this book memorializes the gallant windjammer sailors of a largely forgotten era."

Joan Druett, award winning nautical historian, novelist and author of *Tupaia*

"A much neglected period of sailing history is brought to life by Spilman's fast-moving narrative and apt use of fact and detail."

Alaric Bond, author of the *Fighting Sail* series of novels

Hell Around
the
Horn

a novel by

Rick Spilman

Hell Around the Horn

Copyright © by Richard Spilman 2012
Published by Old Salt Press
ISBN : 978-0-9882360-1-1

To Karen,
for all her love and support

CONTENTS

	Acknowledgments	i
1	River Plate	1
2	Lady Rebecca, Cardiff, Wales	4
3	The Crew Comes Aboard	21
4	Setting Sail	36
5	Trade Winds, Moon Madness and Goats	51
6	Doldrums and Cracker Hash	74
7	Fire Down Below	91
8	Southern Ocean Snorter	102
9	Below Latitude 50 South	113
10	Rogue Wave	132
11	In the Lee of Staten Island	142
12	Fighting the Westerlies	152
13	Reaching the Limits	165
14	Rumors of Mutiny	185
15	Crazy Dane and a Favoring Slant	195
16	A Fair Wind to Chile	200

17   On the Beach Near   216
     Montevideo

     Author's Notes   221

     A Thank You to the Readers   230

     About the Author   231

     Sail Plan   232

     Glossary   233

ACKNOWLEDGMENTS

Thanks to my editor, Broos Campbell, and my proofreader, Karen Lorentz. Thanks also for the insight and support of the members of my critique group - Bruce Woods, Ken Kraus, Kelly O'Donnell, Shelley Nolden, Jael McHenry, and Cathy DiCairano. A special thanks also to the authors Joan Druett, Alaric Bond, Linda Collison and Bob McDermott for their valuable comments and guidance. I would also like to thank the readers and contributors to the Old Salt Blog (http://oldsaltblog.com) for all their encouragement and support.

CHAPTER 1
RIVER PLATE

February 12, 1928

Captain William Jones paused on the bridge wing as the *Mormacmar* steamed up the River Plate. The blue of the Atlantic had turned a dull gray, colored by the silt of the dozen tributaries of the Paraná and the Uruguay rivers that flowed into the Río de la Plata, the river of silver, as the Spanish called it, an optimistic name for a muddy estuary.

He turned and again paced slowly from the bridge wing to the helm where the river pilot stood next to the mate on watch. The mate relayed orders to the quartermaster at the wheel, as they followed the channel markers and began the slow turn into the harbor of Montevideo. It was Captain Jones' first trip on the river and he kept an eye out for the Barra del Indio, the shoal that had marred so many a captain's reputation. He also watched for the fishing boats that swarmed on the river. Running down a local fisherman was no way to announce their arrival. From time to time, the pilot glanced his way quizzically, but Captain Jones just continued his slow pacing.

Then, on the Uruguayan shore, something caught his eye—an old hulk, steel, judging by the deep rust red of the hull. There were many old ships broken by time and Cape Horn on this coast, abandoned by bankrupt or merely indifferent owners. He took the binoculars from the case by the bridge door and trained them on the shoreline. "My God," he murmured softly to himself. "Oh, my God."

Once alongside the wharf in Montevideo, the captain met with customs, spoke with the port captain and port purser, discussed the discharge with the mate and listened to the chief steward about provisions and to the chief engineer about a problem with a feed-pump gasket.

Captain Jones would have liked nothing more than to retreat to his bunk. He had been on his feet for eighteen hours. But he couldn't sleep until he knew for certain. He climbed down the outside stairs to the main deck and found the mate.

"I'll be ashore for a few hours."

"Aye, sir," the mate replied, before getting back to his gang knocking the wedges from the hatch tarps.

The marine superintendent in the office ashore greeted him warmly, called for coffee and sent a boy to find a boat as the capitano required. Within an hour, Captain Jones was a passenger in an immaculate steam launch, all white paint and polished bronze with a diminutive single-cylinder steam engine and a tiny boiler, under the command of a short but proud boatman in a sailor's rig at the tiller. The launch chugged noisily out beyond the breakwater and danced in the short chop of the estuary.

At first Captain Jones couldn't find the old ship. Had he imagined her? Then, around a shallow point on a rocky beach, there she was, an abandoned derelict, but, to his eyes, still lovely. She lay listing slightly to starboard. Only her lower masts still rose above her rusty hull, but even without her rigging there was no doubt that she was a sailing ship. Her lines were long and smooth and her hull was deep with none of the ugly boxiness of a steamer. Even in death, she was a still a windjammer.

He was certain now. She was the Lady Rebecca, his first ship. He knew her too well not to recognize the arc of her bow or the half-deck in front of the poop where he had begun to learn his trade. The launch bobbed in the surf and the boatman called out, "*¿Quieres ir a tierra?*" The captain shouted back, "*Si, a tierra.*" The boatman nodded, pushing the tiller over, pointing the bow toward the beach, as the little steamer chugged toward shore.

CHAPTER 2
LADY REBECCA, CARDIFF, WALES

June 9, 1905

The steel windjammer *Lady Rebecca* lay alongside Bute Dock in Tiger Bay, Cardiff. Her three masts gleamed white, rising from her black hull, soaring up over the dock walls, the cargo cranes and warehouses, seeming almost to reach the wispy clouds in an otherwise deep blue summer sky.

Will Jones, all of 14, a "brassbounder," wearing a snug blue tunic, closed with a row of shiny brass buttons, dropped his heavy sea chest and looked up at the ship in speechless wonder. He stood like a half-tide rock, oblivious to the traffic of sailors, riggers and longshoremen that surged around him on the dock. The young man, with closely trimmed fair hair and a freckled nose, stood up straight and proud as an admiral. He had never actually been to sea, but had studied for two years at the Trinity School of Navigation, so he thought of himself as highly experienced, despite his lack of sea time. His parents had paid the considerable sum of thirty pounds for his apprenticeship aboard the *Lady Rebecca*.

Before leaving home, he had memorized the ship's characteristics from a borrowed copy of Lloyd's *Register of Ships*, until he could recite them by heart. The *Lady Rebecca*—steel, three-masted, a full-rigged ship, 309 feet long, 44 feet of beam, 25 feet of depth. 2,530 tons register, 4,000 deadweight. Main yard—105 feet long. The masthead—180 feet above deck. Now, the figures became wholly inconsequential before the towering mass of the ship herself.

The bowsprit and jib-boom jutted out boldly, reaching high over his head. Will's gaze followed the line of the forestay as it soared up the dizzying heights to the top of the foremast.

The *Lady Rebecca* thrilled and terrified him. She was so massive, so powerful. Standing before her, Will felt very, very small. He wondered whether he had the strength to sail on such a ship. Suddenly, he wasn't so sure. His only comfort was the beautifully carved figurehead of the ship's namesake, a young woman in modern attire wearing a plumed hat, who looked down on him with a gaze that was not entirely unkind.

Will was so caught up in considering the towering ship that he did not notice the man wearing a black coat and a bowler hat standing on the dock a few paces away, watching him with a somewhat wry expression on his deeply tanned face.

"Well, young man, from your jacket you look like the new apprentice. Are you going aboard or are you going to just stand there and gawk?"

The boy jumped. "No, sir. Going aboard, sir."

"Well then, I suggest you do. See the mate. He'll show you where to stow your kit. Then come see the captain. I'll want a few words with you." The man half smiled and with a nod walked down the dock to the gangway.

The apprentice shuddered for an instant in the realization that he had just spoken to the holiest of holies, the captain of the ship. He watched for a moment as the captain ascended the *Lady Rebecca*'s gangway. Will Jones shouldered his sea chest and stumbled down the dock, following the captain's example. Once he reached the main deck, he stopped to catch his breath.

"And who might you be, young sir?" A tall slender man with light brown hair, whose voice was larger than his stature, called down from the poop deck.

The boy straightened up. "William Jones, sir. Apprentice."

"Second Mate Atkinson, pleased to make your acquaintance, Apprentice Jones." He looked the boy up and down. "Well, come along then, I'll show you to your accommodations." The mate dropped down the ladder and walked to a deckhouse just forward of the poop deck. He pushed open the starboard side door to a dark space. "Find a bunk and stow your gear."

"Yes, sir," the boy replied.

Will stepped into the darkness of the half-deck, which smelled of smoke, paint and lye. A dim light filtered through four deck prisms and two dirty portholes. He could just make out a narrow space with two sets of upper and lower bunks on each side and a long table in the middle.

A deep voice boomed, "Who goes there? State your name and rank."

Will jumped and let out a sort of squeak, which was answered by a high-pitched laugh. A young man, in an upper berth, swung his legs out and jumped down to the deck, shaking with laughter. He strode over to the quaking Will and held out his hand. "Jack Pickering."

Will shook the offered hand and said, "You startled me. William Jones." Jack was at least a head taller than Will and considerably broader.

"Well, stow your trap and then let's see if the doctor's got anything for us."

"The doctor?" Will replied.

Jack looked at him sideways then broke into a grin. "You are 'bout as green as grass, aren't you? The cook is called the doctor. You never heard that? I could use a biscuit right about now. Let's see if there's any left." Jack headed out the door to the deck.

Will stood there for a moment, embarrassed. Of course he knew the cook was called the doctor. He'd just forgotten for a moment. "Green as grass, my arse," he thought. He shoved his sea chest into an empty bunk than stumbled out onto the main deck.

Rigging gangs carried blocks, coils of wire and hemp rope across the deck, while riggers aloft inspected, overhauled, refit or repaired the miles of halyards, bunts, braces, clewlines, sheets, topping lifts, outhauls and all the other running and standing rigging in preparation for long months at sea. At the forward hatches, a cloud of black dust rose as cranes dumped vast bucket loads of coal into the gaping holds.

Will looked around. He couldn't see where Jack had gone. The captain had asked to see him when he got aboard. He would have preferred following Jack and trying for a biscuit, but he turned and walked aft.

Will stood outside the captain's dayroom door for a moment before daring to knock. Captain Barker smiled as Will stepped across the threshold. The captain motioned him to a chair and Will sat up as straight as he could be.

The captain's eyes on him were steady and unwavering, the eyes of a man who would stand no nonsense. Still, he wasn't quite as frightening as Will had expected. Not even as frightening as he had been on the dock.

"So, William Jones, you are our new apprentice. A first voyager, I see?"

"Yes, sir."

The captain sat in a chair across from him and leaned forward. "Are you quite sure that you want to be a sailor?"

"Yes, sir," Will replied after a moment's hesitation.

"It is a hard life, m'son. Do you know that?"

"Yes, sir." Suddenly, when challenged, the doubts he felt on the dock vanished.

"I wonder if you know how hard it can be? It is hard work day and night. We'll be rounding Cape Horn in the winter. It will be cold and fearsome tough. You know, you can back out if you wish. Cancel your indenture. It's not too late, if you are not entirely sure."

For a moment, Will tried to imagine the worst that it could possibly happen at sea. He could be washed overboard and drowned or be eaten by a shark. He could fall from a yard in a storm or be killed by falling rigging. He could die of some terrible tropical disease or be killed in a pirate attack. Oddly, each of these seemed preferable to the shame of returning home, turned away from the ship as unsuitable. He would not back out. Not under any circumstances.

"No, sir. I am entirely sure, sir. I want to sail with the *Lady Rebecca*, sir."

The captain smiled again. "Very well, young man. Then sail you shall. I expect you to work hard and to apply yourself. You are to jump cheerfully to do your duty at all times, even when you are cold, wet or tired. Do you understand?"

"Yes, sir," Will replied with determination.

"Then that will do, son. Get to work."

"Yes, sir," Will replied as he scooted out of the cabin. Only when he reached the sunlight on the main deck did he wonder again exactly what he had gotten himself in to.

When the apprentice left, Captain Barker changed into his best shirt with a high starched collar, and a pair of well-pressed trousers with cuffs. After tying his four-in-hand tie and securing it with a silver pin, he put on his vest and jacket and inspected himself in the mirror. A dashing gentleman, indeed. Or as close as you are likely to come, young man, he thought.

Still only thirty-two, captain of a fine ship and now part owner, he was pleased with the image in the mirror. He looked to all the world like a young merchant, as properly he was. This was his third voyage as captain of the *Lady Rebecca*, but it was his first trip as part owner of both the ship and the cargo. When the ship's majority owner, Mr. Shute, couldn't find rates that suited him, he bought coal for his own account, just like in the old days. Shute was his partner now, as well as his employer, and they had agreed to sail without a penny's worth of insurance. His one and only job was to bring their investment around Cape Stiff and to deliver the fine double-screened Welsh coal to a Chilean nitrate port. This trip was his chance. It could either establish or ruin him. All in one roll of the dice.

He looked at his pocket watch, put on his coat and bowler hat and grabbed an ebony walking cane with an ivory handle. He had a crew to sign on.

Fred Smythe, an American sailor of nineteen, of medium build and height, with a full shock of dark hair, tumbled off the Taff Valley train in Bute Station, Cardiff, stiff and sleepy, having spent two days in third class from Liverpool via London. He hoisted his sea chest on his shoulder and headed down Bute Street toward the docks. He was looking for a ship.

At New York's South Street, he had signed aboard the *Shooting Star*, a rather ironically named lumbering Kennebec barque, for a round-trip voyage to Liverpool; but the old ship had opened a seam in the mid-Atlantic causing a leak that kept the crew pumping day and night, sending her to the dry dock for repairs on their arrival. The entire crew was signed off, leaving Fred at loose ends. He had heard that there were ships in need of sailors in Cardiff, so to Cardiff he had come.

Even at ten in the morning, Bute Street teemed like an Asiatic bazaar. The sidewalk bustled with sailors, railway men, shipwrights, boatmen, foundrymen, longshoremen, tavern keepers and doxies of all sizes, shapes and colors. Fred could identify a half-dozen European languages being spoken, but his ear also caught what he thought was Chinese, Arabic, Urdu and Russian.

Every nation and race seemed to be represented, a Cardiff cauldron, a melting pot of souls, jabbering and yelling at each other boisterously. There was a fair share of Welshmen, speaking a blend of Welsh and such heavily accented English that it might as well have been a foreign language. Indian Gujuratis and Bengalis wore softly colored linens, just a bit more rumpled than the Arabs, who seemed to favor white. Africans with skin as black as coal blended in with the local coal-blackened tippers, trimmers and hobblers who worked loading the coal ships.

Fred wondered what his classmates at Yale would think of this crowd. They would no doubt be horrified at the mixing of so many races and creeds with so little care for decorum, yet they might be impressed by the relative harmony evident in all the chaos.

Fred had finished his first year at college when his father died and the family business collapsed. With just enough money to support his mother but none for tuition, Fred did what he had always dreamed of doing. He ran off to sea. He was sick of desks, stuffy classrooms and starched collars anyway. He was sure that what he could learn on the deck of ship mattered more than the ancient history that he was learning in a classroom.

One thing that he had learned for certain was the truth in the old proverb, "be careful what you wish for." There was less romance to the endless toil and miserable conditions that were a sailor's life than he had imagined as a boy. Then again, he had gone to the places of which he had dreamed. He had sailed schooners from New England to the Caribbean and square-riggers back and forth across the Atlantic. As hard as the work was and as miserly the wages, he had few real regrets.

And now, he stood on the street in the famous Tiger Bay, Cardiff's polyglot sailor town where anything was possible, any pleasure or diversion was for sale, and a man could be whatever he wished to be, so long as a crimp didn't dope his drink or a bully boy didn't crack open his skull to steal his purse.

An impressive row of bars and taverns lined the street, all having either opened early or never closed, as both music and drunken sailors spilled from the doors as they swung open and shut. Carts and carriages dodged the inebriated men tumbling off the sidewalks, and Fred was surprised not to have seen any fatalities.

A young lady, heavily painted and perfumed, cruised out from the Anglesea Pub and plotted a crossing course for the young sailor. She grabbed Fred boldly by the arm.

Such beautifully red lips, the exact color of desire, Fred thought. She demanded, "Come, my handsome. Let's have some fun," tugging insistently on his arm.

Fred looked her over. She had bright eyes and a lovely smile, but his glance immediately shifted. Her flowered frock was only partially buttoned in front, displaying her charms to maximum advantage. Ah, the fair orbs of Aphrodite, Fred thought to himself, and it required great presence of mind to not be drawn away.

"Not right now, my sweet," he replied. "I need to find a ship. I shall return this evening. What's your name, my lovely?"

"Lucretia," she replied. "And yours?"

Fred laughed. "Lucretia! Mother of the Roman Republic! How could I stay away? My name is Frederick, dear lady. Until this evening, Miss Lucretia of the Anglesea."

Having failed to slow his progress, the fair maiden released her towline, letting go of her grasp on his arm. "Don't forget me now, Freddy."

"Never, Lucretia, never," he called out, without looking back.

As he walked toward the docks, the street became more boisterous while the buildings became darker with layer on layer of coal dust. Coal made Cardiff one of the largest ports in the British Empire. Fred recalled reading somewhere that eight million tons of the Welsh black diamonds moved through the port every year.

When he finally reached Bute Dock, it didn't take long before he found a ship. Perhaps *the* ship. She was a steel, three-masted windjammer with lines that reminded him of a clipper ship. Her name was the *Lady Rebecca.* She was deeply laden, with two hatches still open and a black cloud of coal dust rising from each, as carts of coal were tipped in. The wharfinger told him that the ship would be signing on a crew that very afternoon. And best of all, she was bound for Chile via Cape Horn.

Somehow, Fred had gotten it into his head that he wouldn't be a real sailor until he took a trip or two around Cape Horn. The Horn was like no place else on the watery globe and any Jack who had rounded it under sail was indeed worthy of respect. And now here she was, a Cape Horner in need of a crew. It was time to find his way to the shipping office. Fred hoisted his sea chest back on his shoulder and headed off.

Captain Barker bounded up the granite steps of the Cardiff Shipping Office. The building was a series of large rooms on either side of the main hall. Sunlight filtered through the high windows as hundreds of sailors milled in and out, checking the chalkboards with the listings of ships and voyages. The crowd ranged from hearty tars in their shore-going rig, eager to get back to sea, to dissipated souls bearing the signs of too much drink, under the watchful eyes of crimps or boardinghouse masters, who would make sure to claim the month's advance owed to their tattered charges, in repayment of debts, real or imagined.

A clerk directed Captain Barker to a room where the board read:

> *Lady Rebecca—twenty able seaman required.*
> *2 PM*
> *Voyage to Pisagua, Chile, thence for orders.*

Several men stood near the board and one spoke up loudly, "Who's going to sail around Cape Stiff on that old windbag? Not me, I'll warrant ya." The sailor spit a stream of tobacco juice at the chalkboard.

Captain Barker clenched his right hand around his cane. If he had been on the deck on his ship, he would have knocked the man down, but ashore, the rules were different. He looked over at the man, sallow with dull eyes, and decided that he was no real sailor in any case.

"And what are you doing here anyway, you stinking cur? You don't look like any sort I'd ever want on my ship. Now, go back to your smoke box, you damned fireman."

The man spun around and looked at Captain Barker, who stood holding his cane in one hand and his bowler hat in the other. The man began to speak, but then just snorted, turned and stomped out of the room. The captain heard chuckles from sailors behind him.

There were many like that steamboat drudge who believed that the days of sail were over. Freight rates had fallen and times were getting tougher, but the wind wagons weren't dead yet. As long as there were winds that blew, there would be sailing ships to sail. Captain Barker had a fine ship and all he needed was a crew.

In a few minutes, a rotund shipping master in a faded blue jacket, waddled in and sat at a large desk at the far end of the room. He bellowed, "*Lady Rebecca*! *Lady Rebecca*!"

The din of chatter stopped and sailors drifted in. Captain Barker scanned the milling crowd. He needed twenty good able seamen. The *Rebecca* was a heavy ship and needed strong and experienced hands. This was his one chance to pick a crew worthy of the ship, a crew that could sail her and who wouldn't be broken by her. It was like picking out cattle at a stockyard, except that this beef had to know its business.

He looked each sailor up and down and asked a question or two. He kept a running track of how many Englishmen he had chosen, as well as how many other nationalities he had sent to stand with the chosen men.

He wanted a thoroughly mixed crew. Better that they fought one another rather than unite to fight his authority. When foreign sailors stepped up, the captain confirmed that each had a rudimentary grasp of English. When he had chosen twenty, he nodded to the shipping master.

The shipping master cleared his throat and began reading the preamble to the Articles of Agreement, then moved on to specific terms and conditions, wages and allotments. Captain Barker walked over and stood next to the master, scanning the chosen sailors with a calculating eye. When the shipping master stopped and put down the agreement, it was the captain's turn to speak.

"Men, I am Captain James Barker. We are embarking on a long voyage by way of Cape Horn. By the looks of you, many here are Cape Horn snorters, so there is no reason that we shouldn't have a happy crowd. All I expect is that you jump to with a will at my orders. Beyond that, it's one hand for the owner and one hand for yourself. All right now, line up over here, one at a time." The captain took a chair beside the shipping master at the table.

The first up was a large man with dark hair that hung across one eye. He had a crooked grin, which he tried to suppress for the serious business of signing articles.

The captain looked up. "Name, age, and nationality."

"I'm, Harry, sir. From Cornwall. I think I'm around thirty."

"Your last name, Harry?

"Yes, sir," the sailor replied.

"Your last name," the captain repeated.

"Yes, sir. My last name is Harhy. I'm G.H. Hahry. That's H-A-H-R-Y. But everyone just calls me Harry."

"Well, I imagine that they would," the captain replied, raising an eyebrow. He handed Harry the pen.

Harry bent down and with great care drew an anchor for his signature. With a self-satisfied grin, he turned, nearly knocking over the man behind him. The sailors took no offense as Harry careened back through the line.

Rolf Jensen, next in line, was a red-faced Dane with a tattoo of a naked woman on his right arm and a ship in the grasp of a giant squid on his left. He grabbed the pen as if it was a marlinspike and left a blotched X as his mark. Behind him came Tony-the-Chileano, Jerry-the-Greek, and Gabriel Isaacson.

Hmmn, the captain thought as Isaacson signed. He had never known a sea-going Jew. Lots of bumboat traders but never a deep-sea sailor. Well, there was Noah, he thought. Isaacson looked fit enough.

The usual assortment of Finns, Norwegians, a Frenchman and a few Liverpool hard cases followed behind.

A young sailor, strongly built with dark hair, added his name among the various Xs and illegible scrawls. In a clear and graceful hand he wrote, Frederick Anthony Smythe. The captain looked down at the signature, and then back at the young sailor. "You look like you've had some education, young man."

"Yes, sir,"

"Where did you go to school, pray tell?"

"A year at Yale, sir."

The captain cocked his head. "I've heard of it. Good school. And an American to boot."

"Yes, sir."

"You sail as ordinary?"

"No, sir," Fred replied adamantly. "Able, sir. Discharge papers to prove it, too, sir."

The captain waved them away. "Very well. Able, it is. Next."

When he had twenty signatures or marks on the articles, the captain stood up. In his best quarterdeck voice, he bellowed, "Crew of the *Lady Rebecca*, you are expected to be aboard tomorrow at seven, breakfast at eight and turn to at eight forty-five, ready for duty."

He turned to the shipping master. "Their month's advance can be drawn on the account of Merrick Shute. I'll send my officers and warrants to sign articles later this afternoon." They shook hands and the captain folded his copy of the articles, put them in his jacket pocket and left the shipping office. There was much to be done before tomorrow. Overall, he was pleased with the crowd he had signed on, though only time and sea miles would tell him what sort of crew they really were.

Mary Barker smiled, watching her six-year-old daughter, Amanda, bouncing with excitement as she looked out the train window as the Welsh countryside rolled by. The lush green of farmland had now given way to coal mines and factories. Amanda's two-year-old brother, Tommy, was slumped against the seat, sleeping soundly. Amanda was too excited to sleep. She had done nothing but talk about going to sea on Daddy's ship for weeks and now they were on their way.

Mary wished she shared her daughter's enthusiasm. She had been on three voyages before but had never taken to the sea. A ship captain's daughter, sister to a sailor and now a ship captain's wife, she would have liked nothing more than to live in Chester on the River Dee, in a small cottage with her children, waiting for her husband to come home. She hated leaving her mother, with whom she was very close. Her mother was not a young woman and Mary wondered darkly if they would ever see each other again.

But James had his heart set on sailing with his family. This was an important voyage for him and for them as well. So if James asked that they go, she knew her duty. Whither thou goest...

She looked at herself in her pocket mirror. She had just turned thirty but feared that she looked older. The sea aged everyone but was crueler to women than men. She put the mirror back in her handbag and tried to think no more of it.

When James met them at the Cardiff train station, Mary smiled as Amanda and Tommy shrieked and leapt to greet their father. He stooped down to grab them both as they charged at him, laughing. His stance was wide, as if he was on the quarterdeck on his ship, braced against a rolling sea. He scooped them up and spun around as they screamed with joy.

A carriage was waiting for them. "I've booked rooms in the Angel Hotel until the cargo is finished loading and your quarters are ready." Mary took James' hand as he helped her into the carriage. The children clambered aboard and they were off to the hotel.

As the carriage clattered along, the captain looked at Mary with concern. She looked tired and somewhat sad. Perhaps she was just weary from the travel by train. Mary was still so pretty, with dark eyes and her hair pulled back in a bun. She had obviously dressed to please him, wearing a new blue dress, not too fancy and quite suitable for travel, but better than day-to-day wear. He began to worry that she was unhappy already and they had not even made it aboard the ship. Nevertheless, he was excited to get under way and would not let feminine fears interfere. All would be well, once the ship sailed.

"We have a new cabin steward. A man named Walter. He comes with good references, so I hope that he will be able to make you and the children quite comfortable. I have also ordered livestock, so that we may have eggs and milk."

Her eyes brightened. "We shall have a cow?"

"Sorry, my love. Cows don't do well aboard ship. We will have goats, as well as chickens." She smiled but he could see the disappointment in her eyes.

"There is one matter that I must discuss with you, however, before you go aboard. You know that I am most pleased to have your brother Thomas sailing with us as second mate. He is a fine young man and a good officer from all that I can tell. Aboard the *Lady Rebecca,* nevertheless, we must maintain discipline. When the voyage is done, we will again be Thomas and James, but until then he is Mr. Atkinson and he will address me as Captain Barker. I do not wish for you to think that I am being brusque with him. That is just how it must be. When he has free time off-watch, he does have my permission to visit with you and the children, but his first duty is to the ship and her crew. As is mine."

Mary smiled broadly. "I may be no sailor, dearest, but I understand well enough." She glanced out the carriage window and then turned back toward him and with a grin. "Do you know what I have taken to calling the *Lady Rebecca*? Your other wife. I am not sure what her owner would think of that. Merrick Shute did name his ship after his daughter, did he not?"

The captain snorted. "An owner's prerogative. He may name the ship for whomever he chooses. I, or rather, we, now own a quarter share of the ship and of the cargo. Ships always seem to own part of their captains. On the *Lady Rebecca*, it is about time that her captain and his family owned a part of her too. I know how hard it is on you to raise a family on a captain's salary. If this voyage goes well, perhaps it will establish us."

She knew that in his dreams James saw himself owning a fleet of fine ships, but that he dared say nothing out loud. One voyage at a time. That is as far as any man could see. James went on to tell tales of steady winds and cerulean seas, of flying fish and sea foam as white as the clouds. This wasn't her first voyage, yet she appreciated his efforts to put her at ease and felt a bit of his enthusiasm about the great venture ahead. Perhaps this voyage would be fine, Mary told herself. Blue skies and fair winds. A dream perhaps, but a nice one.

CHAPTER 3
THE CREW COMES ABOARD

June 10, 1905

Captain Barker slept ashore with his family that night but rose early to return to the ship. He tried not to wake his wife or the children. Nevertheless, Mary reached out and squeezed his hand as he left the bed.

He reached the ship near dawn and took his place on the poop deck. Two hatches were open, the dock cranes ready to resume tipping the huge coal carts into the *Rebecca*'s holds. In the same dock, the *Susannah*, a German barque, bound too for Chile, was also close to finishing loading. She was rumored to be fast. We shall see, the captain thought. The *Rebecca* was very fast as well, so long as her yards weren't braced around upon her stays. Might make a race of it, the captain thought. Wouldn't that be fine? A grand German ship against the

Lady Rebecca, proudly flying the red duster. He'd show the Germans how an English ship could sail.

But they had to finish loading first and they were also still waiting on the last of the provisions and the slop chest order from Jacob the Goat to arrive. He wondered whether the *Susannah* would slip out ahead of them. But then, what did a few hours or even few days matter in race of 12,000 miles?

At seven a.m., a line of bleary-eyed sailors made their way through the dock gate, down along the railroad tracks, to the gangway of the *Lady Rebecca*, duffels or sea chests hoisted on their shoulders. Many appeared to have successfully turned their month's advance into liquid libation. Most barely looked up at the ship, laden as they were by their gear, the early hour and the celebrations of the night before. At least half were still drunk. Several hadn't slept at all since signing articles.

Soon the cranes would again start loading double-screened anthracite coal into the cavernous holds. The sailors trudged to the fo'c'sle house, just aft of the foremast, and tossed their gear onto the bunks. The cook's stove smoked and the sailors dug out their metal cups and utensils from their kit and lined up at the galley house for a breakfast of burgoo and biscuits. The cook, a black Jamaican named Jeremiah, eyed them warily before scooping out a serving to each.

"Send a boy back for de coffee," he said, once everyone had passed by.

A large sailor with a Liverpool accent pointed to Fred Smyth. "Yank, you're the Peggy, get the coffee."

Fred put down his plate and almost said, "Get it yourself." But there was no need to start the trip with a fight, and somebody had to get it. Overall, Fred wasn't feeling too bad. His head hurt, but he had shown at least a modicum of restraint the night before. And the thought of the fair Lucretia brought a smile to his face.

He lugged back a large pot full of a steaming black liquid—sailor's coffee. Hot and bitter, mostly burned biscuit, it had a taste that suggested everything except the fruits of the coffee plant. Fred sat with the rest, finding a place on the deck behind the house, before they had to turn to. Most slumped against the deckhouse, though several lay down on the deck and went to sleep.

Fred looked around at his shipmates, as motley a bunch as ever he'd seen. Fred was one of the youngest of the hands. Some looked like experienced sailors. Some looked to be roustabouts or worse. Some looked too old to still be sailing. Whatever and whomever they were, Fred knew that he would get to know them better in the next few months than anyone he had ever known on shore. In the tiny society of souls aboard a small ship on a boundless ocean, it was unavoidable. Which of these men would he learn to rely on? Which would he stay away from? Who among them would try to become the "cock of the watch"? Who would become a close friend? Only time and sea miles would tell.

He had learned a few of their names at the shipping hall. Harry from Cornwall was large, strong and seemed affable enough. Obviously a sailor. Jensen the Dane also looked as though he knew the sea but was brooding and kept to himself. Fred did admire the tattoo of the naked woman on his right forearm. The kraken devouring a ship on his left had a certain artistic appeal, but seemed a poor choice at the start of a voyage. Fred wasn't superstitious but neither did he believe in tempting fate.

Fred guessed at the nicknames that some would acquire. He had already been called "Yank," which was fine with him. He'd been called worse. There was a Frenchman, François Arno, who would likely end up as

"Frenchie" or "Frankie the Frog." Fred thought that a better appellation might be "Yes Arno," but was sure that would never catch on.

The Irishman, Shaemus O'Malley, hailed from Donegal, and was already being called "Donnie."

The nicknames were generally gracefully accepted, although one could never be sure. On his last ship, he has seen a knife fight break out over whether "Squarehead" applied to Germans or only to Scandinavians.

Santiago was from Chile and was going to home to see his mother and sister, to help them run their shop in Callao.

"Lord have mercy," Donnie responded. "Who ever heard of a sailor tending a shop? What sort'a shop is it? Your mother's not Madame Cashee, is she?"

A dark look crossed Santiago's face. He obviously wasn't too sure how to take the suggestion that his mother was a legendary brothel keeper. Then he grinned, "Nah, me madre, she sells dry goods, not pretty girls."

"If you are Chileno, what's she doing in Callao?" Donnie asked.

"She wein tto work for her uncle," Santiago said with a shrug.

"And what about you?" Donnie looked over to Gabe Isaacson, a skinny young man with a sharp and narrow face. "You look like you should be on a bumboat with the rest of the Jews."

Gabe smiled. "And why aren't you diggin' praties or cutting turf, my Irish friend?"

Donnie shrugged. "Got tired of starving. Not that the grub on a lime-juicer is all that much better."

"Well, I spent enough time on the bumboats. Heard all the stories from all the drunken sailors. Figured it was time I saw for myself," Gabe said.

Donnie laughed. "So you are the famous wandering Jew that we keep hearing about?"

"That's me," Gabe replied.

Frenchie looked over at the German ship *Susannah*, a four-masted barque, across the wet dock, then back up at the three soaring masts of the *Lady Rebecca*. He let out a low whistle. "Ze *Rebecca* is a brute, a ship for strong men. Can we 'andle her, I wonder?"

Fred looked over, "What do you mean?"

"Use your eyes, my friend," the Frenchman replied with a wave of his arm.

Fred looked across the dock. The *Susannah* was a four-poster, the sails spread across four masts. The *Rebecca's* three massive steel masts soared higher. Her sails and yards, on only three masts, were larger, requiring more muscle to raise. Fred looked up at her main yard, steel, like the masts. Gauging from the beam of the ship, the yard, extending well beyond the bulwarks on either side, had to be at least a hundred feet. The topsail, t'gallant, and royal yards above it seemed only slightly smaller.

Frenchie continued. "Ze *Susannah*, she's got four masts and a Liverpool deck, the midship house 'cross the whole beam, that breaks the waves, not like zees' old lady's wide open deck, to scope up all the Southern Ocean and send it crashing down on us, sailors."

When Fred first saw the *Lady Rebecca* at Bute Dock, the ship had reminded him of the graceful clippers of old, just larger and built of steel, rather than oak and yellow pine. What a moment ago had seemed a lovely ship now looked to be a man-killer. He shook his head, wondering what sort of ship he had signed aboard.

"I wonder whether ze *Susannah*'s got Jarvey winches?" Frenchie asked.

"What's a Jarvey winch?" Fred asked.

"You know the Jarvey Patent."

Donnie piped in. "I believe he means the Jarvis Patent brace winch. Never seen one m'self, but I hear tell that they are a wonder. Two men can haul the braces and turn 'round a yard, where it would have taken ten hauling the brace with the Armstrong Patent."

"Alright," Fred replied. "Now what's the Armstrong Patent?"

Donnie hooted. "Why you've never heard of the Armstrong Patent?" He flexed his bicep and pointed to it. That is the winch that hauls the lines on this old barky. Our strong arms. That's the Armstrong Patent."

Fred laughed and shook his head, then finished the last gulp of the bitter coffee.

"Anybody know about the Old Man?" asked Tom, the large sailor from Liverpool. "He's a youngster, sure enough."

Fred smiled. The captain was always the "Old Man" regardless of his age. Nevertheless, on the ships that he had sailed on, the nickname suited the chronology. But not on the *Lady Rebecca*. Captain Barker couldn't be too far into his thirties. Fred had heard talk in the shipping hall that Barker had gotten his first command in his twenties and was the youngest captain in all of British deep-water sail.

The Greek named Jerry spoke up. "Heard he's a driver, a bend it or break it skipper. Not afeared of man nor the devil. Says he once out-sailed the *Preussen*."

"Bah," Donnie replied. "I'll not be believe'n that tale, now. This old bitch could never keep up with *Preussen*, much less show her her heels. Naught but a fairy tale, to be sure. If the Old Man out-sailed the *Preussen*, it was in his dreams. Or maybe the Kraut was at anchor."

Fred had seen the *Preussen* once. Five masts, an immense cloud of snowy white sail, and nearly as fast as the wind itself. She was the largest and most modern square-rigger on the oceans, and the *Lady Rebecca*, smaller and almost twenty years old, wouldn't likely stand a chance against her.

Fred heard a rumor that the Old Man had bet the captain of the *Susannah* that the *Lady Rebecca* would beat them to Chile. Nothing wrong with taking pride in a ship, but hubris was just as dangerous for ship's captains as for the gods of antiquity.

"The Old Man's a fast passage maker anyway. A lucky captain, maybe," Santiago commented.

"We'll may just need some luck rounding Cape Stiff so late in the season," the Cornishman Harry replied. "Cape Horn winter can be a bitch, sure enough."

"He's bringin' his family too. Might soften him a touch."

"Not necessarily," said Tom. "Sailed with McMurry, you remember McMurry? Was a right bastard when his wife made the trip. Worse than when he sailed alone. An' she was meaner than he was. An' almost as ugly."

Another sailor laughed. "Well, that's true enough."

"Cook says that the second mate's the Old Man's brother-in-law. Wonder how that'll turn out."

"Never good having that much family aboard ship. T'ings get so damned complicated wit' families."

Their speculation was interrupted when a large man with gray hair lumbered forward. "Name's Rand. I'm the mate." He walked over and gave a swift kick to the ribs to one of the sleeping sailors. "Get your lazy arses off the deck, there's work to be done."

Around ten a.m., a wagon rattled down the dock, dodging the cranes swinging their loads of coal. The man at the reins had a scraggly goatee and wore a battered captain's cap over a balding pate. Second Mate

Atkinson had been watching out for the wagon and, on its approach, walked over to the half-deck to roust the apprentices.

"Come out, my flock. Jacob the Goat is here and we have slops to stow." He pounded his fist against the house door and the four apprentices trooped out on the deck. Their blue jackets were stored in their sea chests and they now all wore sailor's dungarees. "Down the gangway with you."

While the mate looked over Jacob's tally of foul-weather gear, tobacco, clothing, blankets and soap—all the goods that would stock the slop chest, the ship's store, for the long voyage to Chile and beyond—the apprentices started to untie the canvas that covered the wagon. One second-voyager, George Black, stood back and started giving orders to Will. "Haul down that crate there, youngster."

Paul Nelson, the senior, only a voyage away from completing his indenture, gave George a swift chuck to the back of his head. "And who made you King, George?" He chuckled. "King George. All right. We all work here together, every one of us. Nobody gives orders 'cepting the mates or the captain. So, jump to it, King George."

Will tried not to grin as the elder apprentice, if only by one voyage, was shown his place. The apprentices unloaded the wagon onto the quayside as Second Mate Atkinson, with Jacob looking on, checked the bundles and cartons against the invoices.

"I can see why they call him Jacob the Goat," Will whispered to Jack, looking back at the wizened merchant.

Jack grinned. "I hear he's ornery as a goat besides."

With the accounts in agreement, Atkinson shook Jacob' hand and turned to the apprentices. "Up they go, boys. Into the lazerreto."

When they had finished carrying the slops up the gangway, through the deckhouse and into the lazarette, the provisions wagon had arrived and they turned to at the mizzen gantline, hoisting barrels of flour, molasses, salt pork and bully beef aboard. When Will was sure that they were finished, another wagon arrived, loaded with goats and chickens. "This a sailing ship or a barnyard?" Will wondered aloud. Jack laughed. "Captain's bringing his family along. That's their milk and eggs." As he fought to drive an obstinate goat up the gangway, Will hoped that goatherd would be the least of his duties on the *Lady Rebecca*.

That afternoon, Second Mate Atkinson bellowed, "Apprentices, turn to, the starboard rail by hatch three!" The four apprentices, who thought that they would have some time to catch their breath, lined up along the bulwark next to the hatch. The four boys, ranging in age from fourteen to seventeen, formed a jagged line of varying heights. Will was the shortest. Jack and Paul Nelson, the senior apprentice, towered over him, while George filled in the middle.

"Let's see what we've got here. How many of you have at least one voyage under your belt? Show of hands."

Everyone's hand went up, except for Will's.

"And rounded the Horn?"

Two hands went up.

"OK. That's Paul and Jack. Been around more than once?"

Paul held up his hand.

The mate walked over and stood in front of Will, who immediately felt even smaller than he was.

"So you are our first voyager? Well, that's just fine. Everyone's got to have a first time."

In the shadow of the tall mate, Will felt as if he was shrinking. Atkinson stepped back.

"Gentlemen, into the rigging. I'll go easy on you. Climb the mizzen. One to starboard, one to port. Out to the royal yard, then up to the cap, slap it and sing out. Paul and George, you two first. Up you go."

Will watched as the two apprentices ran to the ratlines and scampered skyward. They climbed higher and higher, disappearing above the top, reappearing again as they climbed the ratlines to the crosstrees. Will's mouth felt dry as he watched. Paul made it to the yardarm first, a tiny shape above the deck, disappearing again, back to the mast. In a moment, Will heard a voice shout out "Paul!" A few seconds later, George shouted as well. They both returned to the deck in half the time they took to climb aloft.

"OK, William and Jack. Up you go."

Will swallowed, and then ran to the starboard ratlines. He grabbed at the ratlines as he climbed, only to have Atkinson bellow at him, "If you don't want to die, William, grab the shrouds, not the ratlines!" Will groaned inside. He knew that, he'd read it, he just forgot. Maybe green as grass wasn't so far off. "Aye, aye, sir," he shouted. When he reached the futtock shrouds, he felt like he was upside down as he forced himself up onto the mizzen top. For a moment he lay on his stomach, catching his breath before jumping up and swinging out on the topsail shrouds. Jack was well ahead of him, almost to the crosstrees.

Will was dizzy. His hands were wet with sweat and his stomach was knotted in fear, but he kept climbing. The shrouds became narrower the higher he climbed until he too finally reached the crosstrees. Jack had already worked his way out to the royal yardarm.

There had been barely a breath of a breeze on deck, yet at the crosstrees, one hundred and ten feet up, the wind gusted. Will could feel the ship move every time the dock crane dropped a coal cart into the forward hold. Suddenly William heard the cry, "Jack Pickering!" followed by a "Yahooo!" as Jack slid down the bare royal mast.

"Get yourself moving, William," came the distant, yet distinct, voice of the mate from the deck.

William began climbing again, shoving his toes sideways in the narrow t'gallant ratlines until they ended altogether at the base of the royal mast. Jack passed by with a huge grin on his face. "Best view in Cardiff!" he shouted as he climbed down. William tried to smile.

There were no ratlines on the royal mast, only a bare pole to be climbed. He shinnied his way up until he could just grab the footropes under the royal yard, thinner than any of the others below. He worked his way out on the footropes until he reached the clew shackle.

The view was breathtaking and terrifying, in equal measure. The deck seemed a distant and narrow place peopled by tiny shapes. Even the other soaring square-riggers in the dock seemed small. He looked down at the red brick Pierhead Building and the clock, Baby Big Ben, in its tower. The wind blew in his hair and tugged at his shirt. Looking away from shore, he could see far beyond the dock walls, out beyond the breakwater to the Severn Estuary and out to the living and boundless sea beyond.

"Hurry up, William," came the cry from the deck. "Up to the cap."

His moment of reverie vanquished, Will held tight to the jackstays and worked his way back to the mast where another twelve feet of bare greasy pole awaited him. He stood up on the yard and hugged the mast for all he was worth, pushing himself higher with his feet, not daring to look either down or up, only out at the blue of the sky, until finally he reached the mahogany cap on the top of the mast. He struck it with his fist and yelled as loudly as he could, "William Jones!"

Captain Barker sat in his dayroom going over the ship's papers. He heard the steward passing by in the companionway. "Walter," he called out.

The light-skinned West Indian stepped into his dayroom. "Sir."

"Would you ask the mate to join me for a few words as his duties permits."

"Yes, sir, cap'n. Right away."

In a few minutes, the mate knocked on the frame of the open door.

Captain Barker swiveled in his chair. "Come in, Mr. Rand. Have a seat."

The large man pulled a chair over and sat down. He took off his peaked cap, revealing a salt-and-pepper mix of gray and brown hair. He was heavyset with an ample waist. Sitting there face to face, he looked far older than he appeared on deck. His wrinkled and leathery face showed the years of wind and brine. His blue eyes looked out from beneath black, shaggy eyebrows.

The captain glanced at his records. Rand had sailed for thirty-five years and yet had never held a rank higher than mate. His papers showed no shortage of experience and, from all that he had seen, the mate knew his business.

"I see you've buttoned up number three hatch. When do you expect to be finished with one and two?"

"Yes, sir. Two'll be done in about an hour. They're bringing in another freight car to top up number one hatch. Long as there is no delay, they should be done by late afternoon. We'll have her scrubbed and clean by nightfall. You can bring your family aboard first thing in the morning, if that suits you."

"That will be just fine, Mr. Rand. Now, as soon as the cargo is finished, I want you to turn the crowd to, to bend all canvas and sort out the running rigging. We should have a favorable breeze and I wouldn't mind setting topsails and t'gallants before the sea buoy. See Mr. Pugsley, the sail maker. I've sailed with him before. He's a good man."

"Yes, sir," Rand replied.

Captain Barker almost ended the interview there, but his eyes kept being drawn to Mr. Rand's service record.

"If I may ask, why have you never sailed as captain?" He could almost read the answer in the man's eyes before he spoke. They were eyes that had seen too many disappointments, too many promises unkept. His gaze seemed to expect the worst—wry, weary and bitter all at once.

The man shrugged. "Dunno. Jus' been unlucky, I guess. Look at the two of us. You sailing captain since you were twenty-five and me in my fifties and never more'n a mate. But Mr. Shute, he promised to find me a command on one of his ships if I get a good report from you at the end of this voyage."

"Well, sir, do your duty. That's all I ask, and I'll be happy to pass a good word to Mr. Shute."

Captain Barker caught a glimpse of motion beyond the cabin port. "Come, Mr. Rand. I believe the *Susannah* is getting under way."

The captain bounded up the stairs to the poop deck, followed a few paces behind by the mate, and stood at the outboard rail as the tall and lovely German ship slipped by. A rotund captain wearing a fine blue coat and a hat with gold braid on the brim stood abaft the quartermaster. He waved when he saw Captain Barker, whom he had met once or twice socially, while their ships were loading.

"Have a good trip, Captain Frederich," Captain Barker yelled over. "See you in Chile."

"We'll wait for you," the German captain responded.

"No need. We'll get there first."

"Ya, sure," the German laughed.

Captain Barker couldn't resist. "We'll beat you by twenty days!"

"Nein, Kapitän. Nie passieren," Captain Frederich shouted back.

"Twenty days!" Captain Barker shouted back for emphasis.

Captain Frederich waved and laughed.

Behind him, Captain Barker heard Mr. Rand say, "No way we'll beat the *Susannah*. She's too fast by half. We'll never catch her."

Instantly, Captain Barker was reminded of the coal box sailor who spat tobacco juice on the *Lady Rebecca*'s name on the chalkboard in the shipping hall. He wanted to turn and punch the mate in the face for his insolence, but thought better of it. He breathed deeply to compose himself, and then turned around.

"We will beat the *Susannah*, Mr. Rand. We are going to out-sail that Fritz, and you, sir, are going to help us do it. Do you understand me, Mr. Rand?"

"Yes, sir." Rand put his hat back on. "If you'll excuse me, sir. I'll see to number two hatch."

Captain Barker watched the mate's broad back was he walked down the ladder to the main deck, and then turned to see the stern of the *Susannah* gliding though the dock gates. The tug *Goliath* had her towline and was easing her out to sea.

"I'll be waiting for you in Chile, Captain Frederich."
He turned to look down the deck. "And I'll be keeping
my eye on you, Mr. Rand."

CHAPTER 4
SETTING SAIL

June 11, 1905

At five a.m., Mate Rand and Second Mate Atkinson pounded on the fo'c'sle doors. Rand bellowed, "Rise and shine, me hearties. Get your useless carcasses out of your bunks. This ain't no pleasure cruise."

If half the crew was drunk when they came aboard, half as many again were drunker on sailing day. They drained the bottles that they had hidden away in their sea chests and duffels. It was a ritual that Fred had come to expect but never really quite understood. On his first ship, he asked a shipmate why everyone drank so much the night before sailing. The sailor looked at him blankly and asked, "Why'd any man go to sea, if he weren't stinkin' drunk?" It was as good an answer as any, he supposed, but as he had suffered enough from the previous day's hangover, he had no wish to repeat it as the ship was getting under way.

The crew stumbled out of the fo'c'sle more slowly than Rand would have liked so he grabbed a sailor by the shirt and threw him a few feet across the deck. A second sailor came flying after him and the rest of the crowd moved considerably faster.

When everyone was out of the cabin, the mate said, "Well, let's see who we got. Sing out when your name is called."

Atkinson stepped up and shouted, "Tom Jackson."

The Liverpool sailor yelled "Aye."

"Make that 'aye, sir,' mister," the mate grumbled.

Jackson laughed. "Well, aye, sir, it is then."

"Otto Schmidt."

"Yah, Mr. Mate," the German sailor replied.

Atkinson snorted. Close enough to "sir," he supposed.

The second mate worked his way down the crew list, receiving an honorific about half the time, and seeming not overly concerned by the lack. His face did grow more troubled when the name he called gave no response at all. "John Williams." He waited. "Williams?" John Williams was apparently not aboard. He moved on to the names of sailors who were present. "Jerry Panagopo ... Panagopoulos."

"Jus' call me Jerry da Greek, sir. Ever'body does."

When he had worked his way down the list, Mate Rand asked, "How many we got?"

"We're seven short."

Rand snorted. "I'll let the captain know."

As Rand walked aft, Mate Atkinson pointed. "You four, stand by the bow lines. You four, the after springs. The rest of you, lead the forward springs to the capstan and stand by."

Rand found Captain Barker in his dayroom, going through the ship's papers.

"Captain, sir. We're seven shy. Seven who signed articles yesterday took French leave, or so it looks. Took your advance money and just skedaddled."

The captain looked up, scowling. "Damned sailors these days. Give me their names. When I send the papers and manifest ashore, I'll be sure they are listed with the constable."

"Make it up with pierhead jumpers?" Rand asked.

Captain Barker shook his head. "I've already been robbed once. Hate to make that twice. But yes, I'll arrange it with the agent." Now he had more bodies to buy. The agent would arrange with a crimp or a boardinghouse master to find him sufficient crew, probably all drugged or drunk, like as not, shanghaied from other ships.

"Well, if that's the way you want it, Captain, that's the way it'll be."

Once the crew was squared away at the mooring lines, Second Mate Atkinson walked aft and pounded on the door to the half-deck, which reverberated like the inside of a bass-fiddle. "Up and out, and be quick about it," he bellowed. Will felt like he had just closed his eyes. They had worked late loading and storing provisions and gear. His muscles ached and he wanted nothing more than to roll over in his bunk and go back to sleep. Instead, he jumped up with the others and pulled on his dungarees.

When he stumbled onto the deck, the second mate shouted, "Paul and George, stand by to handle lines on the poop deck. Will and Jack, get aloft. Cast off the gaskets. Course to t'gallants."

As apprentices, their station when making sail was the mizzenmast, the smallest of the three. Will and Jack climbed the ratlines to the mizzen top. Other sailors climbed aloft on the main and foremasts.

"He's got to be a driver if he is letting the sails hang in their gear before we even leave the wet dock," Will said. Jack only grinned as he laid out on the starboard yard and Will laid out to port.

Will had always heard "one hand for the ship and one hand for yourself," so held tightly to the jackstay with one hand and with the other tried to untie the long canvas strip that held the main course. It was slow work. He glanced over at Jack, who was casting off the fourth gasket where he had just finished one.

"Use two hands, you ninny," Jack shouted over at him. Will colored. Perhaps the old phrase wasn't meant literally. He took a deep breath and let go of the jackstay and leaned over the yard, reaching down with two hands. The square knots in the gaskets were easier to handle now and he was surprised how, between his feet in the footropes and his belly pressed against the yard, he felt moderately secure.

Jack was waiting for him at the mizzen top. "I've seen snails faster'n you," he said with a smile before swinging up the ratlines to the lower topsail yard. Will followed, seething.

On the lower topsail yard, he almost kept up with Jack and did about as well on the upper topsail yard. When they cast off the gaskets on the t'gallant yard, Will stopped and looked below. The deck was a swarm of activity. Aft, the captain and his family had taken to the poop deck; forward, the crew on the fo'c'sle had began stamping around the capstan, slowly warping the ship to the wet dock gate, which inched closer as the ship remained stationary beneath him. Beyond the dock gate, a tug stood by, belching black smoke. Beyond the tug, the Severn Estuary widened into the Bristol Channel, which, in the distance, opened to the sea. The breeze blew on his back as if urging them onward. Will smiled broadly, his eyes now fixed on the hazy line of the horizon..

Captain Barker stood on the poop deck. Mate Rand had the fo'c'sle and Second Mate Atkinson had the main deck. So far, Barker was satisfied with all he saw. Last night he had a nightmare about shipwrecks and storms and woke in a cold sweat, but on this morning there was only a blue sky and a steady light southwesterly breeze, ready to send them on their way once they cleared the channel. He had moved a chair to the poop deck for Mary, who was smiling and holding little Tommy in her arms. Amanda was standing next to her, filled with energy and occasionally requiring a word to stand close and not get in the way of the two apprentices handling the stern lines.

The captain wondered idly on what sort of wind the *Susannah* was sailing, somewhere over the horizon. The last time he raced his ship, against Billy Jackson's *Homeward Bound,* he had won twenty-five pounds, which he had divided up amongst the apprentices. Now he wished he had wagered with Captain Frederich. Bragging rights would have to be enough.

The dock gate swung open slowly. It was high tide, so the level of sea matched the water level in the dock. A sailor on deck threw a monkey's fist tied to a light line to the deckhand on the tug *Sarah.* The tug deckhands secured the heavy wire towing cable to be hauled back to the *Lady Rebecca,* where sailor looped a heavy rope hawser through the steel eye, then made it fast to the bits. The tug bore off and slowly took a strain on the towing cable.

A launch set off from the dockside. Two sailors rowed while the bodies of several others appeared to be piled in the bilge. "Mr. Atkinson," the captain called. "Lower the Jacob's ladder and make ready a gantline. Some of our crew may need help coming aboard." Four of the sailors climbed easily from the launch up the ladder to the deck of *Lady Rebecca*. The next sailor made it halfway up before losing his grip, and had to be shoved up on deck by the sailor behind him. The final man was hoisted to the deck by the gantline tied under his arms.

"Make sure that last one is breathing, Mr. Atkinson. Rather that be sure we aren't paying for a corpse."

"Aye, Captain." The mate shook the comatose sailor, who raised his head. "He'll be fine," the mate called back.

Captain Barker shook his head and snorted. "Sailors these days." On his first voyage as apprentice, a crimp had sold the ship a sailor who appeared to be paralytic drunk. He was thrown into his bunk to sleep it off. Either the man then died or had been dead when he came aboard, because he never came to and the stench gave away his true state. For as long as he sailed as an officer, Barker had always made sure that the crew came aboard breathing, at the very least.

When the launch cast off, the tug throttled up with a belch of coal smoke and slowly the towers and chimneys of Cardiff faded in the summer haze as the *Lady Rebecca* stood into the wide Severn Estuary. In an hour, they had passed the protection of the sister islands, Flat Holm on the Welsh side and Steep Holm on the English, and stood on into the short chop of the Bristol Channel. To Will, Flat Holm looked like the back of a whale with a lighthouse rather incongruously perched near its head. The island looked to be a wild and barren place and he shuddered to think what it must be like for the patients shipped out to the cholera hospital on its rocky shore, to keep the sickness from spreading to Cardiff. Steep

Holm, in the distance, was more substantial, befitting its name. Oddly, in profile, it reminded Will of one of his mother's scones.

As they passed the islands, the southwesterly dropped and then shifted to the north, blowing clear and strong. Captain Barker shouted, "Mr. Rand, let's not waste this wind! Set all sails, 'cept the royals, flying jib, mains'l and cro'jack."

Mate Rand walked forward shouting orders. "All hands to make sail! Clear sheets and downhauls! Ready to cast off bunts and clews! Stand by halyards and sheets!"

Second Mate Atkinson joined in on the chorus as sailors ran to the pin rails, most not needing encouragement, though a kick or punch helped direct the slower movers.

The northerly wind had blown the haze away and soon the sails were replacing the white of the clouds against the sky. The lower tops'l sheets were hauled out, the upper tops'l yards were mastheaded and the sails sheeted home.

Second Mate Atkinson shouted, "Apprentices, overhaul the buntlines!"

Will stood by the mizzen shrouds and looked puzzled. Paul Nelson, the senior apprentice, laughed. "I'll show you how. Run to the stores locker and cut eight lengths of twine, about so long," he said holding his hands apart about eight inches. When Will just stood there, Paul said a bit louder, "Now, Mr. Jones. Now."

"Oh, aye, sir," Will muttered and ran to fetch the twine.

As the sailors hauled on the sheets and halyards, Captain Barker heard a sound that brought a smile to his face. Harry the Cornishman, at the mainmast rail, sang out,

"For I come from the world belooow."

The rest of the sailors along the halyard replied in chorus, *"Whiskey Johnny, Whiskey ooohhh."*

Harry sang back at them, *"For that is where the old cocks croooow."*

"Whiskey for my Johhnie, ooooh."

Harry sang another verse and sailors stomping around the capstan joined in on the chorus, as the heavy upper topsail yard crept skyward, the click of the capstan pawls helping to keep time with the shanty.

A crew that could sing a rope was likely a good crew. Surly sailors who hauled in silence were guaranteed to be trouble. Some captains considered not singing out to be outright insubordination. But here was Harry singing out in rare form. Like the northerly wind carrying them into the open ocean, it was all a good sign. Captain Barker was not one to pay undue attention to signs and portents, but he was loath to ignore them.

The *Lady Rebecca*, now on a beam reach, quickly began to overrun the tug, which swung farther out to try to keep some load on the towline while staying clear of the wake boiling off the sailing ship's bow. Captain Barker told the mate to signal the tug to end the tow. Crew on the fo's'c'le cast off the hawser, letting go the tug's cable. The tug captain waved at them and blew the customary three-whistle blast to wish them a fair voyage. Captain Barker faintly heard the tug captain yell, "Hope ye beat the German," as the tug dropped astern.

"That we shall," Captain Barker yelled back with a wave.

As the sun set, they hauled Lundy Island abeam and the great Atlantic lay before them. When the course was set sou'west and the yards squared, the mates called the crew aft to the break of the poop to choose the watches.

Fred Smythe and the other sailors lined up for inspection as the two mates stood on the poop deck, looking down at them with watchful eyes. The mates had seen the men working now for a few hours and each would choose which would serve in their watches for the rest of the voyage. Behind the mates stood the captain, imperiously—the king watching over his princes.

Whether it was better to be in the mate's or the second mate's watch had been an ongoing topic of conversation since the crew came aboard. Some thought that Rand would be tougher, while others thought Atkinson was too young—and that, as the captain's brother-in-law, he was more likely to be a bucko bruiser just to prove that he was up to the task. Fred had no particular opinion. He had seen good and bad mates in both ranks, and besides, as they would be choosing him and not the other way around, it hardly mattered what he thought.

Rand looked at the crowd and then at the articles. "Harry," he called out, his first pick. Harry moved over to the starboard side of the deck. An obvious choice, Fred thought. Every mate wants a good shantyman on his watch. Atkinson glanced at the articles. "Jensen," he shouted. The Dane moved to the port side of the deck. Not a bad choice either, it seemed to Fred.

Fred watched the mates and the remaining crew, gauging whether the officers valued skill and experience or just brute strength. There were never enough real sailors and, then again, there was never enough beef on a rope to haul the braces and halyards.

About halfway through, the mate called out "Smythe" and Fred took his place with the others to starboard. This suited Fred fine as his gear was already in a berth in the starboard side of the fo'c'sle house, so at least he didn't have to move his kit. And so the choosing went on, until everyone was chosen.

Best of all, by tradition, the captain's watch stood the first watch when the ship sailed. The captain, of course, didn't stand watches so the second mate did in his stead. The mate's watch took the first watch on the homebound voyage. Because he was in the mate's watch, it was Fred's time below, so he could try to get a few hours rest, if he was lucky, before he was due back on deck.

He glanced up again at the mainmast with its massive yards and endless acres of sail. The Frenchman had been right. Even in fine weather, all hands would be needed to tack or wear ship. The old clippers were a third the *Lady Rebecca*'s size and had crews of sixty or more men. The *Lady Rebecca* only had twenty seamen aboard. She was beauty to the eye, but a beast of a ship indeed.

The ship had begun a slow but steady roll in the first hint of the swells off the Bay of Biscay. The arc scribed by the masts across the sky reminded Fred of the pendulum of a clock. It was fitting. When he learned a bit of physics in college, he was awed by Newton's clockwork universe. Simple equations predicted the movement of the stars across the heavens, the rising and setting of the sun and moon, the spinning of the stars. The order and clarity of Newton's clockwork was both humbling and reassuring. Everything was in its place, the heavenly spheres dancing in perfect rhythm.

Ships reminded Fred of Newton. A ship was as reliable as clockwork. Now that the ship's watch-bill had been set, the watches would continue, day after day, week after week, month after month, until the *Lady Rebecca* finally made port. The sailors' lives would be ruled by five four-hour watches, broken only by the pair of two-hour dog watches that daily shifted their labor so that no watch was perpetually stuck in the same spot on the face of the clock. If they stood the morning watch one day, they would shift to the middle watch the next, and then the forenoon watch and so on, moving like the marionettes of a great clock tower on the main square of some Italian city-state.

The routine seemed to soothe the wildest of sailors. Days before, they had reveled in the chaos of their liberty, drunk, debauched and wild. They now settled into the reliable rhythm that they knew so well. Ashore they had been like shooting stars, burning brightly and then dying out. Now they returned to their places in the Newtonian order of the ship, watch on and watch off, day after day, across the limitless sea, beneath Newton's clockwork heaven.

Fred walked forward to the fo'c'sle house. The deckhouse was long and narrow just aft of the foremast, divided on its centerline by a bulkhead, creating two cabins, port and starboard, one for each watch. The deckhouse was considered more modern than the old t'gallant fo'c'sle where the bunks were squeezed in under the fo'c'sle head itself in the very eyes of the ship. At least, the crew was less likely to drown when the ship's bow dove beneath a head sea. With the deckhouse farther aft, the motion was slightly less violent, though it was more likely to flood when hit by breaking quartering seas. The house was lit by a single lantern shared by both cabins, hanging in a hole cut in the bulkhead, casting a smoky yellow glow, but no real light.

Fred elbowed his way through the sudden influx of crew to the upper berth where he had stowed his sea chest and his bedding. He was pleased to see that no one else had moved it to claim the berth for his own. He unrolled his donkey's breakfast, the thin mattress that would make the bunk only slightly softer than bare pine planks, and pulled his blanket from his sea chest. His spare blanket, rolled up, would make do as a pillow. He closed his sea chest and secured it beneath the mess table, where it would also serve as a bench when need be. He climbed up into the bunk, pulled a pencil from his pocket and in the shadows wrote "June 11, 1905" on the white-painted wood. Below it he drew a single vertical line. He would mark every day until their landfall, to help him keep track of time and to make sure that he was paid in full when the wages were calculated. With his housekeeping done, he stretched out in the bunk. There was too much commotion to sleep, but there was no reason that he shouldn't take his ease.

In a few minutes, a swarthy, barrel-shaped man took a lower bunk nearby. He poked his head up and said, "Jerry Papadopoulos," by way of greeting. Fred opened one eye, nodded and replied, "Fred Smythe."

Shaemus from Donegal, whom Fred knew as Donnie, a large Irishman with graying hair, settled into the upper berth just forward his own. He propped himself up and lit a small clay pipe. He was no more loquacious than most from that island nation. "Another voyage, me boys. Anyone willing to lay a wager as to how fast we make it to the line, or how quick we make it 'round?" He paused, but receiving no immediate response, continued, "Been around the Horn twelve times m'self. On the old *Clan Longworth* made it around from 50 south to 50 south in twelve days. Course, on the damned *City of Perth*, it took near enough a month and half." He puffed contently on his pipe for a few minutes.

"Now, there is only one way to sail 'round t' Horn, ye know. Got to grab the westerlies by the balls and just hold on. Then, every time the winds slacken just a wee bit and you get a favoring slant, you crowd on the bloody canvas and grab every inch afore the westerlies start snorting again."

Jerry the Greek looked over and said, "Why you telling us? Why not you go aft and makes sure the captain knows all your smart t'inking? Get us around Cape Stiff right quick. You just tell him hows it's done."

Donnie smiled as he puffed his pipe, the sweet smell of tobacco wafting over Fred's bunk. "If the Old Man needs my good counsel, he knows where to find me. Always happy to help out when I can."

Closer to the door, to catch the last light, Hanson, a Swedish sailor, sat on his sea chest and stitched a patch on a pair of overalls. Next to him was Tom, the Liverpool sailor, who was sitting reading a novel by Bulwer-Lytton.

A bit heavy on the melodrama for Fred's taste but perhaps worth swapping for one of the books in his limited library, buried in his sea chest, as the voyage progressed.

The ship was beginning to roll more deeply in the ocean swells, setting the lamp to guttering as it swung from side to side. At the other end of the fo'c'sle someone broke out a harmonica and began to play as Fred slipped off for a few minutes of sleep before his watch began.

Will and Jack were called aft to help the second mate heave the log. Will held the sandglass and Jack held the log spindle. "Twelve knots," announced Mr. Atkinson boisterously.

The captain, standing by the rail to windward, smiled. "A fine start to a fine voyage," he said to no one in particular. Mate Rand, near the wheel, grumbled, "Good starts often have bad ends."

The captain looked over sternly at his sullen mate, but his visage shifted to a smile and then to a laugh. Things were going too well to let the dour Mr. Rand spoil the day.

The *Judy Adams*, an ugly tub of a steamer that the captain recognized from Port Talbot, was steering to pass them to starboard, the master apparently confident that they would cross well ahead of the *Lady Rebecca*.

"Sir, the steam ship." The helmsman looked over to Mr. Rand, who looked at the captain.

"Hold your course," Captain Barker growled.

The steamer kept edging closer until she suddenly veered off to port, falling back to cross astern of the *Lady Rebecca*. Will could hear derisive laughter from the crew on deck.

The captain smiled and said, "Those smoke boxes think they own the sea. Well, not yet, anyway. Not yet. With the wind behind her, many a steamship'll taste the *Lady Rebecca*'s wake. And mark my words, as long as the wind keeps blowing, there will be sailing ships to sail on it. The wind is still cheaper than coal."

The northerly continued to build. When the bell struck, ending their watch, Jack and Will saw the cook and took plates of salt pork and sailor's biscuit for dinner back to the half-deck. They washed it all down with an oily, dark and hot liquid that the cook claimed was tea.

The ship was rolling along now in the long swells on a broad reach, with everything set save the royals. Even in the half-deck they could hear the hum of her wake beneath the sound of the wind, the low tune rising and falling as she charged from crest to trough.

Jack sat back against his sea chest, popped a square of tobacco into his mouth and started to chew. "Ye know, a sailor's life ain't as bad as they say, don'tcha think?"

Will opened his mouth to reply and then closed it quickly again. His stomach churned and his head spun. In an instant, he bolted for the half-deck door and stumbled across the deck to the leeward rail. He began to retch the net contents of what seemed his entire being from his toes to his nostrils into the rushing waters. He hung on, with his arms wrapped around the leeward stanchion. He wasn't sick. He was dying. He was sure of that.

When it was mostly past, he felt a strong hand on his shoulder. It was Jack. "Come on, old son, let's get you into your bunk. You'll feel better soon enough."

CHAPTER 5
TRADE WINDS, MOON MADNESS
AND GOATS

June 14, 1905 – Three days out of Cardiff

Will tumbled out with the rest of his watch at four a.m. After downing a mug of the cook's coffee, which tasted like burnt biscuit mixed with dirt and grease, they set about scrubbing down the deck. The *Lady Rebecca* was built of steel but her deck was still good English oak. They all rolled up their pant legs, threw their shoes on the hatch cover and set to work with brushes, sand and buckets of water to scrub the deck clean.

At first it was great fun, slipping around as the rinse water sloshed over the deck, but soon Will's shoulders began to hurt and his shins were severely bruised from sliding into the bulwark as the ship rolled. Within an hour, he was cold and very hungry; and the deck to be scrubbed seemed to grow larger the longer that they worked.

When the watch ended at eight a.m., Will dragged himself back to the breakfast, a large dollop of nearly tasteless burgoo, a biscuit and a steaming pannikin of tea. He tried to swallow the burgoo without chewing. The oatmeal and barley were coarse and gritty. "What do they put in this?" Will wondered.

"Maybe better not to know," Jack replied. "Coupl'a months, we'll likely run out and then you'll miss it."

Will took a drink of his tea and then spat. A sodden cockroach hit the deck. "That whore's son of a cook. There's cockroaches in this tea."

"There's always something in the tea. Dirt, wood chips, bugs. Just the way it is. Last trip an old sailor tried to convince me that the cockroaches were relatives of shrimp. Didn't believe him. Still don't. "

"Damned cockroach didn't taste anything like shrimp," Will replied.

Will wandered forward and found Fred at work parceling a shroud.

"The mate told me to find you," Will said.

"So you found me. What does the mate want?"

"I think he wants me to work with you. Said you should show me the ropes."

Fred looked up and raised an eyebrow. The Brits were an odd lot. The apprentice that stood before him had paid, or more likely his parents had paid, to get the position. As an apprentice, he earned practically nothing. He also probably knew practically nothing, yet if he completed his apprenticeship without getting himself killed or sinking the ship, he would most likely sit for an exam and be made second mate. On an American ship, any smart and tough A.B. could become mate anytime, so long as he was an American citizen.

And now, an underpaid seaman was supposed to train the apprentice who one day might lord over him as mate.

That was just the way Limeys did things. Fred shook his head.

Fred put down his serving mallet and looked at the young apprentice. "Ever parceled and served a shroud before?"

"No, sir."

"I'm Fred, not sir. Learn that right quick."

"Yes ... Fred."

Fred moved to a shroud that he had just stripped of tar, worn canvas and marline. The serving and parceling protected both the shroud and rigging that rubbed against the shroud from wear. As the shroud held the mast up against the force of the wind and the sea, Will agreed that it was a worthwhile project.

"First you take the marline and wind it in between the strands of the shroud. See how that makes it smoother?" Fred looked at Will, who nodded.

"That's called worming. Then you parcel. Hand me those strips of canvas. You wrap the canvas around the shroud, same direction as the lay. See the way I am doing it?"

Will nodded again as Fred tied off a piece of canvas. He picked up a tool that looked like a wooden mallet that had been cut out on one side to perfectly fit the diameter of the shroud.

"Then you use a serving mallet to wind the line around it tight, before you tie it off and tar it all over." He tied off a new section of marline on the shroud and pressed the mallet against the shroud. With the line wrapped around the handle, he wound the mallet around the shroud, pulling the line tight over the canvas parceling beneath.

"Got that?"

"I think so," Will replied.

"OK then. I have a poem for you to memorize:

Worm and parcel with the lay / Turn and serve the other way. Now repeat it."

With a moment's hesitation, Will did.

"Come on, then, you do it," Fred said, handing him the mallet. "The only way to learn."

For the next week, Will was Fred's shadow, copying everything the older sailor did. From casting off gaskets to furling sails and rolling the bunts, it wasn't long until he started to think he understood most of a sailor's work. For several watches, he stood next to Fred when it was his trick at the wheel, before he was allowed to steer the ship on his own, with Fred standing by to make sure the apprentice didn't broach the ship to, or leave them in irons.

That first week was its own kind of torture as Will's muscles ached, not yet acclimated to constant hauling and heaving. At first the soreness made it hard to sleep in his four hours off watch, until exhaustion finally overwhelmed the pain.

During the first dogwatch, Fred was showing Will how to tie a block mat from old junk that the ship's carpenter had given him. The mat was put under a block on deck to cushion it when the line went slack, so the block's pounding didn't mar the deck or hurt the block shell. It was simple and pleasant enough work, an initial pattern that kept repeating until the mat was big enough, finished off with a few twine stitches to hold it together.

Will looked up. "You sure know a lot about rope work, Fred."

Fred laughed. "I don't know a damn thing. If you want to see fancy work, you just watch Harry. Now he is a marlinspike sailor if there ever was one." He looked at his young charge. "In the afternoon watch, they have you working in the after house, don't they? What do they have you doing back there?"

Will shrugged. "What else? Cleaning. The cabin, chart room and the dayroom. Steward's got to keep his pantry and kitchen clean, but we do all else."

Fred looked out at the ocean. "I've always had an interest in navigating. How about you?"

"Most assuredly," Will replied. "Before signing on I spent two years at the Trinity School of Navigation. I look forward to putting my schooling to practice."

Fred smiled at the apprentice. "Well, when you find yourself cleaning the chart room, why don't you make a note of our position. Just for interest's sake. I like an idea where I am, from time to time. Would you do that for me?"

"All right," Will replied with a shrug.

June 22, 1905 – 12 days out of Cardiff

They had begun to pick up the northeasterly trade winds. The mornings were warm and the trades, steady on the quarter, were exactly the winds that the *Lady Rebecca* was built for. The sails were set to the t'gallants and they hadn't touched the braces for days. Fred loved to listen to the hypnotic hum of the wake, a steady and soothing hiss, as the miles slipped effortlessly beneath her keel.

In the afternoon, during the two dogwatches, all hands turned to, to sweat up the halyards and any other lines that had stretched in the previous day's sail. It was easy enough work as most lines were steel cable with hemp rope tails. Only the hemp stretched and there wasn't much of it. Harry took the forehand, and the men tailed the line behind him. He sang a favorite halyard shanty.

"*Oooh, Boney was a warrior, a way hey, a warrior, a terrier . . .*"

Fred sang along with gusto as they hauled in unison on the heavy hemp line, "*John François!*"

"*Oooh, Boney fought the Prussians, a way hey, the Austrians and Russhians ...*"

"*John François!*"

And so it went, at each of the three masts, until all the running rigging was taut again and the yards pressed snug against the blocks. As Fred walked forward, he glanced back at the captain watching imperiously from the break of the poop deck, the lord and master of them all. He could almost see a smile on the Old Man's face. Hell, why not, Fred thought, smiling himself as the mighty ship rolled on before the steady trade winds, the sails huge and white against the cloudless blue of the sky and far deeper blue of the sea.

After sweating up the lines, the crew spread out across the deck to enjoy the rest of the second dog watch. Fred sat leaning against the fo'c'sle deckhouse gazing idly up at the sails. In a moment, Donnie, who was sitting beside him, gave him a quick backhanded swat to his shoulder.

"What was that for?" Fred demanded.

"Quit yer looking at that upper topsail brace, " the old Irishman snorted.

"What do you mean?"

Donnie sighed. "The brace is slack. It could use some hauling. If you keep looking up at it like a mooncow, the mate will see you, look up himself and we'll be back up hauling on the brace, and I just set myself down."

Fred laughed and took one last look up at the rigging. Donnie was right. The brace was slack. He averted his gaze and looked out instead at the rolling sea, the waves a deep blue with foaming white crests. If the mate saw the slack brace, he wouldn't be blamed for it.

A short way away, Harry was sitting on the hatch coaming, working on a pair of fancy rope handles for his sea chest. Tom Jackson, the sailor from Liverpool, sauntered over. A stream of tobacco juice squirted from his lip, hitting the deck, just missing Harry's foot. Harry looked up at the tall young sailor.

"Would ya wipe that up for me, now?" Tom asked.

"Wipe it up ya'self. I'm busy," Harry replied, both his hands still occupied with his rope work.

"Now, that is na' friendly at all," Tom replied with an ominous smirk. He kept chewing the tobacco but his fists were clenched.

Fred, watching from a few paces away, had been wondering when the ritual would be played out. The community on a deep-sea ship was primitive. There was always a top dog. The cock of the watch. On some ships, an older sailor was simply deferred to. On others, a young tough would assert his claim. Harry was the experienced hand and a shantyman to boot, so he would naturally be the untitled leader of the watch, but Tom Jackson was the new young rooster. Along with the rest of the crew, Fred could only watch and see who came out on top.

Harry looked unconcerned. "Ya see, I ain't got a rag, so I canna help you."

Tom pulled a dirty rag from his pocket and dropped it at his feet. "Now, wipe it up, ya codger."

Harry smiled. "Ach. I've sailed long enough to know that t'ere is no point in scrapping." He put down his rope work and bent over to reach for the rag.

Tom grinned in triumph and looked around at the rest of the crew to make sure that they had seen his victory. The old man was afraid to fight. He as much as said so.

"You dropped your rag," Harry said. With remarkable speed for a man his size, Harry grabbed the rag in his large fist and sprang up to full standing, using the power of his legs as well as his massive shoulders, driving his fist under the young sailor's jaw. Tom was lifted off the deck, landing on his back near the bulwark. The crew burst into laughter and catcalls.

A moment later there was silence. Tom was not moving. Had the blow killed him?

After what seemed a very long time, Tom opened his eyes and moved his head slightly. He slowly opened and closed his jaw and then brought his hand gingerly alongside his face.

"Best be careful, youngster," Harry said, standing over him. "It's easy to get hurt. An' you dropped your rag." He tossed the rag on Tom's chest.

All eyes were on their horizontal shipmate. Would he spring up to fight the older sailor? Or would Harry give him a hard kick or two, break a few ribs, before he could get up? Fred realized that he was holding his breath. He exhaled slowly.

Instead, Tom chuckled. "'Right ye are. Never can be too careful." He raised his hand to be helped up and Harry took it warily and hauled Tom off the deck. Now was when Tom might start swinging again, if he hadn't learned his lesson, but instead he slapped Harry on the back. "You pack quite a punch and you're a damn sight faster than ya look, ya know." Tom went over to the tobacco juice on deck and scrubbed at it with his rag, then went back to his bunk, chastened and sore.

Harry resumed the work on his sea chest handles. He had finished one, which lay on the hatch cover next to him as he worked on the second. Santiago, who was sitting not far away, motioned at the finished handle. "Can I see?" Harry nodded. "Das as fine work as I've eve' seen," Santiago opined. Harry just nodded and kept working.

Jerry the Greek nudged Santiago, who passed him the handle, and so the handle made its way around the deck with each man expressing his admiration for the fine marline-spike work.

When the handle reached Fred, he turned it over in his hand. It was shaped like a large iron shackle, except much lighter and softer and adorned with beautifully detailed rope work. Harry had taken a length of three-quarter-inch rope, spliced both ends, then puddened the middle with layers of canvas to make it thicker. He covered the whole thing with four-strand coxcombing and Spanish hitching in white cod line, ending up with two three-stranded Turk's heads. He had then carefully bent the becket to shape. The handle "bolt" was leather-covered rope finished at each end with a star knot. Fred let out a low whistle of appreciation and then passed the handle to Donnie.

After a moment's careful examination, Donnie said, "A fine rope handle, to be sure. Pro'lly nobody on the ship could make one better. Course, I once sailed wit' a Frisian named Vanderploeg on the old *Mariana*. Now, he could make a set of handles, I'll tell you. Never seen any finer. Not that ter' is anyt'ing wrong with this handle, now, nothing at all, but the handles that Van made, well, they were near enough to breathtaking, with rose knots and coach whipping and wall and crown knots. Yes, sirree."

Harry got to his feet and walked over to the Irishman.

"Are you saying that I can't make a rope handle as well as a bloody Frisian? You saying a Frisian's better'n me?" Harry still had the marlinspike that he had been using to work the cord, clutched in his large right hand.

Donnie jumped to his feet. "Well, now, I ain't saying anything of the sort! Why would you even ask such a question?"

"All right, then," Harry replied, and snatched the finished handle from Donnie's hand.

"Good work there," Donnie said as Harry went back to where he had been sitting. Harry only snorted in reply.

Donnie sat back down and Fred turned to him. "Why did you do that?"

Donnie grinned. "Just having fun."

"You are lucky you didn't end up with that marlinspike in your gizzard."

"Ach," Donnie replied, "Harry's not a bad sort."

"True enough," Fred replied. "With others you might not have been so lucky."

"The skill, to be sure, is knowing which from which," Donnie said with a smile.

The mate bellowed from the break of the poop deck. "The watch! Take up on the upper main topsail brace!"

As they got to their feet, Donnie said, "Told ya not to be looking."

Fred laughed. "It wasn't me."

At midnight, Fred began his two-hour trick at the wheel. At first, Mr. Rand stood next to him with one eye on the compass and one on the sails. Fred only barely suppressed a grin. This was not his first time steering a sailing ship in the trade winds. In a few minutes, Mr. Rand strolled off to windward.

Somewhere forward, Fred heard a harmonica playing, in an odd but pleasing counterpoint to the drone of the sea and the creaking of the steel yards and rigging. An almost full moon filled half the sails with moonlight, and cast the other half in shadow, shifting back and forth as the ship rolled in the quartering sea. On a night like this Fred could imagine being no other place in the world. He held the wheel lightly, giving a spoke or two now and then in anticipation of the ship's movement, sailing by the set of the sails and by the compass glowing dimly in the binnacle. He reveled in the unimaginable power of the wind, the sea and the mighty steel ship that he could feel gently cradled in his hands on the wheel. The wind, on his back, whispered to him and the sea sang in its magical monotone. He knew that moments like these never lasted. The best never quite made up for the worst—whether icy winds and mountainous seas, or just the bad food, lousy wages and poor treatment. Yet for a short while, at least, none of that mattered, as he steered a mighty wind-ship across a rolling sea and star-strewn sky.

When relieved at the wheel, Fred was sent forward to spend the rest of the watch as lookout. As he rounded the deckhouse, a shadow leapt out toward him. He saw the flash of a knife blade cutting through the moonlight, inches from his throat. He jumped backward and grabbed his own knife from his belt, holding it out in the darkness against his phantom attacker.

But the attack never came. Fred saw a large man lunging about on the deck in the moonlight, fighting an unseen foe. Stepping warily closer, Fred recognized the Dane, Jensen, lurching and slashing at the darkness, cursing in what to Fred sounded like gibberish. Fred watched him for a moment, shook his head and crossed over to the leeward side of the ship.

At the fo'c'sle head, Fred relieved Tom Jackson. "That crazy Dane came near enough to slitting my throat. Son of a bitch."

Tom shook his head. "Yeah. Seen him dancing around. Pretty fair sailor, but crazy queer come the moon. Best give him a wide berth. If I see the mate, I'll tell him."

"You do that." Fred spent the rest of the watch looking out for other ships on the horizon and glancing over his shoulder, watching for a moon-mad Dane with a knife.

The next day, when Fred was off watch and it was near enough to dinnertime, he drifted aft to the galley and overheard the Jamaican cook, Jeremiah, pontificating, as he was prone to do. The large black cook seemed to think of himself as a prophet, yet never a happy one. He was always moaning of bad tidings, while the only bad tidings that Fred was aware of came from his kettles. He was a better preacher than a cook. Jeremiah spoke so often of the gospels that some in the crew were now calling him the ship's sky-pilot or the reverend instead of the doctor.

Jeremiah's voice carried beyond the cookhouse. "He a Jonah-man. That he be. Dancing around like a debil in the moonlight. Got the debil in his heart, that man. He be bringing down the bad spirits and foul winds on us afore this trip is over. Pray for salvation from the Lord on high. But with a debil aboard, maybe not even God Almighty hisself can save us. Mark my words."

Fred heard Harry's voice, "Shut your yammering, ya crazy fool. Don't need no talk like that. Talk like that's what brings the bad luck. That's for damn sure."

Later at the cabin table, as the watch gnawed on the salt horse and biscuit, the talk was of Jensen.

"So what? Most Danes are crazy, for sure," suggested Tony the Chileno. "Jensen's all right."

"Just might be sometin' to it, all the same," Otto Schmidt said. "Not smart to ignore bad spirits. Let's 'em sneak up on ya that way. A crazy man is bad enough, but a crazy man swinging a knife, that's somethin' else."

Harry shrugged. "I just don't like all the bad-mouthing of another sailor. Good thing that Jensen has na' temper. That black bastard talk like that 'bout me, I might slit him from gut to gizzard with his own stinking blade."

Otto pulled out his tobacco pouch, made of the foot of an albatross. Fred smiled. Otto was the most superstitious of the lot yet cared not a whit for the stories in books. Like most sailors, Otto was ready to catch and skin an albatross, the poet's verses be damned.

"Barker 'spose to be a lucky captain. Le's just hope his luck is wit' us," offered Tony.

"Sometimes, hope is all we got," nodded Harry.

Fred sat looking at his tin plate. The cook's talk about Jensen didn't bother him as much as the food the cook was serving. Never enough and what there was was bad. He had never sailed on a British ship before but had always heard that the limejuicers were bad feeders. He was beginning to understand just how bad.

Mary Barker finally sat down to the small writing desk in the cabin. The children were being watched by one of the apprentices and she had some time to herself. She took out her stationery, pen and ink and set about the letter that she had been meaning to start for days.

Ship Lady Rebecca   *June 25th, 1905*

Dearest Mother,

I had promised you and myself that I would write often. I have no idea when I might get the opportunity to mail this letter. If we happen to cross paths with a homeward bound ship, I might be able to post to you. Failing that, I will mail to you the letters I write in one bunch from Chile where they will be put aboard the first homeward bound steamer.

It is just as well that we have seen no other ship thus far, as this is the first time I have managed to put pen to paper since we sailed. The children and I were deathly seasick for the first two weeks of the voyage, the Channel chop and the Bay of Biscay being not agreeable to our land-lubberly dispositions. There is an old sailor's expression that you are not seasick if you think that you may die. You are only truly seasick, if you fear that you will not. Now that I have recovered, I can say that I was truly seasick, in those early days.

Those first two weeks, James was very busy with his duties as captain, but checked in on us as often as he could. Dear brother Thomas was also quite busy as Second Mate, but visited when off watch. I am afraid that the children and I were quite a burden to the steward, a light skinned black man named Walter, who showed us every kindness, as his duties permitted.

The Lady Rebecca has now reached the north-easterly trade winds and the world seems a different place all together. The seas still roll along but the motion is much easier. The sunshine and warmth has been a blessing. I heard an apprentice call these "barefoot seas," as their sea boots are put away and they pad around the decks and scamper aloft wholly unshod.

A shoal of dolphins kept company with us for much of yesterday, swimming along behind the ship, then darting up to play under and around the rudder. They have beak-like snouts and are all a silver grey that by some magic captures the sunlight in the water that flows around them, so that they seem cloaked in flowing sheets of myriad colours. I could watch them swim and play for hours.

Some of the sailors have taken to fishing. One or two good sized tunas have been hauled aboard, much to everyone's glee. The Jamaican cook prepared the fish for the crew with only his usual grumbling and sent a few fish steaks aft, which were delicious.

When the sailors catch a shark, they torment it most brutally. They won't eat shark on the chance that the beast has devoured some poor sailor and feasting on its flesh would make them cannibals, once removed. After cutting off the tail and the jaws they toss the evil thing back into the sea. They nail the tail fin to the end of the ship's jib-boom, the spar that extends beyond the bowsprit, as a warning to all other sharks. I am not sure whether I find their rituals savage or amusing. Perhaps some of each.

We have crossed schools of flying fish. The fish do really have wings or fins that are close enough to serve as wings. Their pectoral fins are broad and many times the width of their slender bodies. They shine in rainbow colours as they glide over the waters. We have had quite a few soar up over the rail and land flopping about on deck. Walter has cooked up several for us. The flesh is not altogether unpleasant but they do tend to be rather boney.

The children seem to have taken to the ship, becoming right little shellbacks. They have become very attached to one particular apprentice named Will, who has been designated their minder to give me an occasional hour or two off watch. I am not sure Will is overly pleased, but the children are happy, so am I as well.

The crew seems to have taken to the children as well. The deckhands are a rough-looking crowd but seem kind-hearted beneath all their grumbling and growling.

Just the other day, I was on the poop deck with James and the children when Pugsley, the sailmaker came to the break of the poop and asked permission to step up. Pugsley is much weather-worn and a bit stooped; a Scot from Peterhead, who always wears a battered bowler on his graying pate.

When James gave permission, he climbed the steps, nodded to James as captain and to me as his wife, but swept off his hat and bowed most gallantly before little Amanda, who immediately broke into a fit of giggles. He then laid at her feet a small package, wrapped in brown paper and twine. When Amanda tore the paper off, she squealed with delight. It was a doll, made of old canvas and stuffed with oakum. The hair is spun yarn and the eyes and mouth are just dabs of black and red paint. It is such a crude little thing and reeks horribly of tar, but Amanda loves it so. The tar might as well be perfume, the way she hugs it. Amanda is never seen on deck without "Mrs. Murphy," as she has named the doll. (I believed she named her doll after a family friend. I hope the real "Mrs. Murphy" never learns of her rather poor likeness.)

I must end this letter, as I hear the bells clang for the change of watch. I must relieve poor Will from his duties of minding the children. I miss you terribly and will try to write again soon.

Your loving daughter,
Mary

June 25, 1905 – 14 days out of Cardiff

After reducing his noon sun sight and plotting their position on the chart, Captain Barker returned to the poop deck with his telescope. Mr. Rand was on watch, standing at the break of the poop as the ship rolled on before the trades.

"Afternoon, Mr. Rand," Captain Barker said, in passing, as he walked to the weather mizzen ratlines. He tucked the collapsed telescope into his belt, swung out and began climbing up to the mizzen top. He usually sent an apprentice or even a mate aloft, but why not make the climb himself? Good to remind the crew that he was as fit as any of them and the day was too lovely to waste on the poop deck.

Once on the mizzen top, Captain Barker braced himself on a shroud, extended the telescope and looked out to the east. The dark smudges in the glass appeared where he expected them to be. The volcanic peaks that rose above the horizon were the Cape Verde Islands, 2,500 nautical miles from Cardiff. The largest should be Santiago, unless the *Lady Rebecca* was farther south than he thought and he was seeing Fogo, the highest of the volcanoes. As he swept the horizon with the glass, trying to get his bearings on the ten islands of the archipelago, a white blob obstructed his view. He refocused the glass and saw that it was the top-hamper of a ship. He couldn't see the deck, but it was four-masted and a barque.

Captain Barker laughed out loud. The rigging was exactly right. It had to be. He shouted down to the deck, "Mr. Rand, I do believe that I spy the *Susannah,* well to the east of us."

Atkinson came on deck, curious about the shouting. The captain called down, "Mr. Atkinson, could you join me aloft. I would value a second opinion."

When the second mate clambered up onto the platform, the captain handed him the telescope. "Tell me what you think."

After a moment's consideration, Atkinson said, "Well, she certainly could be the *Susannah*. The cut of the mizzen topsail looks German."

The captain nodded. "I checked the shipping press before we sailed. I think that is the only Kraut four-poster to sail from the coast anywhere near our departure. It has got to be her. We caught up and have a good bit of westing on her."

He took the telescope back and looked again toward the sails rising above the horizon. Nothing set above the t'gallants. He yelled down, "Mr. Rand, set the royals on the fore and main."

"Aye, sir," Rand yelled back. He turned to the deck and started shouting the orders to set the royals.

"If you'll excuse me, Captain," Mr. Atkinson said as he disappeared over the edge of the mizzen top.

Captain Barker looked down from the mizzen top. "So, we'll never catch the *Susannah*, is that what you said, Mr. Rand? We've caught her and now we'll show her our heels." He climbed back down the ratlines as the royals blossomed on the main and foremasts against the deep blue of a cloudless sky.

In fair weather of the trades, the captain agreed to give the three goats and half-dozen chickens the run of the ship. If they were to provide milk and eggs, he thought it better to free them from their pens. Jeremiah, the cook, was none too pleased when the bearded bandits stole biscuits, lard and old rags from his galley. He menaced them with a cleaver. "I'd cut your mangy heads off if'in you weren't de captain's goats," he shouted at them—a threat that seemed to have no effect whatsoever on the bearded children of Capricorn.

The goats also began raiding the off-watch fo'c'sle cabin, making meals of the foul-weather gear hanging on the pegs on the bulkhead. They also liked seaboots and dungarees.

Mr. Rand, seeming uncharacteristically jolly, came aft and spoke to the captain.

"Well, sir, your goats are giving you a guaranteed profit in your slop chest sales. Crew'll be buying lots of gear if the goats keep it up."

Captain Barker looked back at Rand. "Who did you assign to tend to them?

"John Lindstrom, comes from goat country in Norway, I hear."

"When was the last time he milked them?"

"I'm not sure. I'll check."

"Do so." The captain called for the carpenter. "Mr. Pugsley, please round up the goats and tie them where they will stay out of mischief."

Twenty minutes later, Lindstrom went to milk the goats. He carried a short stool, a rag and a bucket. Rand tagged along to make sure that the job was done. They found the goats tethered with twine just outside the bosun's locker.

On seeing their approach, one of the three goats stiffened, crouched and then launched into a sudden spring, breaking his twine leash and hurling itself headfirst at the mate. Its two other kinsmen followed suit, hitting Lindstrom and Mr. Rand right about amidships and knocking both down on the deck. Lying on his back, the mate bellowed for reinforcements. Soon, a tangled mass of sailors grappled for the three goats, who proved to be far more agile than they might have first appeared.

Curses, laughter and cries of pain rose from the squirming pile until all three goats were well and thoroughly secure. Disheveled sailors and the exhausted goats all splayed out on the deck catching their breath.

Lindstrom got up and found his stool and bucket, which had been kicked across the deck. He sat on the stool and placed the bucket under a now calm she-goat. Reaching below the beast, Lindstrom did what he could, but to no avail. Apparently a diet of oilskins, dungarees and rubber boots was not conducive to the production of milk.

The chickens were more productive. Set free to roam every morning at six, they returned to their pens on their own by six in the evening. Every morning the cook collected the eggs with an allotment going aft and the rest shared with the half-deck and the fo'c'sle.

The chickens took to the captain's son, Tommy, who liked to sit on deck surrounded by them at feeding time, grabbing as much of the chicken feed for himself as he could before his mother or Will stopped him.

Will grated at being the designated nursemaid, but he sincerely enjoyed keeping an eye on Amanda and little Tommy. At home he was the youngest, so having two children to watch out for was a new experience for the apprentice. Both children made him laugh. Tommy tottered around, not quite stable yet so close to the deck that he didn't fall hard or very often.

Amanda was feisty. Were it not for her gender, Will thought she would make a fine ship's captain. She knew how to assume command. She would take Will's hand and say, "Come along, Mr. William," as she took him below to have tea with Mrs. Murphy, the canvas doll that the sail maker had sewn for her. Tommy followed along behind to the mess room. Will gave Walter, the steward, a nasty look when he saw him grinning in the pantry.

Mr. Rand came to the captain's dayroom. "Getting complaints about a crazy man for'ard, Captain. Jensen, the Dane. Starts swinging at shadows from the lamp in the fo'c'sle with his knife and been doing queer things on deck in the moonlight."

"Do you think him dangerous?"

"Hard to tell, sir. Could be harmless, unless he hurts or kills someone."

"Thank you, Mr. Rand. I'll have a word with him. Send him aft when he is off watch."

Not long after Mr. Rand left the dayroom, Walter Gronberg, the ship's carpenter, stood on the threshold. "Scuse me, Captain."

"Yes Chips, come in."

"Thank you, sir. Doing my rounds. The coal in number two hatch is heating up. Just thought you should know."

The captain, who had been updating the log, put down his pen. "How hot is it getting?"

"Round a hundred and ten right now," the carpenter replied, checking his notebook.

"Could just be the warmer climate. Watch it and keep me informed."

"Yes, sir," the carpenter replied with a nod.

An hour later, the Dane was outside the captain's dayroom, twisting his cap in his hands.

"Come in, Jensen," the captain called out.

"You wanted to see me, sir?"

Captain Barker looked at the sailor, who had clearly been sailing for much of his life. His face was weathered and hard, though his eyes looked calm and almost kindly. The tattoos on his arms had faded a touch in the sun. The tattoo of the naked woman with the large breasts on his right arm suggested wild times ashore, hardly unusual among sailors. Barker had been watching Jensen. He was one of the best sailors in the crew—skilled, fast and hardworking. He would like a dozen more like him.

"Jensen, we sailed without a bosun. You seem to have all the knowledge required. Would you be interested in the job?"

The big man shook his head. "Ach, no, sir. Lots of fellers forward better qualified than me. Wouldn't be right. Hate to bother them about it."

The captain leaned forward. "Don't worry about anyone else. I think that you are qualified for the job and it is my decision to make, not theirs."

"Thank you, sir. I just couldn't. No. Think I best stay for'ard."

Captain Barker sighed to himself. Forward was where the problem was. If Jensen was bosun, he would bunk aft and the crew wouldn't have to worry about the Dane. It seemed an easy solution, but Jensen was having none of it.

"Tell me, Jensen, were you injured on any of your last ships?"

"Yah, on the *Daniella*." He raised a hand to the back of his head.

"What happened?"

"A toggle falls from the maintop and cracks me on mine *hoved*, my head."

The captain looked concerned. "Where you laid up long?"

"Was in my bunk a few times. Captain paid me off in Portland." His voice dropped until it was barely audible. "Captain said I was crazy."

"Have you felt oddly during this voyage?"

"Yah, sir," Jensen replied softly. "Sometimes, when the moon gets big."

Captain Barker sat silently for a moment. Jensen didn't seem dangerous, but who could tell?

"Jensen, if the moon or anything else gets to bothering you, come and tell me about it. I'll tell the mate that you have my permission. Will you do that for me?"

"Yes, sir," Jensen replied.

"Then, that will be all."

CHAPTER 6
DOLDRUMS AND CRACKER HASH

July 7, 1905 – 25 days out of Cardiff

The four apprentices sat around the long table in the half-deck. "I miss my mother's cooking," Will mused to himself.

Jack looked over. "What, you homesick already?"

"Nah, just hungry's all. Ma isn't much of a cook but least I was never pinch-bellied."

Jack hooted, and then looked ruefully at his own metal dish, empty now except for a piece of salt horse that was all gristle and bone.

Rations were set by law. It was all laid down in the articles, detailing the quantity and variety of food that had to be served up to sailors. But nothing in the law guaranteed the quality of the stores or whether the weight specified was all fat, bone or gristle, not fit for feeding to hogs. And then there was the skill, or lack thereof, of the cook, who could be relied upon to ruin even that portion that was edible. Will found that he was hungry most of the time.

That morning, it had been Will's turn to wait with a bread barge, a sort of oblong box, at the deckhouse door for the steward to dole out the day's allotment of "Liverpool pantiles." Nicknamed after a type of roofing tile, the hard-baked biscuits that would substitute for bread for the long voyage. Tom, a sailor from the off-watch, waited with his bread barge in hand as well.

Once he delivered the biscuits to the half-deck, Will fetched a billy of tea from the cook in the galley. Twice a week they got a bit of sugar and tinned milk, but they used that in a day, so they had only black stewed tea to wash down the chalk-dry biscuits.

Breakfast was burgoo, pantiles and tea, while the midday dinner was a measly piece of salt beef with pantiles. Pantiles and tea was the evening meal.

On Sundays and Thursdays, salt pork replaced the "salt horse," and each man got a boiled potato. Even early in the voyage, the spuds were rotten or sprouting. And when they ran out, there would be no more for the trip. The cook also made a dried pea soup, almost as gritty and tasteless as the burgoo.

The first few weeks hadn't been too bad. There had been eggs from the chickens but now the birds weren't doing so well. Sea life apparently didn't appeal to them. They had stopped laying and were losing their feathers. The consensus in the half-deck was that they would soon end up on the captain's table.

Jerry the Greek had been lucky with a fishing line, catching two fine tunas, so for a few days, everyone had a bit of fish, but now that they were leaving the trade winds, there was no time for fishing.

Once a week, on Tuesday in the first dogwatch, the slop chest—the ship's store—was open for business. The apprentices lined up with the rest of the crew. The business in oilskins and sea boots was brisk. The goats had eaten through many sets in the fo'c'sle. Each sailor's purchase was marked down in the steward's log to be deducted from his pay at sign-off.

The half-deck had so far resisted the goats' assault. Instead of gear, the apprentices pooled their miserably small slop-chest allotments to buy a pound tin of raspberry jam. The four rushed back to the half-deck, the senior apprentice, Paul Nelson, cradling their prize in his arms. They then took turns eating the jam a spoonful at a time. After the initial lust for sweets had been sated, they took the rest for cracker hash.

The recipe was easy. They took a steel belaying pin and crushed the four pantiles that they had left in a flat pan, picked out the weevils, and then stirred in the remaining jam. They then all marched forward, with Paul Nelson taking the lead, carrying the pan before him, stopping at the galley door where they most politely asked the cook to bake the hash in his oven. They waited outside, peering into the galley from time to time, praying that the oven wasn't too hot or that the cook didn't get too busy or their cracker hash would be burned to a crisp and it would be no use complaining.

Paul leaned tentatively across the threshold of the galley door. "Do you think that it might be ready now, cook?"

"Why you minding my business?" the black cook scowled. "I know what I am about. Be lookin' to your own business, not mine." Nevertheless, he took his rag, opened the oven door and pulled out a perfectly cooked cracker hash. After a minute's cooling, the delicacy was bundled back aft where it was divided evenly.

The jaw-breaking biscuits were now soft and saturated in sweetness. It was the most delicious, glorious repast Will could remember or imagine, surely close enough to ambrosia. In a few minutes the watch bell rang and Paul and Charlie tumbled out on watch. Will stretched out in his bunk and dreamed of cracker hash.

One evening at suppertime, after settling into the meager fare, Will was surprised when Paul Nelson told them all to get cleaned up.

"Put on your best bib and tucker," he said. "And scrub your hands and faces. Tonight, we have been invited to dine with the captain and his family in the mess room."

The apprentices cheered. Will knew that the captain had to be eating far better than they were.

"Dining in the mess room. Ho ha," George said, then turning to Will in a lowered voice, "or should we call that the lady's tearoom? Will Mrs. Murphy be there?"

Will elbowed him hard in the ribs.

"And after dinner, we will provide the evening's entertainment," Paul continued.

"We will?" Will asked.

Paul chuckled. "We are all going to sing for the captain and his wife. A command performance."

"Sing? I can't sing ... well, I can't sing ... very well," Will stammered.

"So?" Paul replied. "We are the closest thing this ship has to a gramophone."

Jack came over. "Don't worry, Will. You'll do fine. 'Course, last trip they did throw poor Johnny overboard when he got too frightened to sing. Isn't that right, Paul?"

Paul swatted Jack with the back of his hand. Jack only laughed. "Come on, get cleaned up. We can't keep the captain and his lady waiting."

In a few minutes, the four apprentices trooped into the mess room, their hands and faces washed and their togs reasonably clean. The old ship had once carried cabin passengers, so there was plenty of room at the table. Captain Barker sat at one end and wore a shirt with a collar and a tie, while his wife, Mary, sat next to him, wearing a blue dress and short jacket. Mate Rand and Second Mate Atkinson sat on the other side of the captain. Will worried for a moment who was watching out for Amanda and little Tommy, who were not present, but any thoughts of his charges drifted from his thoughts as he caught a whiff of the smells from the galley. The aroma was intoxicating. One or more of the chickens had ended its days in a cook pot.

As the youngest apprentice, the lowest in rank at the table, Will was served last. When his plate finally arrived, he breathed deeply and then dug in. The chicken thigh wasn't large but it was nestled between an ample portion of canned peas and potatoes. They had scarcely been at sea a fortnight, yet it seemed like years since Will had tasted chicken, peas and potatoes. He slowed his pace to savor the meal.

The conversation was polite but limited. The captain asked Paul several questions on his impressions of the how the ship was sailing and suggestions regarding changes to the rigging, which, as senior apprentice, Paul handled nicely. At one point the captain even spoke to Will to ask, "And how are you doing, young man?" Fortunately, Will was between bites so he could reply, "Very well, sir. Thank you," without the risk of choking or spewing out his peas.

After dinner the mates went back on duty and the rest went into the main cabin, where the apprentices stood lined up against the bulkhead. Captain Barker and his wife were seated in chairs facing them. To Will it felt a bit like being on the wrong end of a firing squad.

"Thank you, gentlemen, for joining us this evening," the captain said graciously. Will wondered whether he heard a touch of sarcasm in the tone, though wasn't sure. Mary Barker smiled beneficently at them. She was a lovely woman. Will had decided that at the start of the voyage and nothing in her manner had changed his opinion since.

Paul began with a version of "Southern Moon." Will had had no idea that Paul had such a nice voice and was immediately afraid that he would croak like a lovesick frog when his turn came. Everyone clapped when Paul was through. Jack sang a spirited version of "There's an Old Mill by the Stream, Nellie Dean." His voice wasn't as rich as Paul's but his enthusiasm made up for it. Everyone clapped for him too. George warbled through "My Wild Irish Rose." He wasn't much of a singer, but there was polite applause, nevertheless. Will didn't think of George as much of a sailor either, so he was pleased that he was no more skilled as a songbird.

Now, it was Will's turn. He wasn't sure what to sing. Every song he knew seemed to have fled from his mind. After an uncomfortable moment of silence, he sang the only thing he could remember, his mother's favorite song, which she used to sing to him as a child,

After the ball is over, after the break of morn,
After the dancers' leaving, after the stars are gone,
Many a heart is aching, if you could read them all …

When he miraculously made it through, he was surprised by the clapping. Mrs. Barker said, "Oh, William. I do so love that old song. Thank you." Will could feel his face flush, but managed to smile and nod.

For their musical efforts, they were rewarded with chocolate cake that Walter had baked that afternoon. Sitting at the table, making sure to catch each and every crumb, Will looked at the cabin rug, the upholstered chairs and the paneling on the bulkheads and was amazed by the vast distance between the captain's cabin and the half-deck, even though they were separated only by tens of feet.

A few days later, when they came on watch Pugsley called Will and Jack to the mess room. He had a roll of heavy canvas, two pairs of shears, waxed twine, needles, and several canvas patterns laid out on the table.

"What's this?" asked Will.

"Our new supply of oilskins," the sail maker beamed.

"Oilskins?"

"Yes, indeed," Puglsey replied. "Our friends, the goats, have eaten into the slop-chest supplies and the captain doesn't want to round Cape Stiff without a supply of spare skins. So have a seat, gents, and we'll get started."

Pugsley rolled the canvas out on the table. While Will and Jack held the canvas tight, Pugsley traced out the front, back and sleeves of the oilskin jackets, and then began on the pants. When he had four pair marked out, he handed Will and Jack the shears and told them to start cutting.

"Make it neat, boys. I don't wanna be sewing no ragged edges." With that, he nodded and left the mess room.

The shears were sharp but Will's hand was aching after cutting out the first jacket. But he kept cutting.

"Rather be hauling on a brace," Jack murmured softly. Will snorted in agreement.

Pugsley came back to the mess room with a steaming cup of coffee. "How are we doing, laddies?"

He picked up the cut canvas sections, turned them over, and said, "Hmmn, not bad—keep cutting. My turn to get to work."

Pugsley picked up the twine, a heavy needle and a sailor's palm, and began stitching the panels together. He used a wooden rubber to fold the seams over, so that when he stitched them there were no rough edges. Will was amazed at the speed of the sail maker's stitching. All the stitches were even and in perfect alignment. Puglsey looked up and said, "Mind to the cutting, William."

When all the panels were cut, Pugsley put down his sewing and said, "Follow me, gents."

In the galley, a large pot of boiling linseed oil was on the stove. Will and Jack wrinkled their noses at the smell. An oilcloth was spread over the small space on the deck. Puglesy gave each apprentice a stick with a rag wrapped around the end and said, "Rub the pants and jackets with oil. Now, don't go burning ye'rselves, and make sure you get everything covered well. Pay attention to the seams. Else, you just might find yourselves wearing leaking oilskins one day. Hang 'em up to dry over there, when you are done. "

Before they had done with one set, Pugsley brought in another. When Will and Jack finally stumbled out onto deck they breathed deeply the sweet salt air. Pugsley called after them, "Turn to tomorrow to put on another coat. The skins need two more coats of oil."

When they were finally finished, Will was pleased with his handiwork. The oilskins were softer than the black waxy oilskins sold by the chandlers, which always seemed to crack after moderate use. There was something satisfying in seeing work well done. Looking down at his linseed-stained hands, he also hoped that he never had to make another pair of oilskins as long as he lived.

Fred and Tom were in the fo'c'sle discussing books. Tom was a great fan of Edward Bulwer-Lytton, whereas Fred loved Twain. After lengthy negotiations they agreed to exchange favorites with the solemn promise of return when each finished reading. Fred took Tom's copy of *Last Days of Pompeii* in exchange for Fred's well-worn edition of *Huckleberry Finn*.

Just as the transaction was completed, Mate Rand wandered through the fo'c'sle cabin door and sat down heavily on a sea chest. He took out his clay pipe, filled it with a bit of tobacco and began to smoke. Lindstrom, who had been in his bunk, swung down and sat next to Rand, who shared his tobacco. They talked quietly.

Tom, who was stowing the borrowed book in his sea chest, glanced sideways at Fred and mumbled beneath his breath, "No place for a bloody mate." Fred scowled.

"Sailed afore the mast for so long he still thinks the fo'c'sle is his home. No wonder he never made captain," Tom whispered.

Fred climbed into his bunk. Tom shrugged and went out on deck, saying, "Good afternoon, Mr. Mate," as he passed. His slight emphasis on the honorific "mister" apparently went unnoticed.

Fred opened the Bulwer-Lytton and began reading.

BOOK THE FIRST—Chapter I
THE TWO GENTLEMEN OF POMPEII.

'Ho, Diomed, well met! Do you sup with Glaucus to-night?' said a young man of small stature, who wore his tunic in those loose and effeminate folds which proved him to be a gentleman and a coxcomb.

'Alas, no! dear Clodius; he has not invited me,' replied Diomed, a man of portly frame and of middle age. 'By Pollux, a scurvy trick! for they say his suppers are the best in Pompeii'.

Fred groaned inwardly. He'd traded Twain for this? Still, any book was better than none. He put down *The Last Days of Pompeii*, dug into a canvas bag and pulled out his journal and pocket atlas. He opened the atlas to the Atlantic. With the positions that Will had given him, Fred had plotted the ship's course as accurately as he could, given the small size of the atlas page and the dullness of his pencil. The *Lady Rebecca* was making good distance in the trades. Fred traced his finger down their likely course, across the equator and down the South American coast. His finger came to rest on Cape Horn. What was waiting for them in those dangerous waters? He smiled to himself, closed the atlas and restowed it in his bag.

He had to be a little careful with his keeping track of the ship's position. By the customs and traditions of the sea, the crew were not supposed to know the position of the ship or look in on the ship's navigation. Crew that could navigate and knew the ship's position might mutiny. Fred was no mutineer. He just liked understanding where they were in the voyage.

He jumped down from his bunk and looked back at Mate Rand talking quietly with Lindstrom. If a mutiny was brewing, that is where it would start—a mate spending too much time where he had no business being, talking softly, conspiratorially, to a deckhand. Perhaps he was reading too much into it, Fred thought. It would bear watching.

Fred only thought of mutiny during the mid-day meal, when he did his best to chew the gristle that by law was supposed to be beef or pork and soaked his weevily biscuit in his tea so it became soft enough to eat.

They had sailed beyond the trade winds into the doldrums, the fluky band of confused wind or no wind at all, just north of the equator. At six a.m., rather than scrubbing down the decks as usual, all hands were called aft. Pugsley and the apprentices were hauling out the light-air sails from the sail locker. Fred groaned to himself, though the day was no surprise. He had wondered how long the Old Man would carry on before shifting the suit of sails.

Rand shouted out, "Starboard watch, the main mast. Port watch, the fore. Take one down and put one up. Now, jump to it, you lazy buggers."

Fred and the rest of his watch clambered up the ratlines. They were striking the heavy-weather sails and setting the old and patched light-air sails. Every roband, halyard, sheet, outhaul, downhaul, buntline, gantline, lift and clewline for each of the seventeen square sails and nine jibs, staysails and spanker would have to be cast off, and then the heavy canvas sails would have to be lowered to the deck and the old set of sails hauled up, with every line rerun and secured—all the robands retied, and all the sheets, tacks, bunts and clewlines run fair. It was going to be a long and brutal day.

It would have taken half as long and been twice as easy if the Old Man had let them strike all the sails at one time, lowering them all to the deck and then setting the new, but that was not his intention. The captain wanted one sail struck and then reset so he wouldn't lose any time. In the light airs the ship must have been barely making three knots, so it wouldn't have made much difference, but no, the Old Man would keep the ship sailing as fast he could manage, no matter how much sweat and toil he had to squeeze from his small crew. Fred was growing to loathe the captain, perpetually lording over them from the break of the poop deck, but he just clenched his jaw and set to work. There was no other choice.

Will knew something was up but couldn't quite tell what it was. Too many sidewards glances during the first dogwatch, too many whispers and scurrying about. The captain, mate and second mate were all on the poop deck. Mr. Atkinson raised his spyglass to his eye and cried out, "I believe I spy a ship, sir." Will stared out at the empty ocean and saw nothing.

Captain Barker replied, "I do believe that is King Neptune's ship."

In an instant Will knew what was happening and felt more the fool for not figuring it out. They had reached the equator. They had crossed the line. Just as the realization hit him, he was grabbed from behind by two pair of strong hands and dragged toward number one hatch.

Will suddenly noticed that two bosun's ladders had been hung over the sides, port and starboard. From starboard, a huge creature was coming aboard, apparently climbing out of the sea itself. He was blue, with a beard of green seaweed, and he wore a rough crown made of wood and wire. He carried a large staff with what looked like a starfish at its end. He marched from the rail to midships just before the mainmast. It took Will a second, but he recognized Harry in the outlandish garb—bare-chested and painted blue, but Harry all the same.

The captain bellowed from the poop, "All hail King Neptune." The crew hooted and yelled their approbation.

From the port ladder, a second creature climbed aboard. He wore a huge green mustache and an approximation of an admiral's hat. Will recognized Jensen. Then the strangest creature appeared from around the back of the fo'c'sle house. It appeared to be a woman, as blue as King Neptune but with long flowing rope-yarn hair. Her breasts appeared to be coils of rope and she wore a flowing skirt of painted canvas. Beneath the face paint and rope wig, Will recognized Donnie.

"All Hail Davy Jones and Her Highness Queen Amphitrite," the captain shouted. The crew cheered louder still.

Davy Jones bowed deeply, and then took the Queen's hand and stood beside the king. Neptune glanced at his attendants, scanned the deck and sniffed the air. He pounded his staff on the deck and cried out, "I smell slimy pollywogs. Bring them out. We'll scrub 'em clean and make proper shellbacks of 'em."

A moment later, two sailors dragged Fred out to stand behind Will. The only two sailors aboard who had never crossed the equator, they were the ship's slimy pollywogs.

"What in hell," Fred mumbled.

"Pollywogs, be silent," Neptune bellowed. "Step forward."

Will felt someone shove him from behind. Someone shoved Fred as well, who bumped into Will and almost knocked him down.

"What is your name, pollywog?" Neptune demanded, pointing at Will with his scepter.

"Will—"

As soon as he opened his mouth someone stepped up behind him and shoved a paintbrush laden with soap, tallow and tar into his mouth. He choked and spat as the deckhands cheered. His face was lathered with the wretched mix and someone was shaving him with a rusty razor, though he had little enough beard to shave.

Neptune demanded Fred's name as well, but Fred kept his mouth shut until someone behind him grabbed his jaw and shoved a frothy, stinking paintbrush into his mouth as well, sending him gagging to the deck.

Someone tied a gantline from the main yardarm around Will's waist. Suddenly, brutally, he found himself hoisted up off the deck, flying up and outboard until just as suddenly he was dropped into the sea. He flailed in the water for only a moment until the gantline was yanked again and he flew up once more, only to be dunked again and again. Then, like a huge fish at the end of a line, he was hauled back in and dumped on deck. Partially blinded by the soap and slush smeared on his face and by the saltwater stinging his eyes, he could just make out that Fred was receiving the same treatment on the port side of the ship.

What happened next was a blur of dumping water over their heads, and their backs being hit with old rope and stinking mops. And all the while, his ears were filled with wild hooting and chanting from the rest of the crew.

The torment seemed to go on endlessly. When it finally stopped, a very battered Will and Fred were hauled before King Neptune, who tapped their shoulders with his staff and dubbed them "Trusty Shellbacks and the True Sons of Neptune," to the cheering of the crew. The cheering continued when Captain Barker ordered the steward to issue out a tot of rum to the crew, trusty shellbacks all.

"Well, I am an ass," Fred said to Will. "I mentioned to Tony that I had never crossed the line. Should'a kept my mouth shut."

After the sailors' heaven of the trade winds, the doldrums were a maddening purgatory. The days were insufferably hot. The wind was light and shifting, when it blew at all. The sun baked them as they spent all day hauling the sheets and braces to catch every breeze, every williwaw, every faint breath of wind. The afternoons often brought blinding, warm rain but no wind. When the squalls passed, steam rose from the deck as the sun again baked down on them. The nights seemed almost as hot as the days as they labored watch by watch. By the end of the first week, tempers began to flare. Accidental slights became grave insults. Lindstrom and Tony came to blows over a misplaced step and a dropped knife. Even Harry and Jensen sang the shanties listlessly, if at all, at the endless heaving round of the yards. And when the wind died all together there was nothing to be done but wait. And wait they did for days at a time.

Fred slumped against the deckhouse. He had been on windbound ships before, along the coast, where there was no choice but to anchor and wait for the return of a breeze. The doldrums were different.

It was as if they had sailed off the edge of the earth. The sea was a perfect mirror. The *Lady Rebecca*'s masts soared both skyward and seaward, her image reflecting as crisp and clear looking down as looking up. They could have been as easily floating on the sky as on the sea, the heavens both below and above with the horizon lost in the haze.

The only sound was the soft flapping of the sails and the squeaking of blocks. Conversations seemed to have drifted away on the last of the breeze. Were it not for someone humming softly to himself, Fred might have thought himself entirely alone on the ship. The Ancient Mariner came to mind.

> *Day after day, day after day,*
> *We stuck, nor breath nor motion;*
> *As idle as a painted ship*
> *Upon a painted ocean.*

He whispered the words to himself, not daring disturb the silence. After an hour or so of simply starring out at the vast emptiness, the image before him began to ripple and he felt a hint of a cooling breath wash across his face.

Mr. Rand from the poop deck bellowed, "Square the cro'jack." Fred jumped to his feet, joined by the rest of the watch emerging from their resting places, scrambling to haul the braces to swing the yard around to catch the tiniest hint of a breeze.

Once the sails were trimmed, the breeze that for a few moments seemed so promising died away again as quietly as it had arrived.

A bit less than a fortnight after entering the doldrums, Captain Baker came on deck just as dawn was coloring the western sky, and he knew. The winds were still faint but he could feel it in the swell and see it the bank of clouds off their port quarter. He could almost taste the southeasterly trades. He was sure that the royals and t'gans'ls would be feeling them soon. By noon all sails were full and drawing. The wind was still light but the *Lady Rebecca* was again gliding off to the southwest.

The winds grew steady. They had reached the southerly trades at last. In a day's time Captain Barker ordered the light-air sails struck and the heavy-weather sails set once again. The crew grumbled and growled but worked with a will. The southeasterly trades renewed their spirits. The petty arguments and feuds fed by the doldrums seemed to have blown away on the fresh and bracing trades.

Three days later, a grim-faced Rand and the carpenter, Gronberg, pounded on the captain's cabin door. When they stepped inside, Gronberg was holding a shattered glass tube.

"What do you have there, Chips?"

"The thermometer from number two hatch, sir. Burst from the heat."

The captain stood speechless for an instant.

Rand spoke up. "The coal in hatch two is burning. The ship's afire, sir."

CHAPTER 7
FIRE DOWN BELOW

July 24, 1905 – 43 days out of Cardiff

C aptain Barker climbed the ladder to the poop deck, followed by the mate and the carpenter. He was surprised to see a dozen pair of eyes looking up toward him. Half the crew had drifted aft and stood in silence, watching. Had the carpenter talked about the fire or had the mate? He had sailed two trips with Gronberg and knew the carpenter to be a tight-lipped old Kraut, if there ever was one. It had to have been the mate.

With more than half the crew watching him, Captain Barker knew he had to act decisively. He always preferred a frontal assault. "Mr. Rand, call all hands and work the coal out of number two hatch till you come to the seat of the fire. Pile the coal on deck and keep clear of the pin rails. I want not a single pound lost over the side. Do you understand me?"

There was a moment of silence as the mate glared at the captain.

"No, sir. I will not." Rand replied. "No, sir. Rio de Janeiro is only a hundred miles to leeward. If we square the yards and run for the port, we can be there tomorrow. I sure as hell won't sail this ship round Cape Stiff with a bellyful of burning coal. And that goes for every man jack aboard. All I have to do is say the word and they's with me."

Diverting to Rio would cost them both time and money. The gang bosses would gouge the ship for all they could. Nothing like a smoldering hold to drive the price of shore labor skyward. The voyage would be sure to be a loss, once the vultures got through with them. But money was the least of it. A mate didn't give orders to a captain. Ever. To do so was mutiny, plain and simple.

Captain Barker opened his mouth to speak, but was simply too filled with rage. A fire in the hold was bad, but mutiny was far worse. He turned and strode below to his cabin, where his wife was sewing, as the children played on the cabin sole. He unlocked a cabinet drawer and took out a pair of loaded pistols.

"Hello, James. What are you doing?" she asked, seeing the revolvers in his hands.

"I've business to attend to," he snapped. He stormed out, not bothering to close the door behind him.

When he reached the poop deck, the carpenter had returned to the main deck and Rand was standing, looking forward, apparently serene. He had stood up to the captain and the captain had backed down. Or so he thought.

"Mr. Rand," Captain Barker roared.

"Yes, Captain," Rand replied, turning, only to find the barrels of both pistols jammed into his stomach.

"A few minutes ago, I gave you an order, mister. When I give an order, it is to be obeyed." He shoved the guns for emphasis. "Do you understand me, Mr. Rand?"

The mate was now visibly pale, the color seeming to have drained from his tanned face.

"Yes, sir," he replied softly.

"Now, mister, will you sail around Cape Horn on this ship or are you still thinking of Rio?"

"I'll sail with you, Captain."

"Good, because I'll see you in hell before you disobey another order of mine." The captain stepped back and lowered the pistols.

"Now, call all hands and get to work. You know my orders."

"Yes, sir," the mate replied sullenly. Then he turned, and as if nothing had happened, bellowed, with a will, "All hands, all hands."

Captain Barker stood watching the mate. A moment before he had threatened mutiny and now he rousted out the crew as if nothing had happened. The captain wondered whether he would be fighting his first officer as well as the cargo, the wind and the sea all the way around Cape Horn.

Fire. The word had spread in the fo'c'sle like a flame in dry grass. Mr. Rand had told a few men in each watch and soon everyone knew.

Fire. There were few things on shipboard more terrifying. Like the rest, Fred knew the stories too well. Would they end up like the *Cospatrick* that sailed from London for New Zealand in 1874? She caught fire in the lonely South Atlantic and of the nearly five hundred emigrants and forty crew, only three souls were found alive, badly burned, drifting in a lifeboat. The stories the survivors told were too horrible to think about, especially with a fire smoldering somewhere beneath the coal in number two hatch.

Fred stood with the rest just forward of the main mast, looking aft. They couldn't hear what was being said on the poop deck but they could see the pistols in the captain's hands. Fred had kept a running plot of their position in his notebook. They were not far off the Brazilian coast. They could be safe in port in a day. Rand had boasted in the fo'c'sle that he would make the Old Man change course for Brazil. It didn't look like the captain was taking Rand's advice. If the ship was going to burn, they would all go with it.

"I don't think that we will be sailing for Rio," Fred mused to Donnie, who was standing next to him. 'What'dya think the captain will do? Flood the hold?"

The Irishman laughed. "Sure enough, that'd be one way to fight a fire. Sink the bloody ship and the fire goes out. Wouldn't be my first recommendation, however."

Fred looked at Donnie, annoyed. Now did not seem to be the time for sarcasm.

"Then what would you recommend? How would you put the fire out?" Fred asked.

"Well, there are mostly two choices. You could button up all the vents. Seal every opening and try to cut off the oxygen to the fire. Smother it. A good choice, unless it doesn't work and the fire keeps spreading and gets completely out of control."

"And the other choice?"

"You go at it head on. Throw off the hatches and dig down to the hot spot. 'Course, you do that, you are letting a lot of oxygen straight into the fire, which could set it burning hotter and faster."

"So what's the answer?" Fred asked.

"Don't never be on a ship afire," Donnie replied.

"Sounds like good advice," Fred said. "I'll remember that for future reference."

Mr. Rand came bounding down the poop deck ladder as if nothing out of the ordinary had just taken place, as if every order he had ever received was punctuated by the poke of a pistol barrel in his gut.

"Rig a tackle, gantline and vang to the mainstay," he bellowed. "Get baskets and shovels." They all jumped to the flurry of orders. Shovels used for shifting ballast were hauled out of bosun's stores beneath the fo'c'sle head, as were heavy cargo baskets. Pugsley and two sailors hauled out tarpaulins to spread on the deck.

Finally, all that could be done was done, save the opening of the hatch. They all stood around, looking at the covered rectangle but not daring to move closer. Finally, Mr. Rand pushed through the crowd of sailors and swung a mallet to break out the hatch wedges. He pulled back the canvas covering the hatch covers. Tossing away his mallet, he yanked the first hatch cover up, and with an angry shout, tossed it aside.

A column of smoke rose from the hold, white and boiling like a genie from a bottle, and the crew all took a step back.

"Get to work, you lazy bastards," Rand roared. "Get the other covers off and start digging, you motherless whores. Put out the fire or burn in hell with it."

Fred walked over and grabbed one handle of a hatch cover as Jerry the Greek grabbed the other. They both lifted and pulled the pine cover free. Others followed suit, hoisting the covers and shifting the cover braces until they revealed the hot, black and shining coal, with faint wisps of smoke escaping from the obsidian surface.

Gronberg, the carpenter, jumped into the open hatch with a bundle of thin, threaded iron pipes and a mallet. He pounded a length of pipe down into the coal, and then threaded on another and kept pounding until the bottom of the pipe reached the depth he wanted. He carefully lowered down the spare thermometer. He methodically recorded the temperature in his notebook, then began pulling up the sounding piped to move to another spot. Not a word was spoken on deck while Gronberg worked, pounding down the pipes and taking temperatures, working from one end of the hold to the other. The only sound was the ring of his hammer on iron pipe, the relentless drone of the wind and the creaking of the rigging. Finally he looked up. "Mr. Mate," he said at a half a shout, "except for the starboard aft corner, the cargo is cool enough. Starboard aft—that is where fire is."

One of the apprentices let out a whoop, before being silenced by a quick jab from the senior apprentice, Paul Nelson. When Fred looked over he saw Captain Barker, still standing at the break of the poop deck, the distant king watching his servants closely.

"All right, finish rigging the gun tackle and drag those baskets over here." If Mr. Rand was aware of the captain looking over his shoulder, he gave no sign of it. "Eight men with shovels digging, six hauling on the gantline, four piling the coal with hand trucks and two with buckets to cool it down. Now get to work. This weather may not last."

Pugsley rigged the tackle over the hatch from the mainstay. A heavy gantline with a hook at one end was rove through the block and led down to a block at the hatch coaming. Fred, Tom, Harry and three others were on the heaving line as three apprentices and three sailors clambered in the hold with their shovels. Fred and the rest lowered two round baskets, each four feet in diameter made of bent wood with steel straps, on the gantline hook into the hold and were surprised how fast the first was full when they heard the command "heave away."

Harry started up the shanty and all on the line grinned at his choice of song when they heard the first line. They all hauled on the alternate beats.

"*She was just a village maiden with a fair and rosy cheek...*"

All joined in, singing, "*to-me way hay he-hi-ho.*"

"*She went to church on Sunday and she sang those anthems sweet...*"

Then with gusto they all sang the chorus:

"*And there's fire, down below.*"

The heavy basket rose from the hold and Otto and Santiago hauled on the vang to swing it over the tarp on deck, where they dumped it. They swung it back over the hold and lowered it, just in time to begin all over again and haul up the second basket. In the meantime, Otto and Santiago started shoveling the coal into a pile near the hatch coaming while two apprentices doused the coal with buckets of seawater.

"*There's fire in the fo'c'sle and the coal is the crew,*
Oh there's fire down below."

In the short breaks between hauling up the coal, Fred kept looking forward at the shape tied up in canvas just aft of the fo'c'sle head. He knew there was a perfectly good steam engine sitting idle that could haul the coal up from the hold. Donnie saw him looking and shook his head. "You'd think the Old Man would let us fire up the donkey boiler and steam winch instead of having us hauling on this gantline like oxen, wouldn't you."

Fred shrugged. "That would cost the son-of-a-bitch captain his bloody coal." He thought a second. "Let's see. The coal in Cardiff cost ten shillings four pence a ton, and they say it will sell in Chile for four pounds ten a ton. So if we used a ton of coal in the donkey boiler, it would rob the owner of about four pounds. And as we get the lordly sum of three pounds a month, they might as well just let sailors' sweat instead of using steam. Who needs a donkey engine when you have donkeys like us? Unless of course, the coal burns out of control because we can't get to it fast enough. But then we all die, so they don't have to pay us wages."

Donnie muttered, "Well, there's that, to be sure. Are you the bloody ship's mathematician?"

Fred grinned, "No, I'm the bloody prince regent."

"Good to know," Donnie replied, as Harry started singing again and they hoisted another quarter ton of coal from the hold. Fred glanced back at the captain on the poop and swore under his breath.

After two hours, the gangs were rotated and Fred and the others on the line climbed down into the hold along with two apprentices who had been on the bucket brigade. Shirtless and sweating even before they started to dig, they broke up into four gangs of two, shoveling at the four corners of the pit that grew marginally deeper with each shovelful. In minutes, they were all covered in coal dust. The dust and wisps of smoke choked them as they shoveled, and the pit only grew hotter as they dug deeper. Their two-hour trick felt endless until finally they climbed back on deck to haul again on the gantline.

In the evening, they were given a half-hour break to eat. Jeremiah handed out pantiles from a bread barge to the exhausted crew. He laughed at the sailors, covered in coal dust and sweat. "I ain't the blackest man on this ship no mo'. No mo' indeed." When Jeremiah came to Jensen, he glared and tossed him the biscuits. Jensen just ignored him. The cook could be heard to mumble to Otto, "Did ya see? He danced with the debil in the moonlight on that very hatch and now she be afire. Didn't I tell ye?"

Will was slumped on deck next to Donnie and Fred. "Spontaneous combustion, that's what I've heard," he said to no one in particular.

Donnie looked over at the youngster, the smallest sailor aboard, who now looked like a black dwarf. "Load coal wet and it can start a fire all on its own, they say.

The week before we started loading, it rai:
Coal probably sat uncovered in rail cars
takes."

"But how can water cause a fire?" Will asked.

"How should I know?" Donnie replied. "Ask our scholar over here," cocking his head toward Fred, who just shrugged. "Stranger things happen," Fred replied.

"Well, that's true, I guess," Will replied.

In a few minutes Mr. Rand began bellowing. "Back in the hold, you lazy blaggards. Don't want to burn alive just because you sons of bitches are too lazy to get off your arses."

The mates kept them all working until midnight, when one watch was allowed to sleep for four hours while the other kept digging, until they too got four hours rest, before all hands were turned to again, shoveling and hauling. The more they dug, the hotter the coal became, whether because they were getting closer to the fire or whether the digging was feeding more oxygen to the buried flames, they couldn't tell.

Fred kept digging methodically, his muscles aching with each shovelful, blinded by his own sweat and the coal dust. The sulfurous smoke burned his nostrils and made him choke as he dug ever deeper. He was reminded of Dante's *Divine Comedy* and decided he preferred reading of the inferno in Italian to digging at it with a shovel.

The only rest they got in the hold was when they had filled a basket with a quarter ton of coal. They could lean on their shovels while the deck gang hauled it to the deck. Will was in the hold, doling out water to the diggers. He staggered in the smoke.

Fred called over to him, "Be sure to drink some of that water yourself, Mr. Jones. Don't want to have to haul you out of the hatch as well. Coal's heavy enough as it is."

They dug for four days, and each day the pit got hotter as the piles of coal on deck grew. The soles of their feet burned as they dug. They gasped for air in the coal dust and acrid smoke. As he climbed out of the hold at the end of his shift, Fred heard Santiago tell of a voyage to Calcutta where he saw fakirs, Hindu mystics, who walked on coals. "I thought they was loco. Never thought I'd be one of 'em."

On the fourth day the baskets of coal themselves were on fire as they rose from the hold. Extra hands were put on the bucket detail to make sure that the flaming coal didn't set the deck ablaze. Finally, they dug past the embers and ash to where there was no flame. Gronberg climbed down into the pit for his inspection. When he declared the fire out, the steward served out a healthy tot of rum to everyone save the apprentices, who sat glumly along the hatch coaming.

For a few moments, at least, all seemed well with the world. The fire was out, they wouldn't be burned alive on an empty ocean. The only fire now was the rum in their bellies.

Fred kept looking at the sky behind them. It was early afternoon and the sky was a darker blue than it should have been. He snorted wearily, and then muttered, "Damn. Shit. Damn. Damn."

He looked at the poop deck, and there was Captain Barker. Had he moved in the last four days or had he kept his vigil, watching them dig and haul coal from the fiery pit? Fred felt himself growing to hate the man. The bastard wouldn't put into port to use shore crews to put out the fire. He wouldn't burn his precious coal to use the donkey boiler and engine. And now a storm, a real snorter by the looks of it, was brewing and they were rolling along with an open hatch and tons of coal on the deck. "Damn," he repeated to himself.

The captain and the mate could read the weather as well as any sailor, and Mr. Rand soon had the crew hurriedly shoveling the coal back into the hold. At least when reloading the coal, there was less hoisting to be done and they could breath again in the open air. Except when called to shorten sail, they kept shoveling and dumping the coal as the wind rose and they drove ever farther south into the Roaring Forties.

An ominous swell began to roll from the southwest. The wind was rising and the motion of the ship as she rolled along under topsails and t'gallants added urgency to their shoveling. They filled the two baskets and then used hand trucks to roll them over to the hatch coaming to be tipped into the hold. The coal dust that rose as they dumped each load disappeared in the gusting wind. Everyone kept an eye out to weather at the approaching storm. No one wanted to be caught in a storm with an open hatch cover, ready to swallow up the first breaking sea and the next and the next, until the ship disappeared beneath he waves.

What took them four days to dig and hoist only took one to load. As the last coal disappeared into the hold, the hatch covers were dragged in place and the tarpaulin stretched over the hatch, secured by heavy deal planks, as the *Lady Rebecca* pitched and rolled wildly in the swells. Fred finally worked his way to the fo'c'sle cabin. Time to tie on his foul-weather gear before the storm hit.

CHAPTER 8
SOUTHERN OCEAN SNORTER

July 30, 1905 – 49 days out of Cardiff

The apprentices were in the half-deck, sent to get their gear. The lantern swung as the ship rolled, casting weird shadows across the young men's faces. Will had put on his thigh-high rubber boots, oilskins and sou'wester once before, for a photograph before he left home. Now he pulled them out of his sea chest and dressed in earnest for the first time.

"The storm's really blowing," Will commented.

Paul Nelson, senior apprentice, snorted, "This ain't nothing." He was cutting lengths of twine and laying them out across the edge of his bunk. "Come here," he said. Will stepped over.

"Stick out your arm." Will did and Paul began tying a length of twine around his wrist.

"What's that?" Will asked. Paul shook his head. The youngster still had a lot to learn.

"Body and soul lashings. You go out in a howler with your sleeves open or jacket bottom not tied, the wind will fill your oilskins full of water, if it don't blow them off altogether. Now tie your other wrist and your pant legs."

Will looked over and saw that Jack already had his gear on. Will tied his lashings to match Jack's. He tied his sou'wester tight on his head. With his new oilskins, boots and his body and soul lashings tied tight, he felt ready for anything. Then the wind gusted again and the ship rolled, and he wasn't so sure.

Captain Barker stood on the poop deck wearing a dreadnought jacket. They were scudding along under lower topsails, foresail and jib. Lifelines had been rigged along the deck, port and starboard, and double lashings had been put on the boats, the spare spars and the stores casks. Extra tarpaulins were stretched over the hatches and the wedges driven home. Hatches two and three, which would take the brunt of the weather, were covered by three-inch deal planking, all well secured. Short of a full-scale hurricane, Captain Barker thought, the *Lady Rebecca* was ready for anything the Southern Ocean might throw at her.

Mary and the children were below, once again deathly seasick. He felt a moment's guilt, but there was nothing to be done. The captain glanced over at the binnacle.

"Mind your helm, damn it," he snapped at the helmsman.

"Aye, sir," came the reply, as the sailor struggled to keep the ship on course in the confused, rolling swells.

The wind suddenly dropped and then shifted to the southwest. A dark line of rain and wind rolled at them like a freight train. Seeing it coming, Captain Barker shouted, "Brace yourselves."

The blast hit the ship abeam, sending her over, dipping her lee rail in the rushing sea, scooping up an angry wall of green water that surged down the deck as she rose again.

"All hands on deck!" The cry came in rapid succession from the captain, from Mr. Rand and the second mate, Mr. Atkinson.

The apprentices tumbled out of the half-deck house, half running, half sliding. The deck was at a forty-five-degree angle and the deck to leeward was underwater.

"Grab hold of the lifeline," Paul yelled. "Don't let it go." Will slid downhill and slammed into the heavy line, grabbing at it frantically. Jack collided with him a second later. Over the howling of the wind, they could just hear the captain bellowing, "Lee fore-brace." The mate echoed the command.

For a moment Will didn't think that he could move. A wave broke over him and he gasped then choked as icy water forced itself down his throat. He could neither see nor breathe and he held the lifeline in a death grip. He knew if he let go for an instant, he would die, be swept over the side and away into the raging sea. He had never been so battered or so frightened in his entire life. Another wave broke over him and knocked him off his feet.

With the others he hauled himself to the pinrail and grabbed the brace line. On the weather rail, the mate slacked off the weather brace, grabbing hold of the pin rails as green seas broke over the side when the ship rolled to windward. To the lee, Will and the others were knocked off their feet with every wave, relying on the tail-end man to take a quick turn around a belaying pin to keep them from being swept away. Somehow between the waves, they all hauled on the brace line, before the next comber sent them under water again.

When the main lower topsail yard was hauled around, they struggled to coil the line. Will was confused but went along as they tied the brace lines not to the pin rails, but inboard to the lifeline, to make it slightly less likely that the waves would wash the coils free.

Will struggled to stand and took a deep breath of air before he would be dunked again. He felt someone hit him on the shoulder and heard Jack yelling at his ear. "Let's go."

They moved on to the mizzen braces which led to a fife rail aft the main mast, which was even more exposed to the waves than at the main braces. Gasping for breath in the wind that seemed more spray than air, Will again strained with the others to haul the mizzen yard around. They then all trudged forward to strike and stow the fore stay-sail as the Old Man on the poop deck shouted at them to move faster, to quit their dawdling and finish the job.

At last, Will heard Paul shouting at him, "Come on," and they retreated to the break of the poop deck. On the deck above them, Captain Barker shouted, "Helm down." The sailor at the wheel pushed the spokes to windward and slowly the *Lady Rebecca* rounded up in the wind. She lay, pitching and heaving in the seas; yet, balancing between wind and wave, she hove to.

The storm kept building until it felt like a full hurricane was blowing at them. Will lost all track of time. It should have been afternoon yet was as dark as night. Then, when night finally fell, the absolute blackness seemed to swallow them whole, broken only by jagged lightning, illuminating the rolling breakers topped by crests of white foam charging at them from out of the darkness.

The mate's place on the poop deck was to windward while Will, as apprentice, stood to leeward. He took a quick round turn to secure himself to the rail to avoid being washed overboard by a breaking wave or being thrown to the deck as the ship corkscrewed in the sea. Between the waves, he kept an eye on the binnacle lantern. His task was to keep the lantern burning. The wind and driving rain kept blowing it out. He would cast off his lashings and fight to relight the lantern, wondering all the while, why it mattered. The helm was lashed down and the helmsman stood by with nothing to do but hold on and hide behind the weather cloths for whatever limited protection they might afford. Will blew into his hands for warmth, and then struggled with the matches once again in an endless battle with the wind and blowing spray.

On the second night of the gale, Fred huddled at the break of the poop with the rest of his watch. In the darkness and the spray, they didn't see John Whitney, a sailor from Glasgow, step out of the fo'c'sle cabin just as a wave broke and exploded across the deck. They heard him shout as it swept him off his feet. He grabbed in vain for the lifeline but the wall of green water carried him aft, washing him into the scuppers, then carrying him across the deck and finally slamming him against the deck pump, catching his leg on the pump handle. His screams of agony carried above even the roar of the wind.

In the wild darkness, it took four men to reach him. Torrents of water surged down the deck, as Fred, Tom, Jerry the Greek and Harry formed a human chain from the lifeline to where Whitney lay crumpled, crying out as each new wave struck. Harry managed to grab him by his shirt and pull him up from where he lay, with his leg twisted unnaturally beneath him. Whitney screamed as they hauled him slowly out from under the pump, carrying him as gently as they could on the rolling deck, through the cabin into galley where they laid him on a blanket on the table, tying him down so that he wouldn't be thrown off, as the ship twisted in the waves.

Captain Barker took a look at the injured sailor, gently straightening one leg and then the other. Touching Whitney's left leg started him howling in pain. The captain looked at Fred. "Get Chips. We'll be needing a splint."

Fred found the carpenter's cabin and pounded on the door.

"Man's been injured. Captain says he needs a splint."

Gronberg was pulling on his dungarees and oilskins. "You tell the captain, I'll be there right quick."

In a few minutes, the carpenter was measuring Whitney's leg.

"It appears to be fractured in three places," the captain commented.

"Ya, looks like it." Gronberg nodded in agreement. He pocketed his tape, cinched his oilskins tight and left the galley. He hauled his way along the deck, hand over hand, holding onto the lifeline as the breaking waves sent water surging from his knees to his chest, until he finally reached the wood shop forward, where his tools and spare planks were stored.

When he returned about a half-hour later, thoroughly soaked from his trip down the deck, he pulled two pine planks from beneath his dripping oilskins. They fit Whitney's leg perfectly and had slots cut in the planks where sail gaskets could be threaded to hold them in place.

"Nicely done, Mr. Gronberg," the captain said as he began carefully tying on the splint. Whitney, who had been given morphine, slept quietly as the captain gently bound the shattered leg.

"Thank you, sir. Not my first pair of splints," Chips replied.

When the captain was finished he said, "You men, put him in the spare cabin next to the steward."

Whitney would likely live, but he would be out of commission for the rest of the trip. As they carried the sleeping sailor gingerly to the cabin, Fred couldn't help think that the twenty-man crew was down by one and they were still well north of Cape Horn.

One thing that Captain Barker knew for certain was that even a full snorter of a gale would blow itself out sooner or later. After four days, the skies cleared and the wind filled in again from the northwest. Barker took one last look at the rising barometer before climbing the ladder to the poop deck. "Mr. Atkinson, all hands, if you please. Set everything to the royals. I don't want to waste an ounce of this breeze."

Mr. Atkinson bellowed, "All hands." The shout was soon echoed by Mr. Rand, who a moment later appeared from his cabin. With a favoring breeze pushing them toward Cape Horn, even he looked less dour than usual.

"Come on, you motherless farmers," he shouted. "Let's see what the old lady can do."

Will and the other apprentices laid out on the mizzen yards, casting off the t'gallant gaskets and then racing to see who could be the first back on deck.

Harry belted out a favorite shanty as the crew scrambled down the ratlines and formed up at the halyards to raise sail.

"*Me boots and clothes are all in pawn,*"
and all sang back, hauling in time,
"*Go down, ye blood red roses, go down.*"
"*Cause it's mighty drafty round Cape Horn,*"

"Go down, ye blood red roses, go down...."

After the misery of the gale, Will couldn't quite believe the color of the sky that peeked through the broken clouds. It was blue, as deep and clear a blue as he had ever seen. With all sails set, the canvas filled the sky and once again the grand ship rolled mightily over the waves rather than being battered and tossed by the storm. The wind was cold but bracing. Somehow yesterday's gale seemed far, far away as Will grinned like an idiot gazing up at the towering sails.

Beneath the blue skies and the steady northwesterly the *Lady Rebecca* picked up her skirts and danced along at close to fourteen knots. Captain Barker felt like dancing as well. He went below to to the chart table. The barometer stayed high and he smiled as he plotted a course to weather St. John's Point on the eastern tip of Staten Island, the gateway to Drake's Passage and the waters of Cape Horn. By his reckoning, they would round Staten Island on August 7, a passage of over 8,000 miles in fifty-seven days. They had lost a few days in the gale but were making up the distance nicely. Captain Barker was well pleased with his ship, his crew and himself. His only concern was his mate.

At noon, he and Mr. Rand were on deck taking sun sights beneath a clear blue sky. Captain Barker lowered his sextant and jotted his reading into his notebook, and then asked the mate for his meridian altitude as well. Mr. Rand spat it out in a growl, turned and walked to his cabin.

Captain Barker watched his back as he walked away. Had Mr. Rand been a bad mate, his choice would have been easier. There were twelve pairs of shackles in the lazarette, part of the ship's allowance, ready in case of a mutiny. He could simply clap Mr. Rand in irons for the rest of the voyage. Mutinies always need a leader and there was none better than a disloyal mate who believed he knew better than the captain, or perhaps thought that he himself should be captain. Unfortunately, Captain Barker didn't have a spare mate on the lazarette shelf next to the shackles. So far Tom Atkinson had shown himself to be a fine young man and good second mate, but this was only his second voyage as an officer and he could use more seasoning. On the other hand, Captain Barker knew that he might not have any other choice.

If his thoughts were dark, at the least the skies were blue and the wind favorable. He wondered whether Mary and the children would recover from their seasickness sufficiently to come on deck and enjoy the sun. These winds were colder than the trades but perhaps with blankets they might enjoy the brief sunshine, which was all the more remarkable with every mile they sailed south.

As he worked out his position with the sight reduction tables, he saw that they were still making over 250 miles a day. The Falkland Islands lay due east over the horizon. He wondered idly where the *Susannah* might be. She had to be in their wake. He could feel it. Not even a fire had slowed down the *Lady Rebecca*. They had to be ahead of the German ship. Soon they would round Staten Island and all that remained for them would be to round Cape Horn itself. He prayed for fair weather, even though he knew that might be too much to ask for.

Ship Lady Rebecca   *August 3, 1905*

Dearest Mother,

I know my last letter to you may have been dour, and I do not wish you to think that your daughter does nothing but complain. We have faced considerable discomfort and no doubt face more to come, but all the same, I cannot deny the beauty of these waters.

Yesterday, we saw our first albatross. It was such a magnificent bird. It appeared to ride the winds effortlessly on huge wings, skimming along close to the surface of the sea and then rising higher and higher towards the clouds, in an ascending spiral.

Today we sailed past a whole armada of albatross, sitting quietly on the water, disappearing in the troughs and rising placidly as the crests pass beneath them. We could not have been farther than 50 yards away when they decided to fly off. They flapped their wings, which each must be two yards long, and rather comically paddled madly with their cabbage leaf feet to get them into the air. Fortunately, their grace in flight is not diminished by their awkward ascent.

We are also seeing Mother Carey's chickens now. Some people call them Saint Peter's birds as they seem to walk across the water while feeding. They are smaller and a dusky colour, save for white feathers on their tail and the back of their wings.

I must tell you that I have seen the most beautiful sunsets than ever I could imagine in these waters. Near the equator, sunset is like someone suddenly shut the door. The sun drops quickly below the horizon and there is little twilight to speak of. Now that we have reached the higher latitudes, the sun lingers and the colours, as it sinks into the sea, are almost beyond describing. Last night I feared that we might have no sunset as the sun slipped behind a dark and glowering cloud. A few minutes later, myriad arrows of light shot up from behind the blackness in a panoply of hues and textures. I stood on deck watching in reverent awe as the colours faded into blackness, despite being called several times to dinner by our ever patient steward, Walter.

Later that evening, James called me to come again on deck where he presented to me the Aurora Australes, magnificent cascades of blue and green lights filling the Southern sky.

It appears that the heavens have gone out of their way today to lift my spirits.

Your loving daughter,

Mary

CHAPTER 9
BELOW LATITUDE 50 SOUTH

August 3, 1905 – 53 days out of Cardiff

While sweeping up, Will peeked at the chart table. He had come to enjoy his minor conspiracy with Fred, as he regularly passed the position on to his shipmate before the mast. He pulled his notebook and a stub of a pencil from his pocket and jotted down the date, August 3, 1905, and the position—51 degrees 46 minutes south, 64 degrees 10 minutes west.

They had left the Roaring Forties behind and now stood into the Furious Fifties, as the sailors called them. According to the faint pencil marks on the chart, they were roughly abeam of the Falkland Islands, the last inhabited refuge for sailing ships before the Horn.

He finished up the sweeping, took the broom, dustpan and rags back the pantry, and then buttoned his dreadnoughtjacket and went back on deck. He strode quickly to the weather mizzen ratlines and clambered up to the mizzen top. The wind was bitterly cold and made his eyes water as he wrapped an arm around a shroud and peered intently toward the east. At first, all he saw was the gray sea, rollers capped with white crests stretching off toward the horizon, shrouded in low clouds.

Then, as he stared, he thought he saw a dark smudge floating in the blurred juncture between the sea and sky. He blinked several times and wiped his eyes. It was still there. The Falkland Islands. He let out a small yelp. There wasn't much to see, but it was the first land that he had seen since the Bristol Channel. Some place, off to the south and west , was the mighty Cape Horn. His ears smarted from the cold and his cheeks burned with every wind gust. Still, he couldn't help but grin. He swung out on the futtock shrouds and climbed quickly down to the deck.

Ship Lady Rebecca   *August 4, 1905*

Dearest Mother,

This evening James told me that we are now passing the Falkland Islands, the southernmost of all British colonies. Port Stanley in the Falklands is the closest port to Cape Horn, so many ships call there if they are in need of repair. James, however, has a very low opinion of the port. He says that any ship owner whose ship falls into the clutches of the repair yards in Port Stanley will face exorbitant fees and charges, while the ship itself may never be properly repaired. "A pit of thieves and vipers" is, I believe, the phrase he used.

We had a delightful surprise for dinner tonight. The steward-cook, Walter, fixed a stocking-leg duff . It is made with stewed dried apples wrapped in a roll of dough that is boiled in a cheese cloth. With a hot sweet sauce, it tasted nearly as good as the apple dumplings we make at home. Amanda and little Tommy squealed with joy when they tasted it. Walter tells me the name originated in the fo'c'sle where duff is always boiled in the leg of a stocking.

The temperature has been falling dramatically as we sail South. I will often go on deck where I am less prone to sea sickness. On occasion, I have seen the approach of one of the black squalls that strike so fiercely. The wind can blow the breath back into your throat and the sleet feels as if it will cut the skin off my face if I don't I hurry down below to where all is warm and we draw near to the heat of the cabin stove. Above the howling of the wind, I can hear the sailors shortening sail under these terrible conditions. I worry about the welfare of these brave sailors. Of course, I feel so for James and his officers as well, whose duty keeps them out in freezing cold. I can only pray that our rounding will be quick.

Your loving daughter,

Mary

Fred marked the daily entry into his journal. August 6. There were now 55 marks on the bunk bulkhead. Fifty-five days from Cardiff. They had passed the Falklands and would soon fetch Staten Island. A respectable if not overly fast passage. He stowed his journal and dressed for the watch. He could feel the cold even in the fo'c'sle cabin. He rubbed his fingers and his breath spread like a tiny fog bank before him. The ship's bell rang and with the rest of his watch, he turned to.

The mate bellowed to take a pull on the fore topsail brace, so he joined the gang at the lee rail and hauled the brace a bit tighter. The crowd drifted back to the break of the poop. Captain Barker's rules forbade anyone from going below except under orders while on watch, so they stood by, shuffling to keep warm. Fred cursed beneath his breath at the son-of-a-bitch captain, as well within his right to do so. It was every sailor's right to growl.

Fred felt more like a mummy than a sailor now, with all his layers of clothing. At this moment, however, the cold wasn't bothering him. On the near horizon was one of the reasons he had sailed on the *Lady Rebecca*.

The island of Tierra del Fuego rose from the ocean, forbidding and wild. Almost vertical walls of rock soared up from the sea to ragged, rugged peaks topped with snow and ice, the tallest disappearing into the clouds. Black gorges and chasms filled with snow broke the uniform gray of the shore. A wilder and lonelier coast he had never seen or even imagined. Somewhere to the north lay the entrance to the Strait of Magellan, too narrow and winding for sailing ships, fit only for the smoke-box steamers.

Tierra del Fuego, the land of fire. Fred liked the way the name felt on his tongue and repeated it to himself. Tierra del Fuego. It seemed inconceivable that anyone could live in such a barren place, but Magellan had named the island after seeing the fires of the natives ashore. He had acquired that bit of knowledge in the comfortable library at Yale, literally half a world away, yet which now seemed to be a part of another universe entirely.

He stomped his feet, rubbed his hands together for warmth, and stared out at the dark and forbidding shore. Finally, as the sun was setting, the mate returned to the deck, struck the bell and yelled, "That'll do the watch."

Fred took one last look at the distant shore and trudged back to the fo'c'sle cabin.

August 7, 1905 – 57 days out of Cardiff

The weather turned unsettled and gloomy about a hundred miles north and east of St. John's Point. The wind had shifted nor'-nor'east and was dropping. A long bank of clouds lay on the easterly horizon. Captain Barker stood on the poop deck with the mates, discussing the likely change in the weather.

"It'll blow from the southeast and then east, afore the westerlies fill in again," Mr. Rand opined. Captain Barker saw that Mr. Atkinson stood looking engaged in the conversation but offering to no opinions of his own. The captain approved. Better to listen and learn than to open your mouth and demonstrate your inexperience.

"I think you are right, Mr. Rand. If we can round Staten Island and square away with an easterly breeze, we might be around and into the Pacific as slick as a whistle."

Rand shook his head. "Have you ever managed that trick, Captain?"

"No, sir, but no reason that we might not get lucky this time."

"I've never thought it wise to rely on luck, sir," the mate grumbled.

"Well, neither have I, but I am loath not to appreciate it when it comes along," the captain replied.

As Rand had predicted, the wind blew a fresh east by south. Captain Barker ordered the helmsman to sail her full and by, as close to the wind as she would bear with all sails drawing. In the rising wind, they struck the upper and lower t'gansails and the cro'jack and were still sailing close enough to the edge of losing sails or rigging, but somehow everything held together. She plowed along to weather at close to eight knots and by dawn was within forty miles of St. John's Point on Staten Island, the gateway to Cape Horn.

The weather grew thick and they could see perhaps five sea miles. The daylight was halfhearted, yet bright enough through the clouds to see that they were now no longer alone in these waters. There were at least six ships, emerging and disappearing in the gloom, all bound for Cape Horn. Captain Barker recognized two of them, both Frenchmen, the full-rigged *Desaix* and the *Crillion*. If he recalled the shipping reports, they had sailed from Antwerp bound for Frisco a few days before the Rebecca sailed from Cardiff.

Captain Barker stood next to the helmsman, watching the set of the sails and wondering if they would be able to weather St. John's Point on a single tack. He was tempted to square away and take the shortcut between the toe of Tierra del Fuego and Staten Island, through the Le Maire Strait. Wouldn't that be a story to tell? Still, he decided against it. There were rocks extending a considerable way north of Staten Island that would be impossible to see in the overcast. Finding just one rock with these seas running would hole the ship and bring the top-hamper crashing down. Not the way he wanted to end the voyage.

So they stood on, the *Rebecca* shouldering the building seas. All hands were now clustered on the main deck just abaft the fo'c'sle head, staring out into the gloom, looking for the dim shadow that would be the outline of the eastern end of Staten Island.

A cry rang out as the lookout spotted St. John's Point, barely a point to leeward and a scant five miles off. Captain Barker debated with himself whether to stand on and clear the point by the slimmest margin or to bear away. As he considered the question, the six other ships all, one by one, wore about and stood to the north.

Mr. Rand bounded over. "We'll never clear the point, Captain. Can't you see the rocks to leeward? Look at the seas breaking over them. We still have time to wear ship. If we don't, God help us."

Captain Barker turned and snapped, "Mister, I'll be the one saying when to wear ship and when to stand on. We're a full point to windward and the wind is lifting us. She'll come up some yet. The wind striking those cliffs there will lift us farther still. We'll be clear and squaring yards in ten minutes, so stand aside and stand by."

Rand grumbled to himself, and then stamped off to leeward.

The *Lady Rebecca* drove on and the spray from the breaking waves reached higher. Captain Barker shouted forward, "As we pass, hold on, every man for himself. It'll be rough."

As the point drew abeam, the sound of the breakers rose to a roar. They were suddenly buffeted by waves from both sides. The swell from the open Atlantic struck from port while the waves rebounding off the rocks rolled back out and struck them from starboard. The sea seemed to be rising up to swallow them, with spray flying in all directions, in a wild cacophony of wind and wave.

And then suddenly, there was silence. The easy hum of the wind and creaking of the rigging was the only sound they heard. They were past the point. They had rounded Staten Island. Now, Cape Horn was one hundred and fifty miles away and, magically, they had a favoring wind. Captain Barker felt like letting go with a cheer, but only clasped his hands behind him and smiled. He turned to the helmsman.

"Quartermaster, bear off two points, and once the yards are squared bear off two more."

"Aye, sir. Two points and two more when the yards are square."

"Mr. Rand," Captain Barker shouted, "square away and shake out the t'gansails and royals. I don't want to waste one ounce of this breeze."

"Aye, captain," the mate replied.

"And once the sails are set and square, send everyone aft," the captain continued. "It's time we spliced the mainbrace. Have the purser break out the rum cask. A tot for every man."

August 8, 1905 – 58 days out of Cardiff

The next day, the easterly breeze held and the *Lady Rebecca* stood boldly on, south and west, with all sails set. At noon, Captain Barker and Mr. Rand took their sun sights. Once he had reduced them to latitude and longitude, Captain Barker came on deck and commented to Mr. Atkinson, in a voice meant to carry well beyond the poop deck, "Our position is 56 degrees 20 minutes south and 67 degrees 30 minutes west."

Mr. Atkinson broke into a wide grin and replied, half shouting, "Then we have passed the meridian? We have rounded the Horn?"

"Indeed we have, Mr. Atkinson. We will not be properly around until we again reach 50 south latitude, of course, but we have indeed passed the meridian of the cape."

William wanted to cheer, but instead ran to the mainmast ratlines and climbed aloft to see if he could spy the Horn, only to be shooed down a few minutes later by Mr. Atkinson. They were too far south, in any case. Cape Horn was over the horizon to the north and just slightly east. Word spread quickly, and soon everyone aboard had heard the news.

Harry joked with the cook, Jeremiah. "Not such an unlucky ship after all, doctor. Maybe your Jonah bring us this easterly, what do ya think?"

"Aach, don' be bothering me," the cook replied gesturing with his cleaver. "We's not in Chile yet. No, sir. Not by a long shot."

By early afternoon, the easterly wind had begun to die. The sails hung limp and slatting, and the ship slowed until she was nearly becalmed in the long oily swells. The captain's family, who had been on deck since noon, were quickly ushered below. The temperature dropped suddenly again as a bank of low clouds obscured the horizon. Then it began to snow and, for a time, the ship and the sky almost disappeared in the swirling storm. When the snow squall passed, the ship glistened in a sepulchral whiteness.

The captain dropped below to check the barometer and returned looking grave. All eyes were turned toward the poop deck as the captain spoke quietly with the mates. Then came the expected battle cry. "All hands to shorten sail."

The watch below tumbled out on a run. The Cape Horners among them knew what was coming and everyone scrambled to the pin rails. Fred read the deadly earnest in the expressions of Donnie, Harry and the rest and hurried along with them.

"Bunts and clews. Furl the royals and t'gallants. Slack away those bloody halyards, you motherless sons of bitches. Run," Rand shouted, needlessly.

To the bellowing of the commands and the clicking of the patent blocks, Fred grabbed the icy buntlines and hauled with the rest, his hands burning on the snow-crusted lines as the sails slowly gathered up against the yards. Their work on deck done, they scrambled up the ratlines to furl the sails, fighting the snow-covered canvas with frozen hands. Fred tried to focus only on the job he was doing, squatting down on the footropes, trying to pass a gasket to Jerry the Greek, who was bent double over the yard reaching out as far as he could to catch it. The sails were stiff with snow and ice, and furling them was a painful ordeal. The long swells were building and the ship pitched and rolled. Fred shouted curses at the wind as he struggled to pass the gaskets, while avoiding being pitched from his tenuous perch. Both ignored the horizon, which was now wholly a swirl of black and gray and seemed to be rolling toward them at a terrible speed.

In the blackness, around 10 p.m., all sails were furled. The waves grew higher, yet in the relative lull before the storm the ship had almost no headway and so was at the mercy of the swells. The *Lady Rebecca* rolled sluggishly like a sailor on a three-day drunk. Fred braced himself, his back against the fo'c'sle house with his hand shoved under his armpits, trying in vain to warm his fingers. Looking out in the darkness, he saw a vivid, boiling white line rushing toward them. The long swells had transformed into lines of breaking waves, driven by a demon wind.

The captain yelled, "Hard up your helm. Lee braces."

Fred and the others ran to the lee pin rail and frantically hauled the forward yards around so that they would be less square to the wind when the blow struck.

When the wind did hit, Fred was first deafened by the unholy roar, and then was tossed against the shrouds. An icy wall of water washed over him but he held tight to the line he had been hauling, as the rushing water lifted him off his feet. The ship staggered and rolled in the infernal blast. Then she fought her way back up, pitching and rolling like a battered boxer, never quite knocked flat, always rising again.

After what seemed like an age, the squall passed, leaving rolling trains of mountainous seas. The *Lady*

Rebecca lay six points to the wind, doggedly fore-reaching under reefed lower topsails. She was not quite beam on, her bowsprit jutting perhaps twenty degrees forward, presenting her stout shoulder to the sea's onslaught, dropping down in the troughs and rising up again to climb the precipitous, breaking crests.

When the watch was sent below Fred threw himself into his bunk fully clothed. Just behind him came Donnie.

"Well, lad. You've got a tale to tell, to be sure. Rounded Cape Horn, an' twice in one day."

Fred raised his head. "What?"

"We rounded westbound this afternoon, and with these winds pushing us back, we'll likely round it eastbound before dawn. I'm guessin' that this'll not be a fast passage after all." The Irishman grinned wryly and shuffled off to his bunk.

The westerlies began to blow. South of Cape Horn, there was nothing to block the wind, nothing to deflect the waves. Huge and slate gray, the waves grew into massive rolling ranges, each preceded by a long valley. They rose thirty, forty, even fifty feet high, crested by boiling white caps, and each wave that followed was seemingly larger than the last. The Southern Ocean was a vast raceway where the howling westerlies and monstrous seas chased each other endlessly around the bottom of the world.

Fred huddled with the rest of the watch on the leeward side of the poop deck, grimly watching the mountainous waves that rolled at them relentlessly. In the long troughs, the roar of the wind diminished slightly only to rise again to an unearthly howl as the wave lifted them higher and higher. At the top, they were blasted by the full force of the gale, before crashing through the foaming, breaking crest, and plunging down the other side of the wave like a cast-off cork. With each wave, the ship rolled deeply, scooping up tons of green water on the open leeward deck, sending it surging the length of the ship to break against the raised face of the poop deck.

Fred marveled at how the old ship fought the seas, shouldering a roller with a burst of spray and then rising again and again over one towering sea after another, as dogged in her determination as the rolling waves were relentless. The wind was bitterly cold and the spume froze as it struck the shrouds, the running rigging and the reefed sails. All Fred could do was pull his jacket tighter about him and hold on.

The captain stood on the poop deck to windward, their lord and master, staring out into the half-light. A line of dark clouds was bearing down on them.

"All hands to shorten sail," the captain shouted once again. And once again, Fred and the rest of the watch ran to the pin rails. Before they were through, the squall hit with a roar like a million wild beasts. The ship shuddered and rolled, sending the lee rail underwater. Fred held desperately onto the lifeline as the surging icy water, rising up to his chest, tried to carry him away.

When the ship rolled back and the water receded, his face was pelted by sleet. With frozen hands, they belayed and coiled down the clews and bunts and then mounted the weather ratlines to furl the sails, which, held only by the bunts and clews, thrashed wildly. The sailors finally wrestled the frozen sails and secured them with the gaskets and returned to the treacherous, wave-swept deck.

When the squall passed, the sky lightened slightly. Off to windward Fred could see a maelstrom of clouds piled high above the horizon, illuminated by broken shafts of sunlight. At the crest of one wave, Fred was startled to see an albatross serenely rise up from the trough and wheel effortlessly in the gale's blast. It hung there for a moment and then as if by some enchantment flew off to westward, directly into the wind. Fred stood stunned, and then recited a stanza from part of the old poem that his professor had made them all commit to memory.

And now the storm-blast came, and he
Was tyrannous and strong:
He struck with his o'ertaking wings,
And chased us south along.

Tom Jackson looked over at him and scowled. He couldn't hear what Fred was saying over the wind under any circumstances, but Fred replied as if he could, "From '*The Rime of the Ancient Mariner*' by Samuel Taylor Coleridge." Fred grinned. Education was never wasted.

West. To the west was where they needed to sail and to the west was from whence the gale blew. As long as the westerlies blew, they would make no westing. Despite their fore-reaching, the current was carrying them backward. Day after day they slogged on, waiting for a shift in the wind, the favoring slant that would free them from the shackles of the westerlies.

In addition to being carried back on the current, they were sailing south, farther and farther south. Fred could feel it on the air. Inexorably southward, farther from the cape and ever closer to the Antarctic ice. If the westerly gales didn't kill them, there was always the ice. Icebergs could sink ships, the grandest windjammer disappearing without a trace. And worse, an ice sheet could trap a ship, leaving the sailors aboard to freeze or to starve.

Day and night the crew scrambled aloft to take in sails when the wind rose and to shake out the reefs when it eased even slightly. The ice-covered steel shrouds burned and ripped at sailor's palms as they climbed aloft. The frozen sails refused to be reefed or furled without an extended pounding to break off the layers of ice. The sails ripped at their nails and froze their fingers, and the ship, rolling and pitching, threatened to hurl them from their slippery perches onto the deck below or into the icy waters.

When his watch was finally over, Fred threw himself into his bunk. The floor of the fo'c'sle was awash with six inches of water and Fred was pleased to have chosen an upper berth, even if the overhead leaked and he had to rig a bit of canvas to avoid the dripping. The small bogie stove glowed in the far end of the cabin but seemed not to give off any appreciable heat. Fully clothed and shivering, Fred slipped off to sleep. Steam rose from his oilskins, as his own body heat helped to dry his clothing, just a bit.

He awoke to a cold meal. The galley was awash, just like the fo'c'sle, and Jeremiah couldn't keep his stove alight, so they all chewed their salt junk cold. "I never signed on to cook underwater, no sir," became the cook's refrain. Donnie's knack for impersonation brightened the fo'c'sle slightly with a few chuckles as they worked their jaws on the cold beef and pantiles. They were all tending sail underwater, at least some of the time, so Fred could see no reason why the cook couldn't do the same.

The bogie stoves in the fo'c'sles were too small for any practical use, so the steward heated large pots of coffee and tea in the deckhouse aft, which the apprentices then shuttled to the fo'c'sles, dodging the seas surging across the deck. More than a few times, the pots of hot liquid ended up full of cold salt water before they arrived forward.

Fred was again reminded of Coleridge: *Water, water everywhere and not a drop to drink.*

There was no shortage of freshwater. They had more than enough of it in the form of snow and the sleet than they would ever want. Not that they could conveniently drink it.

There was no shortage of freshwater in the tanks of the *Lady Rebecca*, either. The problem was simply getting to it. The tank access was directly behind the mainmast, convenient both to the fo'c'sle cabins and the galley. The hand pump affixed to the tank trunk was padlocked and could only be used in the presence of an officer. The pump was built into a pin rail just aft of the mast.

In fair weather, there was no problem pumping the ten buckets a day of freshwater allowed for drinking and cooking. With water breaking across the deck, it was an entirely different matter.

Lifelines were rigged fore and aft and athwartships. Eight sailors and an officer would make their way to the pumps, holding buckets over their heads. It then became an ugly game of trying to pump frantically between the breaking seas then holding the buckets high enough to keep them out of the seawater. Most buckets made it back to the cabin or to the fo'c'sle more than a little brackish from the spray alone. Of all his duties aboard ship, this was Fred's least favorite. He would rather fight a frozen topsail than walk the deck holding a sloshing bucket above his head while icy waves up to his chest tried to wash him overboard.

"Captain Barker, sir. I believe you need to see this."

The captain looked up from the chart table. "Yes, Mr. Atkinson."

The second mate stepped into the dayroom, followed by Hanson and Lindstrom.

"Show your hands and feet."

Three fingers on Lindstrom's left hand were red and shriveled as were four of Hanson's toes on his right foot.

"Have the steward wrap the affected fingers and toes in warm compresses. Put these sailors on light duty and I will check on them daily."

"Yes, sir," Atkinson replied.

"And speak to Mr. Rand. Have him check on frostbite in his watch. If your sailors are afflicted, he might have problems too."

Captain Barker checked his Board of Trade *Ship Captain's Medical Guide,* but found little enough to be done.

Over the next week, Captain Barker and Mr. Gronberg visited the sailors in the fo'c'sle. Several sailors were showing the signs of frost-bite. Lindstrom's fingers and Hanson's toes were the worst, turning from red to white, and then from white to yellow. One of Lindstrom's fingers appeared to be recovering but the other two were not. When Hanson's toes and Lindstrom's fingers shifted from yellow to the color of a ripe plum, Captain Barker knew what he had to do.

"Mr. Gronberg, Hanson's and Linstrom's fingers and toes have turned gangrenous. They'll need to come off."

"Yah. I'll sharpen my chisels, sir. Best way to do it."

The next day during the first dogwatch, the captain, carpenter and sail maker made their way forward to the fo'c'sle.

"Let me see your fingers and toes," the captain demanded of the two men. Hanson winced as he took off his seaboot and sock. His two smallest toes on his left foot were shriveled and blackened. Lindstrom's third finger on his right hand looked no better. His other fingers were somewhat improved. The captain could only nod to Gronberg. He was right. The blackened fingers and toes had to come off.

With rum to both sanitize the area and sedate the sailors, Gronberg removed the gangrenous toes and fingers. A single blow with his maul and the chisel lopped off the blackened digits, followed by a howl of pain from the sailor. Pugsley followed just behind to expertly bandage the stumps.

The two sailors wouldn't be fit for duty for weeks. With Whitney laid up in the spare cabin and Hanson and Lindstrom in the fo'c'sle, they had seventeen able sailors left. And the west wind still had them trapped. All they needed was a favoring wind shift, just one good favoring slant.

August 20, 1905 – 70 days out of Cardiff

Mary Barker was in the captain's salon with the children. She had been seasick on and off ever since the westerly winds had started to blow. The children were fine, for which Mary was grateful. How often the children are more resilient than the parents, she thought. Or at least their mother.

Amanda was on the couch playing with Mrs. Murphy, that pathetic little doll, while Tommy was on the cabin sole playing with blocks of wood that the carpenter had given him. God bless Mr. Pugsley and Mr. Gronberg, Mary thought. They had been so kind to the children. Mary steadied herself in the chair as the ship lurched and rolled. She never seemed able to grow accustomed to the motion, to which the children seemed oblivious.

She felt trapped. Her entire world now was the children in this comfortable, if simple, salon and stateroom, with light and warmth on a ship that seemed to be a captive of Cape Horn. She didn't know what to do. There was nothing to be done. She shouldn't be complaining or feeling sorry for herself. She had her children for company and the steward, Walter, took care of them the best he could with all his other duties. James checked in on them whenever he could. She couldn't imagine what it had to be like for James, spending so much time on deck in such ghastly conditions. And the poor sailors having to tend sail in the ice and horrible winds—it was almost beyond imagining.

A moment later, the ship took a particularly violent roll and there was a horrible crash. Smoke filled the cabin. Mary spun around and screamed. The last roll had ripped the screws holding down the stove from the deck. It slid across the cabin, hitting the bulkhead and setting it on fire. Mary, still screaming, scooped up Tommy from up off the cabin sole, grabbed Amanda's hand and dragged her into the companionway. Walter rushed past her and then ran out again.

"Help! The cabin's on fire and the stove is adrift," he yelled as loud as he could.

Captain Barker and Mr. Atkinson arrived in the salon at almost the same instant. Red-hot coals were scattered across the carpets, furniture was broken, part of a bulkhead was smashed and burning. It was hard to see or breathe for all the smoke and soot. Barker grabbed a bucket of wash water from the steward's pantry and threw it on the bulkhead, putting out the fire but adding to the smoke. Making their way to the stove, lying on its side, they saw the rivets that had held the top to the sidewalls were broken and twisted. Barker snorted. "Looks like a dying dragon, don't you think?" He shook his head. "It looks beyond repair to me. Mr. Atkinson. Get your gang in here, take it on deck and toss it overboard."

Harry, Fred, Tom, Santiago and Jerry arrived in the cabin with broad grins on their faces. They had been in the mess room, but had never ventured in the captain's salon before, and to see it in such a state was somehow very satisfying. They wrapped wet sacking around their hands, and with a couple of hatch beams they hoisted the broken and smoking stove up and out of the cabin and onto the main deck. Timing it with a roll of the ship, they heaved the stove into the ocean and cheered as it sizzled and sank.

A small spare bogie stove was located in the lazarette, and Pugsley and the apprentices set to repairing the damage to the salon as well as they could. With a bit of new paneling and some paint, the salon was at least in order, if still not quite what it had been. Mary and the children now spent most of their time in the stateroom. The crew spent the next week chuckling over the captain's stove coming adrift. It seemed to lift everyone's spirits forward of the mast.

Captain Barker commented to Mate Atkinson, "If I had known that the bloody stove would do this much good I would have loosened the deck bolts myself." Atkinson laughed freely for the first time in what seemed like an age.

CHAPTER 10
ROGUE WAVE

September 12, 1905 – 93 days out of Cardiff

Captain Barker stared at the chart. The plot of their course was a sickening zigzag, back and forth, trying to capture every favoring wind shift while going nowhere but farther south, ever closer to the ice. In three weeks, by his reckoning, they had gone one hundred and seven miles south and lost twelve miles of westing. There was nothing to be done but to hang on and to outlast the westerly winds.

He reached for his jacket and went up on deck. It was two hours into the first watch, 10 p.m. They were hove to under reefed topsails and a storm staysail. The ship was plunging and rolling in the darkness. Barker made his way over to Atkinson, who had tied himself to the mizzen pin rail behind the weather cloth lashed to the shrouds to give him some protection from the icy spray.

Just then, the moon broke through the clouds and, well to weather, the captain saw a wave — a wave like he had never seen before. It seemed three times larger than the other waves and came from the wrong direction. He blinked and looked again. "Oh my God," he said beneath his breath.

It was a wall of water, stretching endlessly northwest and southeast; the top, breaking and tumbling, roaring toward them at an impossible speed. It towered so high above the other waves that they seemed to be barely swells by comparison. The mighty wave was rushing straight at the *Lady Rebecca* and there was absolutely nothing that he could do. The helm was already lashed down, keeping her bow as high into the wind as it would bear. No change of sail would save them from being hit by this monster, even if there was time.

Barker bellowed with all his might to the watch, "On the deck there, drop everything, jump up into the rigging! Jump for your lives! Climb high! Now!"

The sailors looked to windward and most ran for the rigging. Jerry the Greek stood for a moment, startled, and then turned and ran with the others.

Atkinson, tied to the pin rail, was secure, so Barker ran aft for the wheel and shouted to the helmsman, "Hang on." The captain grabbed the other side of the wheel and waited.

Time seemed to slow. The wave that rushed at them with such ferocity seemed to hang in his gaze for a moment before crashing in upon them. The thought flashed through his mind that no ship could survive such a wave, that they were all dead already. No one could survive such a wave.

The ship slipped sideways into the tremendous trough, momentarily sheltered from the wind, rolling to leeward into the oncoming wave, until the great vertical wall of water crashed over them. The roar of tumbling water was like a thousand cannons. The foaming, breaking crest looked higher than the lower yardarms and it fell upon them in a massive hammer blow that shook the ship, rolling her down, and seeming about to drive her wholly and forever beneath the sea.

The wall of water lifted the captain off his feet. He held on for his life, but the spoke cracked and he was thrown backward, to be stopped by the steel bulwark with a tremendous and painful crash.

The wave rolled the *Lady Rebecca* on her beam-ends. For what seemed an eternity she lay there, pressed by the wave and the relentless wind, like some great animal struck down, lying on its flank. Captain Barker was crumpled against the bulwark, dazed and confused. Everything was on its side. The deck appeared to be a wall, rising nearly vertically skyward. The masts were canted oddly just above the sea, and the lower yardarms were buried in the roiling water.

Then slowly, almost imperceptibly, the old ship began to right herself. She rolled up, knocked back by a passing wave once and again, but she steadily fought back against the wind and sea like a pugilist too stubborn to stay down. The ship wallowed, as if punch-drunk, but she rolled up once again. The reefed topsails and staysail luffed loudly, cracking like gunfire over the howl of the wind. In a minute or two, the cacophony of the sails died down as the fine old ship fell back onto an approximation of what had been her course, seven points off the wind.

Slowly, Captain Barker tried to move. He crawled across the deck, feeling awash in pain, and pulled himself up on the weather rail. He shivered in the cold in the howling wind, as the icy water drained from his jacket and pants. He was bruised from head to toe, but somehow nothing seemed to be broken. He looked over for the helmsman and saw him jammed against the shattered wheel box. Barker yelled, "You all right?" The helmsman raised his hand and nodded.

"Captain, are you injured?" Mr. Atkinson called, looking wild-eyed.

"I'm fine," the captain responded, not yet sure that that was true.

The deck forward was chaos. The rigging looked all out of kilter, yards akimbo. The main t'gallantmast was bent sidewards, probably cracked. The boats on the poop deck were gone. Only the twisted steel davits remained.

Then he heard a cry behind him. One of the crew had been carried overboard and wailed for help. Who had they lost? Barker just closed his eyes and said a silent prayer for the sailor. They couldn't launch a boat in these seas in any case, and now, he thought, looking over at the twisted, empty davits, they had no boats ready to launch.

He turned around and gasped to see the cabin skylight crushed and open to the sky. He ran to the cabin ladder. The salon was flooded. He threw open the door to the stateroom where his wife and children were strapped in their bed. The water was up to his knees. From the moonlight streaming in through the gaping hole in the deck above, he could see that the bed was covered with broken glass and wooden framing.

He shouted, "Mary," but there came no reply. He frantically pulled the wood off the bed, digging down to reach the blankets. Then he heard his wife's soft sobbing. He pulled the blanket back. She was holding both children, who looked frightened beyond tears or speech.

"James?"

"Thank God that you are all alive."

"Is the ship sinking?"

"No," he replied, not sure that it was true either. "We'll be all right." He ran to the locker and pulled out dry blankets and spread them across the bed. He had to try to keep Mary and the children warm.

"Walter," he yelled, calling for steward, and was both gratified and a bit surprised when he heard the steward's reply.

"Yes, captain?"

"Get some hot soup or tea for Mrs. Barker and the children. And more dry blankets."

He turned back to Mary, pale and shivering, beneath the blankets, her eyes wide with fear. "Walter will tend to you now. I must tend to the ship."

As he left, he heard Amanda begin to scream. Little Tommy followed his sister's example as their mother tried to calm them. He could hardly blame the children. If he could have, he would have broken into tears himself, but he had no time for emotion until he knew whether or not his ship would survive.

Fred was asleep when a deep roll to leeward nearly pitched him out of his bunk. Shaken awake, he grabbed the bunk boards to stop from falling when, a moment later, there was a deafening roar, the moan of bending steel and the crack of fracturing timber. The ship rolled back to windward and Fred was thrown violently against the bulkhead. Icy water cascaded into the fo'c'sle, as if they were suddenly all beneath a cataract. As the roar and the deluge subsided, men sputtered and shouted in bewilderment and rage. Fred was sure that he was going to drown. The torrent subsided but he was still pressed against the bulkhead.

Then, finally, the ship began to roll back. Several feet of water, sloshing on the deck, was draining out through the cabin door, which was sprung and hung weirdly by a single hinge. Everything seemed twisted and out of shape. The outboard fo'c'sle bulkhead, heavy wood planks over steel frames, was bowed in and broken. Moonlight streamed in through the broken planks in the overhead casting weird light and shadows across the cabin. Sea chests were scattered, some knocked open, their contents floating in the sloshing brine.

Fred rolled from his bunk, knocking into Donnie.

"What hell was that?" Fred asked.

Donnie just shook his head as they both stumbled out on the deck.

The deckhouse was stove in. The boats were gone. Santiago had been lookout on the deckhouse by the boats. Fred closed his eyes and shook his head. Santiago would never make it home to see his mother or sister. Fred suddenly wondered if any of them would make it to Chile alive.

❖ ❖ ❖

Will hung in the futtock shrouds just below the main top, where he had scrambled after hearing Captain Barker shout. He had seen the wave and was sure that he was going to die. His eyes were closed. His arms and legs were wrapped tightly around the heavy steel cable. The world was rolling over. He no longer hung from the shrouds. Gravity was pressing his body against them. The ship was capsizing. They would all drown. He was sure of it.

Then slowly the world began to right itself again. Up and down returned to their rightful places. He slowly opened his eyes. In the moonlight, the deck was a shambles. Nothing was in its place. Waves were still breaking across the deck. He knew that he wasn't dead only because his muscles hurt and the howling wind was bitterly cold and raw. He still wondered how he could possibly be alive, how the ship could still be afloat.

"Back down to the deck everyone" Mr. Rand yelled. "Work to be done. No skylarking."

As he climbed down the ratlines, he looked along the deck edge and saw a large lump of canvas that seemed to be blocking the freeing port in the bulwark. In an instant, he realized that the lump was a man. He jumped on deck and yelled, "Help me. Somebody's hurt."

It was Jerry the Greek. Most of his body was inboard but one leg had washed through the freeing port and the heavy steel flap was slamming down viciously on his leg as the ship rolled. He wasn't conscious but was moaning, which meant he had to be alive.

Will was shoved aside by the mate. "Get a wedge to block the damn flap. Now haul him out. Easy."

Will staggered back as they carried Jerry to the fo'c'sle.

Captain Barker climbed on number three hatch with the sail maker, Pugsley. The wave had ripped the tarpaulins from the hatches and shifted the deal boards. With every wave that broke aboard the ship, more water flowed into the hold. Number three hatch was the worst.

"Get every tarp we have. We need to seal the hatches or we will all go to the bottom."

"Captain," said Gronberg, the carpenter, standing at the hatch coaming.

"How bad is it?" the captain asked.

"Close to three feet of water in the holds, sir."

Pugsley swore behind him.

"Are you sure?" The captain preferred not to believe what he just heard.

"Yes, sir. Threaded a hose down the pipe to block the water flowing down. Got the same sounding, three times at three hatches."

Three feet meant many hundreds of tonnes of water. It meant the ship floated deeper and had less freeboard. Lower in the water, she was easier for the seas to break over and had less buoyancy to rise up again. She could act more like a half-tide rock than a cork.

"Very good, Mr. Gronberg. If you should see Mr. Rand, send him to me."

In a few minutes, the mate appeared.

"Mr. Rand, get your crowd to stretch the tarps and make the hatches tight. That is our first order of business. Put any free hands you have on the pumps."

"Aye, sir," Rand responded. "Captain, I think the starboard fo'c'sle house is stove in. May have to double up on the port house. And the portside pump is sheared clean off the deck. Not sure about the starboard."

Barker shook his head. "Very well. Get the hatches tight first."

"And a man has been injured. Jerry the Greek is hurt bad. His leg."

"Broken?"

"No, sir, crushed. We got him strapped in his bunk."

"Who did we lose overboard?"

"Santiago, sir. Lookout on the cabin top. He was washed away along with the boats. Wave stove in the deckhouse and swept the cabin top clean."

"The boats . . . ?" He didn't need to finish the sentence. So now they had no boats at all. All swept away by a single wave.

Once back in the cabin, Captain Barker wondered if Santiago hadn't heard him shout his warning or whether the sailor thought he was safe on top of the fo'c'sle cabin. It didn't matter. The man was dead regardless. No one could survive those icy seas. Barker tried not to think of Santiago or anything other than the *Lady Rebecca*.

The enormity of the damage was still sinking in. Three feet of water in the holds and one pump gone. All four boats gone. One man lost and other crippled. Who knew how much damage to the deck and the rigging. He'd find out soon enough once the sun rose. In the mean time he would see to his family. The children were still upset and Mary was doing her best to be stoic, but could only do so much. Why had he brought them along on the voyage? It was a pointless thought which he pushed from his mind. They were with him and he would have to do all he could to keep them safe. He wondered if what he could do would be enough.

At first light, Captain Barker met the carpenter by the portside pump, or at least where the portside pump had been. Perhaps one of the boats had hit it on its way over the side. Whatever had happened, the bolts that had held the pump to the deck had sheared off. The pump shaft was bent and broken. What was left of the twelve-man pump lay crumpled against the bulwark.

"How's the starboard pump?" Barker asked.

"Better'n this one to be sure," said Gronberg. "I think she's OK. She's just not pumping."

"What do you mean?"

"I think the suction be jammed with coal dust. Have to send somebody down to clear it maybe, if things calm down. Be crazy to try it now, with this sea running."

"Thank you, mister," the captain replied, turned and walked aft, holding tightly to the lifeline. Spume flew over the rail and struck him in the side of his face. As he walked, he tallied the damage he had seen this morning. One pump destroyed and the other not pumping. The foremast ready to topple and the main t'gallantmast shattered. And the westerlies showed no sign of abating. Maybe Mr. Rand was right. As soon as he allowed himself to think the thought, he swore out loud, "No, Goddamn it. We are not beaten yet. Not by a long shot."

With daylight, Captain Barker and Mate Atkinson surveyed the damage to the rig. When they worked their way forward, they saw the jib-boom, the spar forward of the bowsprit, skewed oddly upward. "Fractured at the gammoning band," the captain said, and the mate noted it in his notebook.

At the foremast, Barker mumbled to himself. "Bloody Christ." A riveted strap over a butt in two sections of the mast had ripped off. Both the rivets and the strap were gone, leaving a gaping space between the sections of steel pipe. In the running seas the mast sections flexed, opening and closing like angry jaws. He was surprised that they hadn't lost the entire mast and the rest of the top-hamper. "Clew up the topsail and get crew aloft to furl it. We can't afford any load on this mast until we reinforce it."

Captain Barker climbed the weather ratlines on the mainmast. He caught a look of surprise from several sailors. A lot they don't know about me yet, he thought. Still a few tricks up my sleeve.

As he climbed, he looked for problems. The mainmast looked fine, as did the topmast. The t'gallantmast, however, was bent slightly sideways, a six-inch crack at the base. Could it be repaired? He had a few ideas but it couldn't be done in these seas.

When he returned to the poop deck, he turned to Mr. Rand. "Set a course nor'-nor'east. Square away for Staten Island. We'll make repairs in the lee."

"Aye, sir, nor'-nor'east it is. Turning back to Staten Island." Rand smiled smugly.

Barker scowled. "No, sir. We are not turning back. We will make repairs in the lee of Staten Island and then stand on. We are bound for Chile. No place else."

CHAPTER 11
IN THE LEE OF STATEN ISLAND

September 16, 1905 – 97 days out of Cardiff

The world had become quiet and still. In the lee of Staten Island, the endless howl of the wind and the roar of breaking seas were gone. The deck no longer rose and twisted beneath Mary Barker's feet. For the first time in a month, she prepared to venture out from the damp and gloomy cabin that had been both her refuge and prison for so many days and nights. She still felt shaken by the massive wave that had nearly drowned her and the children. The skylight had suddenly burst in a wall of dark water, flying glass and splintered wood. It was boarded over now, making the cabin all that much darker, even with the lanterns lit.

She paused for a moment in front of the mirror. She looked such a mess. She put her hand on her hairbrush and almost laughed. Had they not sailed far beyond the world where such things mattered?

Her hand drew away and then, in an instant of resolve, she grabbed the handle and roughly brushed her hair. A few strokes forced it back into a semblance of order, and perhaps that was enough. Even in this godforsaken watery waste, she would maintain certain standards.

She wrapped a blanket about her shoulders, climbed the stairs to the deck and slowly opened the door. There was no wind. Just a gentle breeze, cold but bracing. She stepped tentatively out on the deck, closing the door behind her.

The sky was overcast but she still squinted, even in the cloud-shrouded daylight. The ship was in a shallow cove. The island stretched out on both sides of them, disappearing in the mists on either hand. It was mountainous, with dark green trees clinging to the darker slopes, rising up to snow-capped peaks that seemed not unlike the scudding clouds moving above them, except that the peaks were still—frozen, literally and figuratively, in space and time.

She wondered if the wave that had so nearly sunk them looked like this island. She had heard the steward call the wave a mountain. High and dark with a foaming crest towering over them, even as the white-crested island peaks towered over them now.

She had only heard the wave, waking a few seconds before it struck. She had cried out involuntarily at the deafening roar and the freezing flood of water that exploded through the shattered skylight. It was all so impossibly loud that she couldn't even hear her own scream.

Now, she could hear the breeze softly humming through the upper rigging, and forward, the gruff voice of the mate urging the men to greater exertion. Now, even the shades of blue, gray and green on the island seemed impossibly vivid. She breathed in the cold but clean dark smell of the shore. She could see, smell and hear again—senses she was not even aware that she had relinquished within the confines of the cabin until now that they had returned to her.

James came up the poop deck ladder. His pace quickened when he saw her.

"Mary, dear. How are you? Are you well?"

"James, I am quite well. Thank you. It feels good to get out of the cabin. I feel as if I have spent a lifetime strapped into that bed. Aren't the mountains beautiful?"

He turned his head and nodded his agreement, and then looked back at her.

"And the children?"

"Sound asleep. First quiet time they have had to sleep in days."

James smiled.

"I see that repairs are under way."

"Yes, a few more days and we will be back at it."

Mary's brow furrowed. "Not back to Port Stanley?"

"No," he replied, more vehemently than he intended. "Where did you get such an idea?"

"I heard Mr. Rand speaking to the steward. He said that he expected us to put into the Falklands for repairs."

"That bastard. He lacks the courage to stand up to me, but is still trying to turn the crew against me. If he wasn't a good seaman I would have had him in irons by now."

For an instant Mary felt a crushing weight on her shoulders. Without admitting it to herself, she held out the faintest hope that she and the children might leave the ship in Port Stanley. But that was not to be. She was as trapped on this ship as all the rest of the officers and crew, bound for Chile, come what may.

"So it is back out into the gales once again?"

He smiled at her. "Don't worry, my dear. All we need is a favorable slant of wind. That is all and we will slip in the Pacific, into warm water and warm weather. The winds can't stand against us forever."

She smiled back at him, not necessarily convinced by his words but admiring his determination. She would pray that he was right.

"If I have learned only one thing in all my years at sea, dear, it is that only way to prosper is to keep to the sea. And so we shall. As long as we are able we shall sail on to Chile. To that I am committed."

"Captain?" She heard her brother's voice. He stood at the edge of the poop.

"Yes, Mr. Atkinson. Be with you presently." Barker surprised his wife by leaning over and kissing her on the cheek. "I must get back to my duties."

She watched him walk away, and realized that that was the longest conversation they had had since arriving in the Southern Ocean. This wasn't what she had imagined her life to be, after her brother introduced her to the dashing young ship's captain at the social after Sunday services years before. There was a certain status to being a captain's wife and she dreamed of joyous homecomings and a comfortable house with flowers by the walk. If someone had suggested that one day she would find herself trapped on a ship and nearly drowned by a monstrous wave or nearly burned to death by a stove adrift, what would she have thought? Would she have called that person crazy? And if so, what did that make her now?

She pulled the blanket tighter around her shoulders and gazed up again at the mountains before going below to check on the children. She and James each had their duties to perform.

The pump suction had to be cleared so they could use the pump to start emptying the ship of the hundreds of tons of water dumped aboard by the giant wave. Will understood as much. What he wasn't convinced of was who should do the clearing.

"Why does it have to be me?" Will demanded.

"Cause you're the smallest, Willie. Now stop complaining." Paul Nelson glared at him.

"George is almost as small as me."

"He's a good sight bigger'n you—and besides, the mate said you, so down you go. Orders are orders."

Will had a rope tied around his waist just in case he needed to be hauled out, and a small shovel with a short handle. "But..." He could see that it was no use so he clenched his jaw and climbed down the ladder into the access trunk. It was cold and black and the light from the deck seemed to grow dimmer with each step down the ladder. Finally he reached the water. He pulled the shovel from under his arm and tried to reach down to the pump suction. Nothing. He reached as far as he could, hanging on the rungs with one hand and dragging the shovel through the water with the other. Still nothing.

He stepped lower on the ladder. He could feel the icy water seeping into his boots. He reached down again but still couldn't reach it. He reached farther and his fingers slipped from the rung. He let out a yell as he fell into the black water.

His head slipped under the icy blackness and he fought to grab the ladder to pull himself up. Shivering and gasping, he found that he could stand but that the water was up to his armpits. The water burned and numbed him at the same time. It was impossibly cold. He was sure that he would die that instant. But he didn't. He only shivered. He had dropped the shovel but, reaching down, he felt it. With fingers he could barely control, he scraped and dug at the bottom of the pipe that was the pump suction. The coal dust felt like concrete as he jabbed at it. Finally, the shovel blade hit only the iron of the pipe.

He tried to climb back up the ladder but his legs wouldn't work. He yelled, "Pull me up," but nothing happened. He yelled again, with still no response. It occurred to him that if someone didn't haul him out soon, his lifeless body would be clogging the pump suction next.

"Help! Help! Somebody! Help!" He screamed for all that he was worth and saw a shadow across the distant beam of light from the trunk access on deck.

"You say something, Willie?" the shadow yelled down.

"Help! Help! Haul me up!"

He felt the rope around his waist tighten and he was lifted slowly through the darkness back to the deck. Paul Nelson and Jack dragged him out and lay him shivering and close to insensible on the deck.

"We should get him some rum," Jack suggested.

Second Mate Atkinson gave Jack a kick. "Get him blankets and a pannikin of hot tea. That'll warm him up better'n rum. Take him to the fo'c'sle and prop him up next to the bogie stove. Get some hot tea or coffee in him and he'll be fine."

He turned to Paul. "Grab that shovel. We're going to fire up the boiler and use the steam engine to drive the pump."

Fred followed Gronberg up the ratlines. The carpenter moved quickly for a man of his age, Fred thought, without quite knowing what that age might be. Tom, Donnie and Hans clambered up right behind Fred and the carpenter. While the main and topmasts were steel, the t'gallantmast was pine, and was now cracked with a noticeable cant to starboard. Gronberg climbed into the crosstrees while the rest split on either side, balancing on the ratlines.

It took several hours to downrig the sails, t'gallant yards, halyards, bunts and clews. Once the mast was bare, the carpenter rigged snatch blocks at the topmast head and secured a line beneath the foot of the cracked t'gallantmast. The sailors each took a strain on the line, lifting the spar as Gronberg knocked out the pin from the mast jaws with a mallet. "Easy, *meine kinder*, easy," the carpenter said softly.

The pin moved freely but the mast jammed. Gronberg hauled back and started pounding furiously at the foot of the mast, shouting, "*Wertlos ficken syphilitische Hure—bewegen!*" The mast squeaked, shifted slightly, and then started smoothly rising. Gronberg grinned. "See, alvays the gentle touch." Clear of the jaws, Gronberg threw a rolling hitch on a gantline around the mast and the sailors started lowering the cracked mast to the deck.

Once the spar was down, Fred glanced over and saw smoke rising from near the fo'c'sle.

"What the…?"

Tom laughed. "The Old Man finally decided to use the steam winch. Trying to pump out the hold is my guess."

"I wish him luck. Wish us all luck," Fred replied.

The galley was dry now and Jeremiah was no longer cooking up to his knees in icy water. Most of the damage done by the wave to the galley stove had been put right, but the cook's mood was still dark. It didn't help that he had to open his coal bin to let the mate start up the steam winch. The cook took a proprietary interest in the coal he used to fire his stove and they had no business raiding his bin, which he freely told them, not that they ever listened. Worse than that, no one listened to him about the devil's wave.

Harry and Fred had been collecting their mess's serving of salt pork and peas.

"Ye know, that wave, that wave from the debil. That wave come to pull his own down ta hell. Long as we got that Jonah onboard, the debil will be reaching up to catch us. Sure, that's the truth."

Harry looked over with a sneer and said, "You be quiet, ya black bastard. Any more talk about the devil and Jonahs and I'll throw you over side to the devil hisself. Sure we could get one of the 'prentices up here, cook better than you." He sniffed at the pork and peas and made a face, and then turned and walked back to the fo'c'sle.

Fred did all he could not to laugh out loud.

Jeremiah was seething and mumbling to himself. He looked up at Fred and said, "That man, he don't know. I speak God's truth. Going against God's truth jus' bring trouble. You'll all see."

It took the better part of two days to rig the new stays to the foremast, but when it was done even Mr. Rand declared it a good job, so long as they didn't crowd on the canvas forward. Captain Barker sent Rand and his watch to work on the gammoning on the jib-boom.

Gronberg and the second mate's watch were kept busy shoring up the damaged bulkhead on the starboard fo'c'sle house with timber. The mate's watch had shifted to spare bunks in the portside house but could now move back, even though the outboard bulkhead was still bowed inward.

Most important of all, the hatches were tight and the steam winch had been pumping for a good ten hours between breaks to refill the boiler feed water.

Captain Barker paced the poop deck, watching the high clouds tumbling over the mountain peaks of Staten Island. Every few minutes he dropped down into the chart room to check the barometer. It was rising. It was definitely rising. Captain Barker could feel it. The wind would be shifting. They were getting a slant. A favorable slant of wind that would carry them west.

Second Mate Atkinson called to him from the deck just forward of the poop.

"Sir, the pump suction locked again."

"How much water is left in the hold?"

Atkinson pulled out his notebook from his back pocket. "Still almost two and half feet, sir. Should I send someone down to clear it again? "

"No." The captain shook his head. "Secure the boiler. I think that we will be seeing a wind shift soon and we will be getting under way."

"Yes, sir," Atkinson replied with an energetic nod.

The easterly wind filled in and the *Lady Rebecca* slipped south around St. John's Point and squared up on a westerly course across a confused sea. Captain Barker took his place on the poop deck, looking unashamedly pleased. By the afternoon watch, Mary and the children, wrapped in blankets, joined him on the deck, to marvel at the favorable breeze and watch the pale sunlight shining on the dancing waters.

The easterly wind died by midnight, leaving the *Lady Rebecca* becalmed. By the next dawn, the westerlies were back, blowing a full gale. A weary crew struck and furled sails, and the *Lady Rebecca* slogged along under reefed topsails, slowly working southward against the relentless westerly wind.

CHAPTER 12
FIGHTING THE WESTERLIES

September 21, 1905 – 102 days out of Cardiff

The barometer fell steadily and the westerly gales continued to blow. There was nothing to be done but shorten sail and fore-reach south until they got a favorable slant. When any favorable wind shift came, as it must sooner or later, they needed to make as much westing as they could before the westerlies tried to drive them back again. It was neither complicated nor elegant but it was the only way to round the Horn in the winter.

They had already spent forty-four days before being driven back to Staten Island. How many more days would it take to outlast the prevailing winds? Captain Barker stared at the chart as if there was some secret to be revealed, but he knew the only secret was to hang on, to endure at whatever cost.

He grabbed his dreadnought coat from the hook and climbed the ladder to the deck. He took his place to windward. Mr. Rand, the mate on watch, was just forward by the leeward mizzen shrouds, a dark shape across the windswept deck.

By now, Captain Barker was sure that the crew must hate him as the cause of all their misery. He couldn't change that under any circumstances, so at least he would spend every waking hour, when he was not otherwise attending to ship's business, there on deck. If he asked them to face the wind and storms, so would he. The wind and the spray were bitterly cold but he was their equal. Let the crew look aft and curse his name. That was their right as sailors. As long as they did their duty, their opinions were rightly their own.

He glanced over at Mr. Rand. Now there was a puzzle. There was no doubt that the man was a skilled sailor. He knew his job and he did it well when he chose to. He worried that Rand was plotting against him. That was usually the source of mutinies—an officer who turned the crew against the captain. A mutiny always needed a leader who would goad the crew on and then step up to take command. Was Rand that officer? Did he have the nerve and the backbone to try and take over? That was the real question. So far, he had always backed down. Would he continue or would he finally show some courage?

If it came to that, Captain Barker was sure he had Mr. Atkinson on his side and, in all likelihood, the apprentices. Two men and four boys might just be enough, if it came to a head.

He had worried about signing on Tom Atkinson. He was a young man, inexperienced and being his wife's brother might cause complications in the rigid discipline that had to be maintained aboard ship.

Cape Horn could age a man and Mr. Atkinson had learned quickly. If he ever spoke more than a word to Mary, he did so discreetly, which is all one could ask. Mr. Atkinson had turned out to be his strong right arm. He was sure he would make a fine captain when his day came.

It was early in the afternoon watch in the gray half-light of the Southern Ocean. A squall was coming. He could see it in the darkening of the horizon and the steady rising of the wind in the rigging that progressively stepped up by a half an octave or so. Captain Barker looked out to see if any sailors were exposed but saw that the watch was all huddled abaft the fo'c'sle house—as protected as they could be, given the conditions.

When the squall hit, the *Lady Rebecca* staggered. She rolled deeply to leeward, scooping up tons of water on her broad deck. A wall of water surged aft as she rolled back, sweeping the deck and breaking against the poop. Captain Barker turned his head so that he wouldn't be blinded by the flying spray.

There was a boom like a cannon blast and the main upper topsail exploded into streamers and shredded rags. For a moment they all stood and looked at the naked bolt-ropes and strips of canvas being lashed by the breeze. Then Mr. Rand shouted, "The watch on deck— cast off the sheets and haul bunts and clews." He bounded down the main deck ladder and continued shouting orders until he was at the mast.

Captain Barker watched his back. Now that was the sort of mate that he could use a few more of. And the mate who refused orders and tried to turn the crew against him, he could use one less.

Will sat shoulder to shoulder with his watch mates in the mess room. It was the largest place below deck to spread out canvas, and it was barely sufficient. Pugsley had a roll of 44-pound, 24-inch by 38-foot No. 1 cotton duck canvas that he was cutting into panels for a new topsail. Their spare set of sails was depleted and the westerlies kept reducing sails to tatters.

The more experienced sailors sewed the seams while the apprentices sewed the bolt-ropes to the canvas under the watchful eye of the sail maker. Will wore a sailor's palm on his right hand, a heavy strip of leather that fitted around his hand with a hole for his thumb. A steel grommet was fastened in the palm, which was where Will placed the end of the threaded heavy needle and, with all the force he could muster, pushed the needle through the two layers of canvas and the hemp bolt-rope. He would then yank the needle free and begin another of the countless stitches it would take to anchor the bolt-rope to just one side of the new sail. He was careful to judge the stitch spacing with his thumb so that Pugsley would not make him cut out and the redo the hard-fought stitches.

Will's hands, arms and back ached. His hands were cracked and bloodied from climbing icy rigging, and with every stitch he winced. Still, being belowdecks was better than being in the weather. The packed-in sailors, working around the sail, warmed the mess room with their body heat, and so while it wasn't warm, neither was Will freezing, which was indeed a welcome change.

Harry was sitting across the table, sewing a well-rubbed seam with perfectly symmetrical herringbone stitches. He looked up and said, "This weather, worst I've seen in all my years at sea. And that ogre of a wave. Aach. I tell anybody 'bout that wave, they call me a liar, for sure."

Frenchie, across the table, laughed. "You are a liar. All sailors are liars."

Harry smiled. "Maybe so. Maybe so. At least we've missed the ice. So far anyway. An old shipmate of mine sailed on the *Florence* out of Glasgow. Ever told you this story?"

He paused for a moment and getting no response carried on. "Well, they was homeward bound and got set way south when the fog set in. Couldn't see nothing. The wind was too light to blow it way. So the mate sends the bosun to the fo'c'sle head with the foghorn. An' the bosun starts cranking and horn blows loud and long, then he stops and listens and sure enough way off in the distance, he hears another foghorn. Calls back to the mate that there is a ship out there.

"So he keeps cranking and then listening and the ship seems to be getting closer, and pretty soon everybody can hear the other foghorn. The mate sends a boy down to tell the captain that there is a ship in the fog. The captain sends a message back to call him when it is in sight. Course, with that fog, they might never see him. And the bosun keeps cranking the foghorn and the other foghorn keeps getting closer, till suddenly, the captain rushes up on deck. 'You idiot,' he yells at the mate. 'That's no ship, that's ice.' He orders the wheel hard over.

"Only a few minutes later, what had looked like a solid wall of fog turns out was a solid wall of ice. A bloody ice island, tall as the maintop. The other ship they'd been hearing was the echo of their own bloody horn off the ice." Hanson across the table nodded his head. Ice could do that.

"They'd just begun the turn, but the wind was so light they barely had steerage. The jib-boom crunches into the ice and is torn clean off. The sudden yank on the forestay brings down the fore t'gallantmast too. They get swung around so they are right alongside the ice wall, pretty as you please, just as if they were tied up on the Mersey docks with the gates open at high tide.

"Once they cleared away the mess of rigging, they launched the boats and towed the ship away from the ice. I hear tell that that was a bloody long row. They say that that wall of ice seemed to run on forever. When they finally found clear water, the captain set a course for the Falklands and they limped into Port Stanley. The ship was sprung forward, so they were pumping for their lives the whole way in. The underwriters condemned her right then and there. Not worth the cost of repair."

"Least not at Port Stanley prices," Frenchie piped in.

"Sure, sure enough. Sold her as a coal barge. Still there, for all I know. They all got a steamer ride home."

"Wouldn't mind a steamer ride home, myself," Hanson mumbled.

Will just shivered involuntarily and hoped that the *Lady Rebecca* never sailed that far south.

Fred was two bunks down from Jerry the Greek, who, with his leg crushed, was insensible half the time and moaning in agony the rest. The captain or the carpenter checked in on him every few days for what good they could do. It didn't take long for the smell from his berth to tell the tale. The leg was infected and becoming gangrenous. Everyone knew that odor.

Gronberg took off his cap when he entered the captain's dayroom. Captain Barker looked up from the chart. The light from the lantern above the chart table swung in an arc with the roll of the ship.

"Captain, Jerry the Greek is gonna die unless you do somet'ing right quick."

"Is it that bad?"

"Well, sir. He's feverish and the leg is stinkin'. If it doesn't come off soon, he a dead man. The gangrene is set in, and it'll spread. I've seen it happen."

Captain Barker looked down at the chart again for a long moment, before looking back at the carpenter. "Have you ever amputated a leg, Mr. Gronberg?"

The carpenter blanched. "No, sir."

The captain thought, *Well, neither have I*, but saw no need to say so.

"All right. Get your sharpest saw. Take it to the cook and have him sterilize it in boiling water. And have him sharpen his best knife. Make sure it is really sharp. Have him sterilize that, too. And get the sail maker. I may need Mr. Pugsley's sewing skills for the stitches. Have him heat up a can of tar on the cook's stove. I'll meet you in the fo'c'sle."

When the carpenter left, the captain pulled down his copy of the *Ship Captain's Medical Guide*, to consult the appropriate sections. After reading what little there was, he put the book back and sat, suddenly painfully aware of the motion of the ship as she rolled and pitched in the running seas.

He stood, grabbed his coat, and unlocked a cabinet next to the chart table. He took out a flask of strong rum, which he slipped into his pocket.

Captain Barker was struck by the smell of rotting flesh as soon as he stepped into the fo'c'sle cabin. Gronberg, Pugsley and Jeremiah the cook were waiting for him. Jerry was in his bunk, barely conscious, covered by a blanket.

"Get another lantern over here," Barker said. "I need to see what I am doing." He pulled the blanket back. The sailor's lower left leg was shades of mottled blue, black and green to just above the knee. The stench almost turned his stomach and he wanted nothing more than to turn and run out of the cabin back into the wind. He steadied himself. As captain, he was the only medical officer aboard the ship. This was his duty to perform. He could be sick once it was over.

"I need a pile of blankets to raise up the leg." Pugsley handed him several folded blankets and he reached down and lifted Jerry's thigh and slid them underneath. He looked over at Pugsley, Gronberg and Jeremiah, who were looking back at him expectantly.

"Mr. Pugsley, I'll ask you to secure a tourniquet, right about here," he said, motioning with his hand across Jerry's thigh. "Once I cut away the leg, you'll tie off the large veins and arteries with twine. Any additional bleeding once the tourniquet is released you will cauterize with hot tar. Please strap him down as well as you can."

Pugsley stepped forward with a length of hemp rope and wrapped it around Jerry's thigh.

"Mr. Gronberg, you will assist me. Please stand by to hand me the saw after I cut the flesh and muscle.

"Jeremiah and you—Fred, isn't it?"

"Aye, sir."

"You and Jeremiah hold him down the best you can. I want him absolutely still." Barker looked up at the lantern swaying as the ship rolled. "Well, as still as possible, at any rate.

"Jeremiah, the knife." The Jamaican cook handed him a large butcher knife that flashed in the lantern light.

"Did you sharpen it as sharp as you can possibly make it?"

"Yes, sir, Cap'n. That could cut the whiskers of Satan hisself."

"As long as it cuts flesh cleanly." Barker inspected the blade and then handed it back to the cook. He took the flask of rum from his coat pocket, opened it and handed it to Gronberg.

"If you will do the honors," he said, holding out both hands.

For a moment the carpenter looked confused.

"Pour some rum over my hands."

"Ah yah, of course, sir." He poured a dollop as Barker rubbed his hands together quickly.

"Now pour some over the knife. Good. That should do. Mr. Pugsley, is the tourniquet ready?"

"Aye, sir."

Baker took a deep breath. Nothing more to be done but to start cutting. He considered taking a drink of the rum, but thought better of it. He looked at Jerry's face, pale and drawn, and wondered whether the amputation might kill him anyway. He took another deep breath and braced his legs so that he was pressed against the bunk to resist being tossed about by the roll and pitch of the ship as much possible.

"The knife, Jeremiah."

He worked as quickly as he could, first slicing and peeling back a strip of skin that could be sewn over the stump. As he cut, Jerry cried out but Fred and Jeremiah were at his shoulders pressing him down against the bunk.

"I think he's passed out, sir."

The captain kept cutting into the leg, slicing through muscle, tendon, arteries and veins, using his full strength until he hit bone and then moving around to slice away beneath the femur until all the muscle was cut and only the white bone remained. The tourniquet reduced the flow of blood from the severed arteries and veins to an ooze.

Captain Barker realized that he had been holding his breath. He exhaled deeply and then inhaled again. "Mr. Gronberg. Splash the saw with rum and hand it to me, if you please." He passed the knife to the carpenter and took the small handsaw.

He sawed as quickly as possible. The femur is the largest bone in the body—he had read that in the medical guide. He would probably have never had thought of it were he not cutting through the unfortunate sailor's leg. His arm was sore when finally he was through and the severed leg dropped on the bunk.

"Mr. Pugsley."

"Aye, sir." The sail maker held out his hands to be doused in rum, and then stepped forward and deftly began tying off the larger arteries and veins. The flow of blood slowed.

"Jeremiah, get the hot tar from the galley stove and be quick about it." He motioned to the leg. "And someone throw that over the side, please."

For a moment no one moved. Jeremiah took a step backward. Then Fred snorted, "Get out of my way," grabbed the mangled leg and made for the cabin door, returning a few minutes later, with one fewer limb.

Captain Barker realized that he was drenched in sweat, which began to drip into his eyes. He took a rag from his pocket and wiped his face and hands.

When the cook returned, Pugsley eased the tourniquet and dabbed the bleeding stump with the tar. He then took a rum-soaked needle and thread and sewed the flap of skin over the stump.

"You have a fine hand with a needle, Mr. Pugsley," the captain commented.

"Why, thank you, sir."

The captain looked at Fred. "Is he still breathing?"

"Yes, sir, he is."

"Nicely done, sir," Gronberg said.

Barker exhaled deeply. "Thank you all for your assistance. Clean up a bit here. Jeremiah, boil some cloth for dressings. We'll want to bandage him up in a few hours. Then Gronberg, Pugsley and Jeremiah join me in the mess. Perhaps we can find a better use for a tot of rum."

Fred returned to the fo'c'sle as the captain was turning. "Fred, you are off watch, are you not? Why don't you join us in the mess in a few minutes as well."

Fred had ventured into the cabin, the realm of officers and apprentices, only twice, once to help pitch an errant stove overboard and once when stitching a new sail. The mess room seemed larger when it wasn't filled with canvas and sewing sailors. When he arrived, the captain was pouring large tots of rum for the carpenter, the sail maker and the cook. Fred gratefully took a glass when offered.

"Well, we should know in a day or two if Jerry is on the mend or not," the captain suggested, apparently trying to make conversation. He remark was greeted with four "Yes, sir's," to which the captain responded with a wan smile and said no more.

"James." They all turned. At the other door to the officer's mess stood Mary Barker. She wore a simple dress and her hair was pulled back from her face. Fred had seen her only at a distance, a figure on the poop deck. Now, up close, he was struck by how pretty she was and also how tired and worn-out she seemed. Just like everyone else aboard the ship.

He wondered what it must be like for her and her children to be stuck in the cabin for weeks on end. As hard as his life as a sailor was, he wondered what that sort of confinement must be like in a small cabin in heavy seas. He searched his memory for a line from Samuel Johnson. "*Being on a ship is being in a jail, with the chance of being drowned.*"

"I'm, sorry, James, I didn't realize that you were entertaining."

"No need to apologize, dear. Come in and join us."

"Oh no, I must look a fright."

"You look wonderful."

"I should see to the children. Good afternoon, gentlemen."

That evening, Fred couldn't help wonder what sort of man would bring his wife and children to sea, in waters such as these.

At dinner that evening in the mess room, Mary was amazed by her husband's appetite. She thought that the amputation might have lessened his desire to eat. Just hearing about it had lessened hers. Still, he ate the stewed canned beef and potatoes with a will. Her brother, Thomas, was dining with them and ate heartily as well.

"What will the poor sailor do with only one leg? How will he live?" she asked.

James looked up. "Let us first pray that he does live. If the leg gets infected, he may yet die."

"Oh," Mary replied.

"I think he will pull through," Thomas said. "The captain did a fine job and was ably assisted by Pugsley and Chips."

"Thank you, Mr. Atkinson," the captain replied. "Only time will tell."

"Those poor sailors," Mary commented, looking down at her plate. "I hear that some are suffering from frostbite."

"Unfortunately so," the captain said. "Several are not fit for duty. Too many sailors would rather spend all their pay on drink and debauchery than decent clothing to protect themselves against the weather."

"The pierhead jumpers are the worst," the second mate added. "They came aboard with the least and are suffering for it."

"And most are too proud or too bullheaded to take any help," the captain said. "On a past voyage, I recall seeing a sailor at the helm, shivering terribly. His coat was thin and totally unsuitable. I offered him a spare overcoat and was ready to call for a relief at the wheel while he put it on, but he just brushed me off. 'No, sir. No need.'

"You know, my dear, I've sailed half my life and I still find deep-sea sailors to be an odd lot. Some of the best lack any ambition, whatsoever. They spend their money as fast as they can ashore, drinking themselves insensible, then go and find another berth. Their only home is the ship they are on at the moment. They are as fond of routine, as ribbon clerks ashore. They will keep working like plow horses as long as they get their full whack, but don't give them anything but sailor's grub. On the *Devonshire Hall,* I once sent a whole chicken forward for the crew, only to have it sent back. A surly sailor returned it saying, 'This ain't proper sailor food. All's we wants is our salt junk and Harriet Lane.'"

Harriet Lane had been murdered and dismembered near the docks in London in 1872, and ever since then sailors had called canned meat by her name. An odd sort of immortality.

"Poor Harriet Lane," Mary murmured.

CHAPTER 13
REACHING THE LIMITS

September 27, 1905 – 108 days out of Cardiff

One morning, the wind shifted slightly more northerly and eased just a bit. All hands were called to make sail, and for the first time in a week they set the topsails and t'gallants. For a few hours, at least, the helmsman steered more west than south. By that nightfall, the gales had returned and the wind veered back to where it had been for countless days.

"All right, you lazy bloody farmers. Furl the upper fore t'gansail," Mate Rand bellowed. Fred walked toward the ratlines in the darkness to furl the sail. He once would have run but he was wearing out. They were all wearing out. Behind him was Gabe Isaacson, a merchant's son, another misfit like himself who had no more business going to sea than he did. For that alone, he liked Gabe.

Fred and Gabe climbed the windward ratlines up to the foretop, up the topmast ratlines to the crosstrees and up the t'gallant ratlines to the t'gallant yard. The sheets had been eased and the bunts and clews hauled so that the sail was partially gathered up. Their task now was just to finish the job, to tie the gaskets and properly furl the sail. The wind, however, tossed the sail wildly and Fred and Gabe, who laid out to starboard, doubled over with their stomachs on the yard and their feet jammed in the footropes, reached down to grab the dancing heavy sail, slick with spray and cold and slippery as ice.

Fred would just get two handfuls of sail under control, bunched up under the yard, when a gust would yank it from his grasp. "You motherless son of a bloody whore, come back here," he screamed for no other reason than it felt good.

When he finally got the outer portion of sail bunched up, he fed the gasket, a six-foot-long canvas sail tie, between the yard and the sail and then threw one end forward. If he was lucky the wind would blow it back and he could catch it and tie the sail tightly in a bundle. It took several tries but he finally got the gasket tied.

Gabe was working closer to the mast and was struggling to tie the gasket as well. Fred had moved down the yard to help him when a mighty gust hit the ship. Just at that moment Gabe was reaching down to grab the gasket. The ship rolled and the wind pulled the sail from Gabe's hand. He grabbed for the jackstay on the yard, but missed.

Fred hung on unbelieving as he saw Gabe slip. He didn't fall so much as he was carried away by the wind, like a leaf on an October breeze. He just disappeared into the darkness and was gone. Fred shouted, "Man overboard," though for what reason he wasn't sure. Gabe was beyond their help. There was nothing to be done.

For a long while, all Fred could do was stare at the place on the yard where Gabe had been. Then below him, he heard the mate. "Finish the job. The sail won't furl itself."

Fred moved down the yard, wrestled the thrashing canvas and tied in the gasket. When he finished, he moved to the mast and helped Donnie and Frenchie, who had laid out to port, roll the bunt of the sail up over the yard and tie it tightly.

Their job done, they climbed down the ratlines to the deck.

The mate was waiting. "Who'd we lose?"

"Gabe," Fred replied.

"Damn shame. A good sailor."

"That he was."

With considerable reluctance, Captain Barker opened the Official Log Book. It was nothing like the daily log, where the mates recorded the wind, temperature, daily course and any other thoughts that might be pertinent or be useful. In accordance with the Merchant Shipping Act of 1894, the Official Log Book was the legal document that he would present to the British consul within forty-eight hours of their arrival in Pisagua, Chile, to be reviewed, judged and certified. There was something galling about being judged by a clerk who had never been aboard a ship save alongside a dock, but such was the way of the world.

Like most captains, Barker wrote as little as he could in the Official Log Book. No need to trouble the consul with unnecessary details. Recording deaths, however, was an absolute requirement. Santiago's name was already recorded. *Carried away by a monstrous wave.* To this he added, *Gabriel Isaacson, carried away from the yard, lost overboard.* That and the date was the entirety of the record of a life lost. Later, Isaacson's possessions, which probably were few enough, would be sold to the crew, which would be logged as well. All neat and tidy for the consul's review.

There had been no attempt to rescue Isaacson. To launch a boat at night in such seas would be suicide and, in any case, they had no boats. Captain Barker had heard his cries for help from the poop deck, but could do nothing for him, except to murmur a prayer for the Jew's soul.

Barker looked at the crew list. Of the twenty sailors he had signed on, two were lost overboard. Two were crippled. Jerry the Greek might yet live and Whitney was mending, but neither were of any use in working the ship. Five more were not fit for duty with frostbitten fingers or toes.

They had been fighting the westerlies for close to fifty days now and only about half the crew was fit to carry on. Sitting alone in his dayroom, the doubts crept in. How much longer could they take the beating from the Southern Ocean and survive? Were they beaten already? Every year, stout sailing ships simply disappeared in the water south of the Horn. Would the *Lady Rebecca*'s name be added to the list? Was it time to admit that they had lost the fight?

The other choice was to turn and run before the wind, to sail east, the other way around the world. It was the long way, but the wind and the current would be behind them. It would take another 40 days at least, but there would be no more slogging into the relentless westerlies.

There were two reasons not to square away and run before the wind. The contrary winds would not blow forever and they would round up into the Pacific and on to Chile when the westerlies eased. That would probably be weeks faster than turning east. The other real and absolute reason why he wouldn't even consider going east was that that the *Lady Rebecca* was too low in the water. She still had two feet of water in her hold in addition to 4,000 tons of coal. She just didn't have the freeboard to lift her stern in a following sea. As heavily laden as she was, there was every chance that she would broach to, to be overwhelmed by a wave and rolled on her beam-ends. She had survived one monster wave already. She wasn't likely to survive a broach.

Captain Barker closed the Official Log Book and returned it to the shelf. He looked at the chart and the barometer. There was nothing left to do but carry on. "All we need is a one good slant," he said to himself. "Just one good slant." They weren't beaten yet.

Every sail change was now accompanied by the call, "All hands!" Too few sailors were fit for duty in each watch to hoist and haul, so off watch or on, every one dragged himself from the fo'c's'le, night and day tend the sails. Fred had just slipped off to sleep when he heard the call. He clambered out on deck, grumbling and swearing. The only thing that brought a smile to his face was to hear Harry begin to belt out a shanty. The sound of the deep voice rising above the wind always lifted his spirits. As long as Harry was singing, Fred would fall in and haul with a will.

"*Oh, they calls me Hanging Johnny,*" Harry sang out.

"*Oh hang, boys, oh hang boys hang,*" the crew sang in reply.

"*They says I hangs for money,*" Harry sang.

"*Oh hang, boys hang,*" sang the crew, hauling in time on the brace.

"*Now let's hang all mates and skippers.*"

Fred sang in full voice to endorse the sentiment. "*Oh hang boys, hang.*"

With a grin, Harry sang out, "*Oh, we'll hang 'em by their flippers.*"

"*Oh, hang boys hang.*"

The line was taut and the Mate Atkinson shouted, "Belay."

Once they had the line coiled the mate, shouted, "The off-watch is relieved." Fred glanced at the mate and then back at Captain Barker, standing like a statue at the break of the poop, and sang to himself, "*Oh, let's hang all mates and skippers.*" But he was bone tired and hanging the officers felt like too much work. He heard Harry laugh, joking with one of the other watch. Fred wasn't sure how he kept his spirits up but was grateful that the Welshman managed. He seemed to be carrying the entire crew now. Fred sang again softly as he dragged himself back to his bunk, "*Oh, hang boys, hang.*"

"Captain." The captain had come on deck after logging their position and checking the barometer at the change of watch. The weather was unchanged.

"Yes, Mr. Atkinson."

"Mr. Rand is in his cabin, sir. Says he is too sick to stand his watch."

"I'll speak to him. Would you mind taking over his watch while I am below?"

"Aye, sir," Atkinson relied.

Captain Barker wondered whether he should fetch his pistols, but decided against it. He went below decks straight to Rand's cabin and pounded on the door.

"Rand, it is your watch."

"Come in, Captain," came a voice from behind the door.

Captain Barker carefully turned the knob and opened the door. He found the mate lying down on his bunk.

"I'm sorry, Captain, but I can't turn to. I've got a pain in my back that is hurting something horrible. I can't half stand up."

Barker stood silent for a moment. Was this Mr. Rand's form of personal mutiny or was he really hurt? Or did it matter? If the mate, a licensed officer, swore that he was not fit for duty there was very little a captain could do beyond recording it in the log book. In the old days, a master might adjust a mate's attitude with a belaying pin, but that wasn't his style nor did he suspect that it would be particularly effective.

He took a breath and kept his voice low and even. "What is hurting you, Mr. Rand?"

"Feels like somebody stuck a marlinspike in my upper back. Hurts like hell."

"May I see your back?"

Rand grimaced as he sat up, pulled off his shirt and turned his back to the captain.

"Hmmp, looks like a pimple to me."

"I don't know, sir. It hurts like the very devil."

"All right. If you are not fit for duty, rest in your cabin. Let me know when you recover."

"Yes, sir. Thank you, sir."

He turned and left the tiny cabin, closing the door behind him, disgusted, but dismissing Rand from his mind. He climbed the ladder to the poop deck and shouted, "Mr. Atkinson! Please ask the senior apprentice to see me in the cabin!"

In a few minutes, Paul Nelson waited at the threshold to the captain's dayroom.

"Come in, young man. Have a seat."

"Thank you, sir."

Paul Nelson looked at him straight in the eye, unlike many shellbacks, who would avert their eyes in the presence of the captain. He was a good-looking young man, with jet-black hair and deep blue eyes. The senior apprentice reminded the captain of himself at nineteen.

"Well, Paul, by the end of this voyage, you will have completed your apprenticeship, is that correct?"

"Yes, sir. It is."

"Mr. Rand has taken ill and I could use an acting third mate. Would you be interested in the position?"

"Why, yes, sir. Thank you, sir."

Captain Barker smiled. "Don't be so quick to thank me, young man. You'll still be expected to haul and go aloft like any other sailor. You'll be casting off the weather braces rather than hauling on the braces to leeward. Other than that your duties will be the same, with a few more added."

"Oh, yes, sir, I understand."

"You are in the mate's watch. Your watch now. How do you get along with that crowd?"

"I've no problem with any of them, but…"

"Yes?"

"Well, sir, I like him fine, but some of the watch are bothered by Jensen. He's not even in our watch but some think he is crazy and bad luck."

"And what do you think?"

"Well, he may be a bit crazy. He keeps saying that the sea is crushing his soul, and that sort of foolishness."

"Do you think he is unlucky?"

Paul Nelson shrugged. "He is a good sailor, sir. And lucky or unlucky? I don't know. I'm not superstitious like some of the rest."

"Does Jensen have problems with his watch mates? Do they work together?"

"Well enough, from all I've seen. Jensen's biggest problem is the cook. He is a poor enough excuse for a cook and he's always talking about gri-gri and the devil. I've told him to put a stopper in it more than once."

Captain Barker sat back in his chair. "Ah, cooks are a bad bargain in the best of cases. Do you think I should have a word with him?"

"No, Captain. I think we can keep the cook in hand."

Captain Barker smiled. "Very well, then. Now understand, if Mr. Rand recovers, he will take over his watch. You'll still be acting third. I am sure we can find duties for you to perform."

Captain Barker stood up and a grinning Paul Nelson jumped to his feet as well. The captain held out his hand, which the young man shook with enthusiasm.

"Very well then, Mr. Nelson. Get back to work."

"Thank you, Captain Barker. That I shall."

There was always a few inches of water sloshing about in the apprentice cabin in the half-deck. There were two doors to the half-deck, port and starboard, where the cabin extended out from the break of the poop deck. Opening the door to windward let in a blast of wind and spray. The door to leeward was more sheltered, except when the ship rolled the lee rail down and scooped up a deck-load of water that came crashing back against the break of the poop.

The apprentices had worked out a signal at the change of watch to get the timing of opening the door just right. The apprentices coming off watch would signal those coming on that it was clear to open the half-deck door by stomping on the poop deck above the half-deck. When the apprentices heard the stomp, they knew it was safe to come on deck, in the long trough between the breaking waves.

Will was about to go on watch. He put the letter that he was writing to his mother away in his sea chest. The chest was tied with marline to the mess bench to keep it out of the water sloshing around on deck. The half-deck had bunks for twelve, but, as there were only four apprentices aboard, their sea chests on the benches didn't get in anyone's way.

He heard a thud on the deck above him and he pushed open the lee door, but hadn't taken a step out before a wall of water knocked him back, head over heels. He crashed into Jack Pickering, who was just behind him, and bounced over the table and benches until he hit the back cabin bulkhead with a crash.

"Son of a bitch." They were both thrashing about in the icy water. Will pulled himself up. Nothing seemed to be broken or too badly bruised. George Black ran in through the door.

"Are you all right?"

"What happened?" Will demanded. "Why did you stamp all clear when a wave was right on us?"

"I didn't," George replied, lending a hand to pull Jack up to his feet. "The ship rolled and I slipped and fell on my ass. That must have been what you heard."

"Useless bastard could have gotten us killed," Jack grumbled.

Before anything else could be said, they heard Mr. Atkinson calling for them. "Apprentices turn to!"

Will and Jack trudged out onto the deck and clambered up to windward before the next wave hit. The mate sent them up the mainmast to shake out a reef in the upper topsail.

When the watch was finally over, Will was tempted to give George Black a taste of his own medicine, but thought better of it. He stomped on the poop deck during the lull, and then ran down the ladder and got the door shut behind him before the next wave.

In the guttering lamplight, Will saw that his chest had broken free from the lashings and was on its side, open, in the sloshing water. He might have knocked it down himself when the wave washed over him. He grabbed it by the handles and drained it. All the letters he had written were a sodden mass. His other clothes were soaking wet and his blue linen jacket with the fine brass buttons was ruined. The buttons had started to turn a sickly green and the fabric was wrinkled and discolored.

For reasons he didn't fully understand, he began to sob and then to cry, holding the jacket that he had once worn so proudly. It all seemed so long ago, a lifetime at least, or more like a silly dream that wasn't real, that had never really been real. The wind howled just beyond the cabin bulkheads and he heard the next wave hit the half-deck door like a hammer blow. The past was a pretty dream and the present was only exhaustion and pain that never seemed to end.

He folded the blue jacket and put it in the bottom of the chest. He hung his spare trousers and shirt up on a bulkhead peg, to let them dry out at least a little, though encrusted in salt, they would never really dry. He took the letters and his notebook and shook them gently. He put the notebook on top of the blue jacket and smoothed the letters out as best he could on the bench and then put them away as well. With a roll of marline, he lashed the chest back on the bench before crawling into his bunk, hoping that he would feel better with a few hours of sleep.

"Captain, a ship on the horizon."
"Thank you, Mr. Atkinson, I'll be up presently."

When the captain came on deck, Atkinson pointed toward a shadow that rose and then disappeared in the seas off to the southwest.

"Not carrying any sail from what I can see. Seems to be lying a-hull." The ship drifted sideways to the seas. Waves in succession broke over the deck, which seemed perpetually awash. The strange ship rolled wildly, her bare mates and tattered sails scribing arcs against the sky.

Captain Barker squinted out through the incessant spray. Mr. Atkinson was right. Definitely a ship. What sort of madman would lie a-hull in seas such as these, he wondered. In a bit, with his binoculars, he could see that the ship had a reefed spanker set. The aftermost sail helped to hold her bow closer toward the wind.

They were on a crossing course, or near enough to one. The *Lady Rebecca* was fore-reaching on a starboard tack and the unknown ship was on the port tack, drifting toward them.

They hadn't seen another ship since they left Staten Island. Word spread among the crew and soon everyone able, on watch and off, was on deck trying to catch a glimpse of the strange ship. Slowly the distance between the two ships diminished until finally the *Lady Rebecca* crossed the strange ship's bow. Captain Barker could read her name, *Clan William*.

There were several blown-out topsails fluttering from the bolt-ropes still bound to the yards. The fore royal mast was shattered and hanging by the halyard, caught in the t'gallant shrouds. Other than that, there did not seem to be anything too terribly wrong with her. Yet, she appeared to be abandoned. Not a soul could be seen. No one was on deck and her boats were gone.

"Mr. Atkinson, would you be so kind as to get the Very pistol and two flares from my dayroom?"

When the mate returned, Captain Barker chambered a flare, took aim and fired. The flare passed in a high arc directly above the *Clan William*. He took the second flare and aimed slightly lower so that this time, the flare almost hit the ship. He stared at the empty deck, looking for any sign of life, but saw none. Abandonment was the only explanation. But why?

For a fleeting instant Captain Barker thought of her value as salvage. He chuckled bitterly to himself. All he needed was a few spare crew and sound boats, the two things he unquestionably lacked. Maybe some other captain would be luckier.

On deck, Jeremiah the cook started praying loudly in a language that Fred couldn't decipher. Harry shouted over to him, "Aw, shut your gob."

Jeremiah glared. "Can't you see? That's the debil's own ship. The *Flying Dutchman* come to take our souls to the watery hell. You can mock all ye want but the debil'll hear you an' maybe come getcha. You mark my words."

Harry only laughed. "She looks abandoned to me. No Dutchman sails without a crew."

They all watched the derelict ship drifting off astern until the waves seemed to swallow her up.

"She be the debil's ship. Mark my words. The debil come. That Jonah man, he . . ."

Harry strode over to the ranting cook and knocked him down with the back of his hand.

"For the last time, shut your damned trap."

Jeremiah hoisted himself up, glaring at Harry but not saying a word. Only when Harry rounded the cookhouse on the way back to the fo'c'sle did the cook mumble to himself, "You mark my words."

When the squall struck, Fred was soundly asleep. His body reacted before his mind to the call for all hands. He rolled from his bunk and stumbled out the cabin door into the pitch black darkness. A shape that he took for Jack was just ahead of him and just above the wail of the wind, he heard Harry's voice behind him, saying something to Donnie.

Fred had only taken a step or two on the deck before he heard a voice cry out. He turned to see the breaking wave, the boiling white crest just visible in the night. Along with Jack, he dove for the leeward lifeline, hitting the heavy line with his chest, knocking the wind from him. He grasped desperately for the line with both hands as the icy water tried to wash him over the side. As the breaker passed, the ship rolled down and scooped up a deck-load of water to leeward. Fred gasped for air as the surging green water rushed aft, submerging him again, trying to pull him off the lifeline that he held onto with all his might.

When at last Fred got to his feet, still holding tightly to the lifeline, he saw Jack and Donnie, but Harry was gone.

Mr. Atkinson appeared at the door, his oilskins dripping on the cabin sole. It was past three in the morning but the lamp still burned and Captain Barker stood at the chart table.

"Captain, we have an injured man. He was caught by a breaking wave. Struck his head on the poop deck ladder. "

Captain Barker grabbed his coat. "Who is he?"

"It's Harry, sir."

Captain Barker stopped for a moment. Why Harry? Harry was the best sailor on the ship. He never complained, worked hard and did his job, and his shanties kept the others hauling along as well. Why did it have to be Harry, of all men?

"Is he hurt badly?" Barker almost didn't need to ask the question from the look on Atkinson's face.

"Yes, sir. I think so."

Barker followed the second mate to the messroom where Harry was laid out on the table. Paul Nelson, the apprentice Will and Fred were standing next to him.

Harry was bleeding from his scalp. His breath was shallow. The captain examined his head carefully. "His skull seems to be crushed. See how it is indented near the gash?"

The second mate looked over his shoulder. "Is there anything we can do?"

"Pray, perhaps." Captain Barker closed eyes. He didn't know of anything else to do. The old ship surgeons used trephination to relieve the swelling but that was beyond his skills or tools.

"All we can do is wait and see," the captain said. "If he survives the swelling he may be all right. If not … Well, we shall just have to wait and see. Put him in the spare cabin."

Harry survived a week before breathing his last. Pugsley sewed him into a sailcloth shroud and weighted the feet with several links of heavy chain. In the second dogwatch, the crew assembled for a burial at sea. They clustered at the poop deck rail as Captain Barker read from the Book of Common Prayer over the white bundle that had been their shipmate, resting on a grating.

"Man that is born of a woman hath but a short time to live, and is full of misery. He cometh up, and is cut down, like a flower; he fleeth as it were a shadow, and never continueth in one stay. In the midst of life we are in death: of whom may we seek for succour, but of thee, O Lord, who for our sins art justly displeased."

Captain Barker looked up from the prayer book. "Harry was a good sailor and a fine shipmate. No higher praise can be said of any man. Join me in prayer.

"Our Father, which art in heaven, hallowed be thy Name." At first there was only Captain Barker's voice carried on the bitter winds. "Thy kingdom come. Thy will be done on earth, as it is in heaven." Progressively mumbles and murmurs grew as the men said the prayer themselves. "Give us this day our daily bread. And forgive us our trespasses, As we forgive them that trespass against us. And lead us not into temptation; But deliver us from evil." Every man aboard joined in on the last word. "Amen."

Barker nodded. Atkinson and Jensen lifted the inboard end of the grating and the body slipped into the sea. Jensen looked down and said, "Goodbye, shantyman." Fred looked down at the rolling water. Harry's body left no mark. He was simply gone.

Captain Barker put the prayer book into his jacket pocket and turned to Mr. Atkinson. "I believe that we could use a reef in the upper main t'gansail."

"Aye, sir. Reef the upper main t'gansail."

The moment of mourning was lost in the familiar rhythm of heavy labor, but this time, at least, the hauling was done without a song. They worked in silence in the memory of the shantyman.

At dinner that evening Fred went to pick up the mess pot and bread barge from the cook. Jeremiah was scowling.

"I tole ye. That man Harry mocked the debil and the debil came up and got him. I tole ye true."

Fred exploded. He reached out and grabbed the cook's collar. "Shut your mouth, you foul son of a bitch. Don't you ever speak of Harry again or I'll take your knives and slice you up into your own stew pot, not that anyone but the sharks would eat your worthless stinkin' hide. Do you understand me, you worthless bastard? I am sick to death of both your hoodoo and your rotten cooking."

Fred could feel the blood in his face and he realized that he was close to lifting the cook off his feet with his hands on his collar. "Do you understand me?" he repeated.

"Yes, suh," was the cook's only reply.

Fred let go of his collar, grabbed the mess post and bread barge and went back to the cabin.

The next day, Fred stood huddled with Frenchie and Donnie at the break of the poop deck. There was nothing to do but wait for the end of the watch. As Captain Barker's infernal rules said they had to stay on deck regardless, they hunched down behind the canvas weather cloth for what little protection it offered.

Fred was tired, worn out, used up. His muscles ached. He was always hungry, often thirsty. Salt sores on his wrists, ankles, elbows and knees tormented his every move. But he kept on because there was no other choice. His body seemed to move by rote, more by habit than thought.

All he could do now was watch the long and endless rollers, the mountainous white-crested waves that slammed into the ship, lifting them, rolling them, sending green water breaking across the decks and leaving a rime of sparkling ice clinging to the rigging and the house front.

Fred finally understood a saying what he had heard in a Liverpool pub years before. An old sailor had said, over too many pints of porter, "There ain't no law below 40 south latitude. Below 50 south, there's no God."

He had acknowledged it intellectually, but now he knew its truth in every atom of his being. It coursed in his bloodstream and had seeped into his bones, tendons and muscles. Looking out over the Southern Ocean with the bitter westerly wind screaming in his face, it was obvious. There was no room for God on this ocean. The westerlies would blow him away or the crashing waves would have crushed him and pulled him under.

God might live in the chapel at Yale, where the swell of the organ and raised voices filled the chamber with sublime song. It was easy to feel the hand of a God there, warm and dry beneath the glow of stained glass.

There just might be a place for God even in the sailors' chapel on the East River by Water Street. The floating chapel, built onto a barge so that it was even closer to the ships than the brothels, bars or the boardinghouses. Beyond the hectoring sermons, in the rough singing of the psalms by men just off deep-sea ships, there was a sort of peace that felt almost, if distantly, divine.

South of the Horn, there was only the howling wind. Organs, hymns and psalm singing had no business here. They would not survive the gales.

One ship might make a fast passage around the Horn, while another, equally sound and strong, could be crushed and disappear in the icy depths. It was all as one. They were not in a struggle with an evil sea, nor would they be saved by its benevolence. That was all for the poets on shore, who never ventured closer to the ocean than the sand of the beach, who spun their fancies into poems to amuse patrons drinking brandy sitting beside a warm and glowing fire.

Fred finally understood the true horror of this place. The monstrous waves and the howling wind were neither cruel nor kind. There was no good or evil in the Southern Ocean. It was far, far worse than that. The wind, the sea and the sky were simply and completely indifferent. Nothing mattered. Ships and men—their hopes, dreams, fears and aspirations—were of no consequence whatsoever. They mattered less than the flotsam or the foam.

In the distance, he saw the great swooping flight of an albatross, rising up above the swells and then dropping down into the shelter of the troughs. Some sailors said that albatross were the hosts to the souls of lost sailors, so it was unlucky to kill one. Other sailors scoffed, catching and killing the birds to make tobacco pouches from their leathery feet. Were those the souls of friends out there, carelessly wheeling in the wild westerly wind? That seemed too much like the stories his mother once told him at night, soothing tales that helped him sleep but meant nothing in the light of day. And if his shipmates were not carried aloft on the albatross wings, where were they? The heaven or hell of the chapels? Davy Jones' Locker or Fiddler's Green? Or were they just carried along in the icy waters? Food for fish and crabs.

He realized that he could have slipped from the rigging just as easily as Gabe, or been swept overboard like Santiago or had his head stove in like poor Harry. It didn't matter how good a sailor he was, how educated or how ignorant, how virtuous or how craven. The wind and the sea didn't care. There was no God to pray to below 50 south latitude. No God at all.

Second Mate Atkinson appeared from below and shouted, "That'll do the watch."

Fred, Frenchie and Donnie trudged down the ladder to the main deck and worked their way along the weather safety line to the fo'c'sle.

Fred knew that Mr. Rand was sick and not fit for duty, so he was surprised to see him in the fo'c'sle, sitting on a sea chest by the bogie stove, talking quietly with some of the crew. The day before, Fred thought that he had seen him heading for the other cabin as well. It was hard to tell. Fred had been furling a sail when he saw the shadow moving across the deck below, indistinct in the spray in the near dark.

Fred didn't care to listen to what was being said. His one and only concern was to rest when he could, eat what little there was to eat and to turn to when his watch rolled around. All the same, it bothered him that a mate would invade the fo'c'sle, which was sailors' territory. The mate had no business being there, and if he was strong enough to make it forward he should be on duty, like the rest of them. Fred threw himself fully clothed in his oilskins into his bunk and slipped gratefully into a dreamless sleep. In four hours, if he was lucky and no one called "All Hands," his watch would start all over again, in the endless cycle of what seemed an endless voyage.

CHAPTER 14
RUMORS OF MUTINY

October 5, 1905 – 116 days out of Cardiff

M r. Rand turned to on the poop deck at the start of the morning watch. He appeared haggard but stood ramrod straight when he presented himself to the captain.

"So, Mr. Rand, are you fit for duty? Have your aches and pains subsided?"

"I am fit as I am likely to be, Captain. My back still hurts like the very devil, but laying up hasn't made it any better, so I figures that getting back to work might take my mind off the pain."

The captain looked him up and down for a moment. "Very well. Paul Nelsen has been appointed acting third mate. He is in your watch. Utilize his services as you see fit."

"Aye, aye, Captain."

Mr. Rand climbed down the poop deck ladder to the main deck. Captain Barker could hear him bellow even above the wind. "Starboard watch. On deck with you."

The next evening, the barometer began to drop. For weeks it had been hovering between 27.50 and 28 inches of mercury but now it fell to 27.3, lower than Captain Barker had ever seen it in his years at sea. The falling barometer foretold an increase in the wind, but if the reading could be trusted they would soon face a hurricane's blast. He ducked down and unscrewed the inspection cap on the barometer to make sure that the chamois bag that contained the mercury wasn't leaking. It was fine and tight. After all the storms and gales, now the wind would really blow.

When he came on deck, Barker found that the wind had indeed strengthened. The ship was having a bad time of it. Looking forward, through darkness in the blinding spray, he wondered how long the fore course would last before being ripped to shreds in the wind. He shouted to Mr. Rand, "The fore course."

Rand nodded and bellowed above the wind, "All hands, all hands! Haul up the foresail!"

Both watches scrambled across the heaving deck, slipping in the rolling water and howling darkness to find the clew garnets and buntlines. Atkinson and Donnie were sent to the fo'c'sle head to tend the tack and Fred and Frenchie stood by the capstan to slack off the sheet.

On the mate's signal Fred and Frenchie slacked off a couple of fathoms on the sheet. The surging of the wire cable against the capstan drum reverberated through the deck. The mate shouted to each watch. They could only just hear him over the wind, but knew what to do. The starboard watch hauled away on the weather clew garnet and the port on the weather buntlines. Fred and Frenchie kept slacking the sheet as Atkinson and Donnie eased the tack.

With the wind howling at seventy knots and the sail and lines strained to almost breaking, the fores'l was hauled up to the yard in good order. No wild out-of-control canvas or snarled lines.

"Now get up there and furl it," Rand bellowed.

Barker shook his head. It was as pretty a piece of sail handling as Captain Barker could recall. He had to give that much to Mr. Rand. He was a consummate seaman. Barker wondered if he would ever fathom the various sides of his mate.

Over the next week, the westerly winds continued to howl, yet the *Lady Rebecca* was making slow but steady progress in her westing all the same. The crew, however, seemed different. They were either reaching the limits of their endurance or something else had happened. Their glances aft at the poop deck seemed more hostile. Captain Barker sensed an anger building in the exhausted sailors.

On one hand, he was afraid that he was beginning to imagine things. The burden on him was as great as that on the crew. All the days and nights looking for the slightest shift in the wind, the countless hours in the icy cold wind and spray, were taking their toll on him as well. He kept pushing back his own doubts and uncertainties until his resolve had hardened to steel, yet now he was afraid of letting it blind him to something that he didn't quite grasp.

At the end of the second dogwatch, Mr. Atkinson stood outside the captain's dayroom.

"Sir, there is something I need to discuss with you."

"Come in. Have a seat."

Thomas Atkinson sat down and took off his cap. He looked considerably older than he had when they set off from Cardiff. Perhaps it was just the constant windburn that had darkened his face and deepened the lines around his eyes. Or perhaps it was the burden of command settling on the young man's shoulders.

"Sir, I have been hearing a rumor. I don't usually bother myself with such things but I've heard it more than once. Crew seems to believe it."

"All right," Captain Barker replied, "What is it?"

"The rumor is that we buried Harry . . . alive."

Captain Barker sat back, stunned. "But that makes no sense. How could anyone believe such a thing?"

Atkinson shrugged. "I agree. It is crazy talk. Why would they believe it? I think everyone is just so worn out that they might believe anything that someone told them."

"And who might have told them something so outrageous?"

Atkinson shook his head. "I couldn't say, sir."

"But you do have suspicions, do you not?"

The second mate paused for a moment before answering. "I would rather not say, sir."

"Consider where your loyalties lie. With your shipmates or the ship?"

Mr. Atkinson sat silent for another moment. "I think Rand is spreading the story. He still thinks that we should square away and run back east. I have heard him say as much when I passed by the fo'c'sle."

It was the captain's turn to be silent. Earlier in the voyage he would have exploded in rage. That seemed a very long time ago. Now, he was merely thoughtful, calculating.

"Go get some rest, Mr. Atkinson. And thank you for your candor. I'll take matters from here."

Captain Barker waited until the first dogwatch the next day so as not to disturb anyone's rest. He called all able hands to the mess room, where he stood at the far end of the table. The ship's log lay open before him. His pistols were on his belt but he wore his coat to cover them. He wanted them close by, just in case, but would rather not be too provocative. As the men filed in, they lined the far bulkheads. They all looked thin and haggard, as weather-worn as the old ship herself. There was silence as the captain looked at his crew and the crew, their captain.

Then Captain Barker spoke. "What's the nonsense I hear about Harry being buried alive? That is a serious charge and a damnable lie. Who believes it to be true?"

The only response was silence.

He turned to the sail maker and the carpenter. "Mr. Pugsley, you sewed Harry into the shroud. What say you?"

Pugsley took off his hat. "He was dead, sir. No doubt about it."

"Mr. Gronberg, you assisted in the burial."

"Ya, he was gone. Dead and gone."

"So who believes that we buried Harry alive? Speak up now, damn you," the captain said, raising his voice more than he intended.

Jensen shook his head. "We are all used up, cap'n. We're all so tired. Gets easy to believe anything you hear."

The captain looked around the room. "And who told you this damnable lie?"

There was silence. Some sailors stared straight ahead. Some averted their gaze.

"Who told you that Harry was buried alive?" the captain demanded. "I will have an answer!"

Fred looked around the mess room. No one was willing to speak. But who were they protecting?

Standing fast for another shipmate was one thing. Protecting an officer was something else entirely.

"First time I heard it, it was from Mr. Rand," Fred replied.

"Rand?" the captain roared. "Where is Mr. Rand? Where is the mate? "

Will spoke up. "Believe he is in his cabin, sir."

"Get him, now," the captain growled.

The apprentice hurried off.

The captain opened the logbook. "I will not have the charge stand that we buried a shipmate alive. I've entered into the logbook that Harry died of an accident and was buried in accordance with the practices of the sea and all pertinent regulations. I want every man to step forward and enter his name or mark in the log that he witnessed this and knows it to be true. I will not tolerate such monstrous lies on my ship. Now step up, each and every one of you."

The sailors shuffled forward, one by one, without a word, and signed or marked the logbook. Then they fell back where they had been.

When they were all finished, Captain Barker demanded, "And has he been telling you any more lies?" His question was again met with silence. "What has Mr. Rand been telling you?"

Jensen finally spoke up. "He told us that if we all told you to square away, sir, that you would have no choice."

Captain Barker shook his head. "Is that what you think? That we should turn around and sail before the wind?"

Again no one responded.

"That is no choice and you are all good enough seamen to know it yourselves. You should know what would happen if we squared away and ran back east in these seas. We are too deep in the water. The stern would never lift to the waves. We would be pooped and worse. The ship would sink and we would all die. I have my family aboard this ship. Do you think that I would keep on if I thought we had any other choice?"

No one spoke. The worn and weary men at one end of the mess room stared back at the captain. Then a shadow appeared at the mess room door. It was Rand.

"So you have finally joined us, after telling so many filthy lies to these men," the captain said, struggling to keep his voice even.

Rand ignored him but turned toward the men. "Here's your chance, boys. Grab him."

No one moved.

"That is mutiny, men, and this is a British ship." Captain Barker opened his coat, putting his hand on the butt of one of his pistols while the crew glared at him in unfocused anger.

"Come on," Rand yelled, but again no one moved. Mate Atkinson moved closer to the captain and was now facing the crew, as were the apprentices. Pugsley and Gronberg stood between the two groups, not joining either side.

Fred didn't know what to do. For weeks now, he had decided that he hated the captain. Hated him with all his heart and soul, yet now, looking at Rand glowering in the doorway, he felt an even greater contempt for the mate. Rand was still hanging back. He seemed to be waiting for the crew to rush the captain and take his guns away, but he himself was standing still. If he wanted a mutiny to make him captain, he lacked the courage to lead it.

Time seemed to have stopped. No one moved or spoke. The captain looked ready at any instant to pull his guns and shoot the first man that approached him. Fred glanced at his shipmates. At least some of the crew appeared ready to rush him across the short length of the mess room. Otto appeared to have taken a step forward before fading back. Jeremiah glared but waited for someone else to take the first step. There were several grim faces that Fred could not read.

The only sound was the howling of the wind and the clanking of a pot in the steward's pantry that slid back and forth as the ship rolled.

Then a small voice came from the side door that lead to the captain's cabin.

"Mr. Puglsey, Mrs. Murphy is sick. Can you make her better?"

It was little Amanda, the captain's daughter, holding the canvas and oakum doll that the sail maker had made for her at the beginning of the voyage, which now seemed an age ago. The stitching had come loose and most of the oakum had fallen out. The little doll's face was oddly flattened and one arm looked about ready to fall off.

Pugsley looked over, startled, and then smiled. He stepped over and bent down. "I'll see what I can do, Miss Amanda."

The look of concern on the little girl's face turned to carefree glee. With two hands she carefully handed the precious doll to Pugsley. "Don't you worry, missie. We'll have her right as rain in no time."

Other sailors were smiling as the little girl left the mess room.

The messroom was silent again.

After a moment, Captain Barker raised his voice. "So, men, will you keep sailing? We are bound to get a slant soon. These westerlies cannot blow forever."

Jensen shrugged. "We just want to get to port, captain. I guess Pisagua is as good as any."

Captain Barker turned to Rand. "Mr. Rand, you are confined to your quarters until further notice."

The big man looked like he was about to speak, but simply turned and left the mess room.

Captain Barker turned to the crew. "Mr. Atkinson, would you speak to the steward. Direct him to serve out tots of rum in the lazarette. I do believe that we all could use one." He was greeted with a smile or two, but mostly just grim nods of agreement. As the crew shuffled out of the mess room, Barker thought, *God bless you, Mrs. Murphy*.

An hour later, Mary and the captain ate alone in the mess room. The second mate was on deck. Mr. Rand was in his cabin. Tommy was asleep and Amanda was happily playing with the newly repaired Mrs. Murphy, which, as promised, Pugsley had quickly re-stuffed and stitched. Walter served and removed the dishes without saying a word. Few words passed between the captain and his wife until coffee. Mary had heard most of what had happened earlier in the mess room and Walter had filled her in on what she had missed.

She looked at her husband and asked, "Is it worth it, James?"

At first she saw a flash of anger in his eyes, but it soon faded to resignation. He was so tired. She could see that in the lines in his face. He had had such hopes for this voyage and now it had almost ended in a mutiny.

"We have no choice but to keep at it. All we need is a slant. Just one good favoring slant of wind."

Mary stirred her coffee with a spoon. "But what if it doesn't come? Or what if you have too few men left to sail the ship when it does? What if we run out of food, water and men before we get the favoring slant?"

She immediately wondered whether she should have spoken. She knew that there were no answers to her questions. What was worse—a mutinous crew challenging his authority, or a doubting wife?

James sat still for a moment, staring out into space. He seemed lost in thought or perhaps he was just letting the sound of the wind on deck carry his thoughts away. The tension around his eyes seemed to ease. After a moment he turned to Mary and reached out to put his hand on hers.

"My dear, we must keep on. It is simply too dangerous to turn before the wind. We are too deep in the water. The westerlies cannot stop us forever. We will get the slant. What we must not do, is to give up. Then all will be lost. We all just have to hold on." He smiled. "Just you wait. We will round up into the Pacific and we'll all be complaining that it is too hot. Imagine that."

The next day the wind shifted to the north and they hardened up on an almost due westerly course. The sun even broke through and Captain Barker managed his first sun sight in weeks. They were finally west of Cape Horn again, a fact that Barker made sure Second Mate Atkinson relayed to the crew.

The wind stayed fair for three days before the westerlies filled back in and another series of gales drove them back, taking much of the distance that they had gained.

CHAPTER 15
CRAZY DANE AND A FAVORING SLANT

October 14, 1905 – 125 days out of Cardiff

T he ship, which had been difficult to handle with twenty sailors, was now being sailed by six and the four apprentices. There were so few sailors fit for duty that Captain Barker finally ordered the second mate to fire up the donkey boiler and use the steam winch for hauling, now that muscles were no longer adequate to handle the sails. Keeping the boiler topped up with fresh water proved almost as difficult as the sail-handing itself.

A tot of rum became a daily ration. Captain Barker had hoped it would be viewed as a reward, but at best, it seemed only to help everyone left just hold on, which perhaps was enough.

Five men were down with frostbite, but three were suffering simply from exhaustion. The oldest three sailors—Hanson, Lindstrom and Schmidt—had nearly worked themselves to death and were all now in their bunks, barely hanging on.

One westerly gale followed the next. Captain Barker resumed his vigil on deck, watching for the slightest hint of a favoring wind shift. The few remaining sailors watched the stony-faced captain on the poop deck and swore softly as they turned to. Captain Barker knew the men were cursing him and hardly blamed them. He cursed at the westerlies. Beneath his best stoic exterior, he raged against the winds. All they needed was a slant.

Jensen waited outside the captain's dayroom.

"Yes, Jensen," Captain Barker said, motioning him in. "Have a seat."

"Thank you, sir." He took of his cap. "Captain, my head is paining me again. From when I was hurt on the *Daniella*. When the shackle hit mine *hoved*."

"If you are sick, I have medicine." The standard medicine dished out was a strong laxative.

"Nah, that won't do me no good, sir. Don't think that there is any medicine that will help."

"Then what is it, Jensen?"

Jensen pulled a sheaf of papers from beneath his coat. "If you could put these in the ship's safe, sir, I would be grateful."

"What are they?"

"Just my discharge papers. Nothing really, but they are all I have. My sea chest is afloat half the time. I just want them to be safe."

Captain Barker took the papers, and smoothed them with his hand. "I'll take care of these, Jensen, and give them back to you at the end of the voyage."

"*Mange tak*, Captain." The big man got up and left the cabin.

Barker sat for a moment before turning back to his desk. Jensen was the best sailor left on the ship. He only wished that the demons that haunted the man would finally give him peace.

The wind shifted again, clocking a point to the northward and dropping in intensity. They set the t'gallants and made good distance to westward for a day until, maddeningly, another line of westerly gales drove them back again.

From the poop deck, Captain Barker could see the dark shapes of the crew bent double over the yards, furling the main t'gallants. He heard a loud crack like a rifle's shot and saw the sail billow up wildly like some mad beast. An instant later he heard the cry, "Man overboard." Barker murmured a prayer under his breath for the soul of the man carried off by the wind. There was nothing else that he could do.

The remaining sailors fought the flogging canvas until at length they tamed it and tied the gaskets. The captain could see that there were three men climbing off the yard, where not long before there had been four.

In a few minutes Mr. Atkinson climbed wearily up the poop deck ladder.

"Who did we lose?" the captain asked.

"The Dane, Jensen. A gasket broke. The sail pitched him off the yard."

The captain just shook his head and paced off to windward. He thought of the puny stack of paper sitting in the ship's safe. The only record of a man's life. How could Jensen have known? He had fought both the sea and his demons for so long. Somehow he knew the end was close at hand.

The next morning the wind shifted northerly again and the *Lady Rebecca* sailed along on a beam reach. It was Fred's turn to fetch the tea and bread barge. He tumbled from his bunk in the crowded fo'c'sle and went on deck. At the galley door, Jeremiah was beaming as he passed out the pantiles and steaming pots of tea.

"Nobody listened to me, when I tol' ye that he was a Jonah. Nobody listen to old Jeremiah but I tol' ye, didn't I? And now he's gone, the debil has his due and the wind is so fine and fair. I tol' ye."

"Shut your trap," Fred growled. "Nobody wants to hear your blather."

Jeremiah scoffed. "But I was right, don't ye know. Debil had his due."

Fred put down the bread barge on the galley doorsill, pulled out his sheath knife and in one quick motion brought the point up under the cook's chin. "If I hear you say another word about Jensen, so help me God, I'll cut your throat from ear to ear. You understand me?"

Fred saw anger in the cook's eyes so he jabbed the knife closer. "You understand me?" he repeated.

"Yes, suh," the cook responded. Fred wasn't sure whether he sensed resignation or defiance in the tone but didn't care. As he made his way back to the fo'c'sle, he marveled at how close he had come to killing the cook.

When he delivered the bread barge and the tea to the watch, it was clear enough that Jeremiah was not the only one relieved at the death of their shipmate. The mood had lifted in the fo'c'sle. Donnie was talking about the whores of Chile again and how glad they would be to see them.

Frenchie opined, "Things be right again, now that ze Dane is gone." Several others agreed.

Fred seethed. "He was fine a sailor, a shipmate and a friend."

After a moment's silence when Fred wondered whether he would be in the center of a brawl, Donnie murmured softly, "Well, never do to speak ill of the dead. Mind you, I do think our luck has changed."

Fred just snorted and left the fo'c'sle, stepping out on deck with his bread and pannikin of tea. The wind was on their beam now. Every sail they could carry was set. Instead of the roar of green water rushing down the deck, Fred could hear the hiss of the bow wave as the *Lady Rebecca* shouldered the swells. Sunlight, shining through breaks in the clouds, made the spray that still broke over the bow shine like a shower of diamonds, before it disappeared off to leeward. Fred raised his tea to the wind and said softly, "Farewell, Jensen, you damn, crazy, son-of-a-bitch Dane." For whatever reason, their luck had changed and now they had a favoring slant. That was all that mattered.

Three days later they rounded 50 degrees south latitude and sailed north by west into the wide Pacific Ocean.

CHAPTER 16
A FAIR WIND TO CHILE

October 23, 1905 – 134 days out of Cardiff

Will stood his trick at the helm wearing a dry shirt, open at the neck. It was the first time in months that his clothes were not wet and salty. They were making good progress up the coast of Chile, having left 50 degrees south latitude in their wake a week before. They had been seventy-one days sailing from 50 degrees south to 50 degrees south, seventy-one days rounding the Horn. The gales were behind them. All sails were set and drawing as a gentle westerly wind carried them northward. If it hadn't been for the toll taken on the ship and the crew by more than three months of the Cape Horn winter, it might have all seemed but a distant and terrible dream.

The sick and injured had been brought out on deck and were laid out on the hatches in hope that the fresh air and broken sunlight would do them some good. The rest of the crew had been busy at the washtubs, which had been broken out for the first time in months. The ship's shrouds were festooned with drying clothes, no longer salt encrusted, finally washed in something approaching freshwater.

By the middle of Will's watch, the clouds began to clear, and he stared out at blue sky for the first time in what seemed like forever. Only the shout from Mate Atkinson, "Watch your helm, dammit!" shook him from his reverie. "Aye, sir," he replied, focusing again on the compass but incapable of suppressing the smile on his face.

The captain's wife and children came up on deck. The mate hurried to get Mary Barker a chair. Amanda squealed, "Look, Mommy. The sun is shining on Daddy's water!" Little Tommy clapped his hands and chortled.

Will laughed out loud. The sun was indeed shining on a deep cerulean sea. Had there ever been a color so beautiful?

The captain and Mary were eating alone in the messroom. Captain Barker felt free to spend less time on deck now that they sailed on warmer waters and gentle winds. He and Mary spoke of the children and of times at home. He had already agreed to send them home from Pisaqua, as Mary had asked. It would pain him to lose his family's company during the long voyage that remained, but they had gone through enough, and as much as he would miss her and the children he couldn't say no.

When Walter brought them coffee, Mary turned to him and asked, "So what will you do with Mr. Rand? I imagine that you cannot keep him locked in his cabin forever."

"I intend to bring him up on charges in Pisaqua. Mutiny is a serious matter. Even the threat of mutiny."

Mary smiled. "But there was no actual mutiny was there? A threat is not quite the same thing. And I understand that he was an adequate mate, for most of the voyage at least."

"You may be a touch too soft-hearted, my love. Some things cannot be so easily overlooked," the captain replied.

Mary sipped her coffee, then took a different tack. "How long will the proceedings take? And will there be expenses involved?"

"Well, that is a consideration. I hadn't given it much thought. Pisaqua is a small port. Empaneling an Admiralty court could take some time. And there would be legal expenses."

"I just thought," Mary suggested, "that we might not wish to delay the ship further or add to our costs. Perhaps you might discharge Mr. Rand in Callao and hire a new mate in his stead. That might serve us all for the better."

James Barker smiled. He wondered whether his wife's concerns were merciful or merely mercantile. Nothing wrong with either. She had a decent head for business, another reason to be sorry to be sending her home.

After a long absence, Mary Barker sat down again at her writing desk in the cabin. She hadn't written for so long because she had had nothing to write about, save her own misery and hopelessness. She finally felt like writing again.

Ship Lady Rebecca   *October 25, 1905*

Dearest Mother,

It had been my intention to send these letters to you on a passing steamer or sailing ship that we might cross on our voyage. It now looks like I will be the courier after all. Rather than these being missives from your wandering daughter, they may perchance serve as a diary of this most horrible voyage.

I have not written as often as I had meant to, but then the children and I did spend months on end strapped into our berth in the dark and wet cabin, so there was both little opportunity to write and even less to say. James, aided by the cabin steward, did what he could to see to our care, but there was not much that either could do.

We hope to arrive in Pisagua, Chile, in a few days, all depending on the wind. James has told me that the winds off Chile can be difficult and drop away all together. I hope and pray that this wind holds. After so many months of too much wind, the prospect of being delayed by the lack of it would almost be too much to bear.

James has promised to put the children and me on the first steamer bound for home. The steam ships transit the more sheltered Straits of Magellan rather than rounding Cape Horn. Also by then, it should be approaching Spring in the Southern latitudes so we can anticipate a less violent and far faster passage.

How I long to see you and the cousins again. How I long simply to be in the company of women again. It has been too long since I could speak to anyone other than the steward, to James and on occasion, to Thomas. You will be pleased to know that Thomas is well and has apparently served the ship most ably during these difficult months.

Once I return to England, it is my intention to never again go to sea. James is my husband and a fine captain, but I believe that I have truly seen hell around the Horn, and if it is within my power, I shall stay happily ashore henceforth.

Your loving daughter,

Mary

Captain Barker compared his latitudes with Mate Atkinson's sight, and gave the order to turn east toward the Chilean coast. Will was almost too excited to sleep. He left his bunk before dawn and climbed the ratlines to the main crosstrees to try to catch a glimpse of the shore. Acting Third Mate Paul Nelson saw him climbing; he smiled and shook his head, remembering his first landfall and how excited he had been.

At first, Will saw nothing but unbroken horizon. Then a brown haze seemed to float on the water. It grew to a low smudge. Finally, he could just make out an indistinct line. "Land ho," Will called out. He looked down at the poop deck and saw the captain walk over to Nelson. Not long thereafter, Nelson joined Will on the crosstrees. Nelson used Will's shoulder as a brace for his telescope. "There's Chile, all right. Just where she's supposed to be." Will yelled "Yahooeeee!" Nelson just laughed.

October 28, 1905 – 139 days out of Cardiff

The harbor at Pisagua was a little more than a shallow cove on a dun-colored coast. The town was the same drab brown as the hills that rose above a barren and featureless landscape. Were it not for the other sailing ships at anchor in the roadstead, it would be have easy to sail past the harbor without noticing the nondescript hovels of the town.

Donnie, Frenchie and Fred all stood by the rail watching the ships at anchor grow slowly larger and more distinct as the *Lady Rebecca* stood into the anchorage. The town of Pisagua itself was in the shadow of the sun rising over the hills behind it.

"Doesn't look like much, does it?" Fred commented. After four and a half months at sea, he had hoped for more than an assemblage of dusty shacks on a treeless sunbaked hillside.

"Don't, 'cause it ain't," Donnie replied. "Nothing there, really, and the whores are about as ugly as the town. Just wait till we call at Callao. Now that's a sailor's town. You know what Pisagua means?" He cast a sideways glance at his shipmates. "Means piss water. Good name for it, too."

"Alor," Frenchie replied. "You make that up. Didn't he make that up?"

Fred shrugged, "*Agua* is *water* in Spanish and *pis* means *piss*, so I guess it could be right."

"*Merde*." Frenchie shook his head. "We sail round Cape Horn in ze winter, all for piss water?"

Captain Barker stood next to the helmsman as the *Lady Rebecca* ghosted under topsails into the anchorage. Mr. Rand, recently released from confinement on promises of good behavior and the understanding that he would be leaving the ship in Callao, assumed his station on the bow in charge of the anchor. Captain Barker looked over the anchorage and chose his spot. He said a few words to the helmsman, who spun the wheel, slowly bringing the bow into the wind. He nodded to Mr. Atkinson at the break of the poop. Atkinson bellowed, "Main, loose the halyard, up bunts and clews."

Barker yelled, "Mr. Rand, let go the anchor. Three shots."

Rand responded, "Let go the anchor. Three shots, aye." He yanked back the hand brake and a gritty red cloud rose up as the rusty chain flew through the hawse. At the third shackle, linking each fifteen-fathom shot, he hauled back on the brake and then secured the devil's claw to the chain.

"Back the fore topsail," Atkinson shouted. The ship began sailing backwards, snubbing the anchor chain. "Loose the halyard. Up bunts and clews. Furl the topsails. A harbor furl, if you please."

Paul Nelson sent up the yellow "Q" flag, requesting free pratique from customs.

Mary Barker came up on deck. The captain walked over to her. "Welcome to Chile, my dear."

"When may we go ashore?" she asked.

Captain Barker chuckled. "Unfortunately, we are a bit short of boats, at present. We have the signal up for customs, so they should be sending out a boat shortly. I am sure that we can arrange for additional boats from shore or from the ships in the harbor. Please try to be a bit patient, my dear. I know that that is not easy after so many months at sea."

Within about an hour, a boatload of Chilean customs officials and an English-speaking pilot put off from the mole in a small steam launch and headed for the *Lady Rebecca*. After completing all the preliminary customs documents, they agreed to carry Captain Barker to shore to visit the British consul and the shipping agent.

As they pulled away from the ship, the captain did all he could to retain his composure. The *Lady Rebecca* sat low in the water, her freeboard less than four feet. The black hull had been scrubbed free of paint by brash ice and was now an ugly rusty red. The jib-boom was canted up while the derigged fore and mainmasts made her once lofty rig look stunted, almost crippled. He knew his ship's condition in minute detail and yet the one thing he couldn't do while sailing her was to take her all in, in one glance. Now the sight of the damage to his beautiful ship took him full aback.

He turned away. The damage to the ship was not the only damage he had to account for. Tucked beneath his arm was the official log with an account of the deaths and the injuries incurred during the voyage. He also needed to find a doctor as quickly as possible, for he feared that several of the sick would die if they did not receive medical attention soon.

He was responsible for his ship and its crew and both had suffered grievously. He squared his shoulders and straightened the blue jacket that he had saved these months precisely for going ashore. He had done all that he could do. Five or six ships simply disappeared every year attempting to round Cape Horn. He had brought his ship, its cargo and most of his crew to port. All else were the hazards of the sea. He had done his duty and if he had any doubt of that, this not the time to show it.

Captain Barker's first order of business was to present the official log to the British consul in Pisagua, an elderly gentleman named Morris, who worked behind a large desk in a small but comfortable office near the nitrate docks.

"Sir, Captain Barker from the *Lady Rebecca*, one hundred and thirty-nine days from Cardiff, with a cargo of coal."

"Hunh," the consul snorted. "There was talk that you might have been lost. I understand that your agent received several telegraphs from your Mr. Shute when you were overdue, inquiring as to your arrival. Looks like you had a difficult passage, Captain. Any loss of crew?

"Four, sir. All properly logged. We also have injuries. I would like to see to it that those in need of attention are brought to a hospital to be looked after."

"Four dead. My word. You did have a difficult passage. Well, I shall review the log and take the appropriate action. As to the sick, we do have a hospital of sorts. Not much to speak of, really, but it may serve."

"Thank you, Consul Morris."

The old gentleman merely nodded and Captain Barker left to find the ship's agent.

The shipping agent was a florid little man named Johnson who greeted Captain Barker warmly.

"So sorry, sir, to hear of your dreadful voyage but you have arrived and the mines are in desperate need of your coal. I regret to say, however, that several German ships have swept the coast clean of nitrates. I have been telegraphing Mr. Shute in search of alternative cargoes."

The last statement struck Captain Barker like a hammer blow. For a moment he felt like he could not breathe. They made money transporting the coal but if there was no backhaul cargo, the voyage might still be a loss. As part owner of the ship and cargo, the loss would be his. All his dreams of establishing himself in one voyage vanished in an instant.

Barker did all he could not to show how the news affected him. His ship was damaged and would require repair, and now they had no homeward-bound cargo. He saw his dream of a highly profitable voyage slip further from his grasp.

"I have confidence in Mr. Shute." It seemed all that he could really say. "Do you happen to know when the *Susannah* arrived in Iquique?" He wanted to get all his bad news at once.

Agent looked dour. "I am afraid, sir, that she is overdue. There have been no reports of her anywhere on the coast."

Captain Barker felt an instant's elation and then a deep dread. Suddenly, the idea of racing one square-rigger against another seemed a game played by children when compared to the fury of the Southern Ocean. The *Susannah* overdue? Given how terrible their own voyage indeed was, he would say a prayer for Captain Frederich and his crew.

Will wore what passed for his best uniform, a white shirt and pants, as clean as he could get them. Captain Barker had purchased four boats for the ship and now he and Jack had to row him to shore and back on ship's business.

He was tanned and, at long last, warm. Hot, actually, but that was just fine with him. Unlike the rest of the crew, who were stuck working on the ship, he and Jack had time ashore. They were supposed to wait by the boat but had learned how long the captain took on his rounds so they could wander the streets a bit and still be ready to row the captain back. They were even earning some pocket money smuggling pisco, the local hooch, back to the rest of the crew.

The worst part of the job had been rowing Lindstrom, Hanson and Jerry the Greek ashore to the hospital. Of the three, Jerry looked in the best shape. Shore labor was brought out to unload the cargo, while the rest of the crew were set to work on repairs. Pugsley got the pump cleared and Will enjoyed seeing the old ship floating on her lines again. Slowly her rust-streaked sides were returning to black as his shipmates on bosun's chairs scraped and painted the hull. Once again, Will has happy to be at the oars of the captain's launch.

It had only been five months since he stood on the dock in Cardiff, and yet he felt that he was entirely a different person. His shoulders were broader and waist narrower. He wore his belt was several notches tighter and had no problem hauling the oars to carry the captain across the harbor. He was different physically, but that seemed to be the least of it.

What he had lived through was only beginning to sink in. Only now were the months of storms, danger and death coming into focus. He had been too tired, too frightened and too overwhelmed to think about what he was doing or where he was. Now, in the warmth of the Chilean sun, he could marvel at his own survival and feel proud that he had carried on regardless. He smiled, thinking about the fourteen-year-old boy who had stood on the Cardiff dock five months before. He was only a few months older, but was no longer that same boy. He felt like a different person entirely. He had survived the worst of Cape Horn. No more need be said.

Within a fortnight, a squat German steamer chugged into the harbor. Two days later, all the apprentices turned to to row the captain's family ashore to meet the steamer. Paul Nelson who was still acting Third Mate volunteered to help row as well. Captain Barker, Mary and the children were in one boat, with a second reserved for their luggage. The wind had picked up, raising a short chop in the roadstead. Will and Jack, rowing the captain's boat, took special care to see that his wife and children stayed dry.

At the dock, Mary forced back tears and Amanda and Tommy hugged their father's legs until they were pulled away by their mother. Captain Barker maintained the same stoic demeanor that he wore while pacing the bridge. Will wondered if he could really be so unfeeling.

Mary and the children stepped away and came over to each of the apprentices. She gave Will a hug and little Amanda looked up and said, "And you take care of yourself, Mr. Will."

"I will be sure to contact your parents, William," said Mary, "and tell them that you are a fine young man who will make a fine ship's officer if that is the course you choose."

"Thank you, Mrs. Barker. Thank you very much. Have a good voyage home."

"Thank you, William."

Mary spoke quietly to each of the apprentices, lined up on the pier, and turned to see James having a few words with the mate from the steamer, who was directing his sailors on the loading of their luggage.

James looked older than she remembered him in Cardiff. He was still a young man but his face was weathered and there was something in his countenance that seemed worn and weary. Nevertheless, at his core, he had the same vigor and determination that he always had. Seeing him now, she was amazed by that determination, the absolute, indomitable strength of will. She wondered whether it was his greatest virtue or his greatest flaw.

They had said their goodbyes in the cabin, so little more need be said. He smiled at her. "I hope the voyage is comfortable, my dear."

"Thank you, James," she replied squeezing his hand.

His only hint of emotion was when he picked up both Amanda and little Tommy at once and hugged them tightly, for the longest time, not wanting to let them go. He seemed to be whispering something to them. Finally, he let them down. Amanda started to cry and a few moments later Tommy followed her example. "You both obey your mother. I will look forward to seeing you when I return home."

His eyes seemed to glisten slightly and Mary wondered whether it was tears or just the wind. It didn't matter. She took her children by the hand. They turned and walked up the gangway to the steamer that would take them home.

A week later, Mr. Rand knocked at the captain's dayroom door. Once they had rounded up into the Pacific he had returned to duty as if nothing had ever happened. They agreed that he would leave the ship at Callao. The captain had in turn agreed to remove any reference to mutiny from the ship's log, always wondering if he had made the right choice in doing so. Avoiding additional cost and delay overbalanced the scale of justice.

"Come in, Mr. Rand."

"I've changed my mind, Captain. My back still is hurting me something awful. I thought it would get better in the warmer weather but it hasn't. I think I'd like to see a doctor after all.

Captain Barker accompanied Mr. Rand ashore to see a physician that the agent had recommended. After a period of time, the doctor came out to speak to the captain.

"How is he, doctor?"

The doctor shook his head. "That man has the largest carbuncle that I have even seen in his upper back, next to his spine. It must have caused him terrible pain. We will have to operate immediately if he has any hope of survival."

Barker was stunned. "I had no idea. He complained of pain, but..."

"You had no way of knowing. A remarkable case. I am surprised he walked in here unassisted."

"How long will he be in hospital? I expect to sail within two weeks."

"Then, sir, I suggest that you find yourself a new mate. If he survives the surgery, he may never walk again."

Once back out on the street, Captain Barker stood for a moment, amazed at Mr. Rand. An excellent seaman who bore up under such physical pain, yet lacking the moral stamina to do his duty. A puzzle indeed. The best of mates and the worst of mates, Captain Barker thought, with a silent apology to Mr. Dickens.

The cargo of coal was finally discharged. The *Lady Rebecca* looked very much like her old self, notwithstanding her damaged masts. Will and Jack rowed the captain back from shore. He had the ship's papers and the official log signed by the British consul. Will was nearly dying from curiosity as to what it meant, where they were bound, but as still only an apprentice, thought it best not to ask. He had already heard ashore that Hanson had died in the hospital and that Lindstrom was still in a bad way. Jerry the Greek, however, was on the mend after an operation on his leg. They would be left in Pisagua with passage money home.

When the captain climbed aboard, Will followed close behind and tried to get as close to the break of the poop deck as he could so that he could hear the captain talking to the second mate.

Will walked quietly forward to pass along the news.

"Have you heard?" Fred asked Donnie.

"What?"

"Callao for repairs and then bound for Australia in ballast to load wool. The apprentice just told me."

"Australia, is it? Well isn't that a fine kettle of mutton?"

"What do you have against Australia?"

The Irishman laughed. "Nothing at all, though if we call at Sydney, there are a couple of Sheilas who might not be happy to see me."

"Hah," Fred replied. "You think they remember you?"

"Every time they look at their young'uns, they pr'olly do. Hear that they bear a strong resemblance."

"And you know what else?" Fred asked. "The *Susannah* finally arrived in Iquique yesterday. The agent got a cable. Two hundred and seven days from Cardiff."

Donnie hooted. "What? Two hundred and seven days? That must be some sort of record for the slowest rounding ever. So the Old Man beat the German by a month after all. Son of a bitch, I don't believe it. Amazing."

Fred stood at the rail, looking to seaward. In the weary days, slogging against the westerlies off the Horn, he had promised himself that he would jump ship in Chile and wander a while in South America. Now, he had changed his mind. He felt no great love for the captain, but he no longer hated him, as he had for months in the Southern ocean, well, Barker was a real seaman, and that deserved respect. And like every sailor, Fred was fond of the ship. She had carried them all through the worst of gales. And Australia sounded interesting. Perhaps it was time to add the Antipodes to his world tour.

That afternoon the provisions arrived, along with a crimp's boat with six new sailors, all drugged or drunk, by their appearance. All hands turned to to secure the hatches and to store the provisions and gear.

Just before sunset, the crew began the long stomp around the windlass to raise the anchor. Donnie began singing, at first almost as if to himself. Since Harry had died, the ship had had no real shantyman. After a verse, he raised his voice and sang out, "*Ooooh, I wish I was in Madame Gashay's down in Callao...*"

After a moment's pause, the rest answered back, "*Horrah, me yellar girls, Do'na let me go me,*" and Donnie bellowed, "*Where the girls will grab and they never let ya go. Horrah, me yaller girls do'na let me go...*"

The clank of the capstain and the click of each link of the anchor chain in the hawse kept time with the shanty until the chain was finally up and down, and the backed fore topsail broke the anchor out of the muddy bottom. With the anchor hove and catted, *Lady Rebecca* bore away, her topsails filling in the light air. Soon her t'gansails and royals were sheeted home and the fine ship stood northward up the coast to Callao, as Pisagua faded into the mist astern.

CHAPTER 17
ON THE BEACH NEAR MONTEVIDEO

February 12, 1928

The launch grounded on the sloping sand beach with a soft hiss. Captain Jones leapt over the gunwale. A wave broke over his polished black shoes, soaking them and the bottom of his slacks, but he barely noticed. He couldn't take his eyes off the hulk on the beach before him. The *Lady Rebecca* sat with a slight list to port. The paint on her hull had been replaced by rust, but, save for a large hole cut near her stern, she seemed intact, almost ready to sail again.

He stood looking up the sweeping lines of the hull, lines you would never find on a boxy steamer. The *Lady Rebecca* had been the perfect balance, wresting every ounce of power from the wind, while slipping through the water as gracefully as a dolphin. And she left no trail of smoke to smudge the sky.

The hole in her hull had, no doubt, been cut to make sure that she would never again leave the beach. It seemed almost cruel, but Captain Jones understood. If she floated free in a winter storm, she would be a serious hazard to navigation. Better that her hull flood on the beach than float away to be run down by a steamer in the river, perhaps sinking them both.

It was all just as well. The *Lady Rebecca*'s time was past. There were still a few great windjammers on the oceans, but too few. When the Laeisz Flying-P ships and the handful of others owned by stiff-necked Finns and Swedes finally furled their sails, there would be no more. The majestic clouds of sail that once graced every ocean would be gone forever.

Even old "bend 'em or break 'em" Captain Barker had understood as much. He went into steam at the end of their voyage on the *Lady Rebecca*. He was still young enough and all the steamship lines were looking for young captains with sail experience. No one understood the sea like the captain of a wind ship.

He had followed his captain's example. When he finished his apprenticeship, he signed on as a mate aboard a steamer. It was the only way. There was no future in sail. Anyone could have seen as much. Still, he had started out on a windjammer and had sailed around the Horn. That was, in itself, a worthy boast.

Life on a steamship was different—uniforms and regulations, schedules that could not be missed, nothing quite like the rough and tumble world of the windjammer. But the sea was the same, as constant and changeable as ever, and just as unforgiving of fools.

Oddly, his voyage on the *Lady Rebecca* had been a sort of brutal gift. In the almost twenty-five years since, the seas had never been as vicious, the waves never quite as high. After fighting frozen canvas with bleeding hands, bent double over a t'gallant yard, high over a raging sea in a Cape Horn snorter, nothing aboard a steamship was ever as frightening or as exciting. He had survived his ship being torpedoed by a German submarine during the Great War and had drifted in a lifeboat for a week before being picked up. He had learned to resist the old sailor's refrain, "Ah, I've seen worse than this." He had, so there was no need to say it.

He had also learned not to tell the story of the mighty wave that struck them off Cape Horn in 1905, because no one believed him. He knew the story was true. The ship, the waves, the storms and the men who lived and died, they were all more true than anything else he had ever known, even if no one believed or understood.

At least two sailors understood, because they were there. As he was passing by his parents' house in Devon just before signing aboard the *Clan McCollough*, as a newly minted mate, he found a letter from Fred Smythe waiting for him. They began a long exchange of letters, not more than once a year but the years had added up. Fred had moved to the Northwest of the United States, worked as a cowboy for a time, then as a teamster, until finally settling down as an insurance broker. An insurance broker! Who could have imagined sailor Fred behind a desk wearing a suit and starched collar? Over the years all of Fred's letters were always addressed to "Apprentice William Jones." Captain Jones always wrote back letters addressed to "Able Seaman Fred Smythe."

He had kept in touch with Captain Barker, as well. Barker retired after a long career straddling sail and steam. He rounded Cape Horn forty-one times before he finally came ashore. There he kept busy giving lectures for rich yachtsmen about the great days of sail. No doubt they sat in rapt attention, like children at a magic show, listening to the old captain spin his tales.

Only last month, just before sailing on his current voyage southbound, Will had gotten a letter from Captain Barker. A group of writers and artists had just purchased an old square-rigger, the *Sophie*. They were going to rename her *Tusitala*, in honor of Robert Lewis Stevenson. The Samoans called Stevenson *Tusitala*, the storyteller. The new owners had asked Barker to be the captain of the newly renamed ship. Captain Barker had asked, he presumed in jest, for Jones to join him as mate. "Be just like old times," Barker had written.

He had written back congratulating him without responding to the offer. It could never be like old times, nor would he want them to be. He did have to laugh. The new owners planned on trading the *Tusitala* between New York and Hawaii, by way of the Panama Canal. They wouldn't be risking their ship around Cape Horn. That time had passed.

Captain Jones stepped closer and put his hand on the rusted steel plating of the *Lady Rebecca*. It felt warm to the touch, like a living being, though he knew that it was only the warmth of the afternoon sun captured by the rusting steel.

Behind him the boatman called, "*¡Señor, hora de ir!*" *Time to go*. It was time. He took his hand away from the steel and saw that is was covered in rust. He stepped down to the water's edge, bent down and washed his hands in the sea. The swirling rust looked to him, for an instant, like blood in the water. Then another wave came and washed it away.

Captain Jones gave the launch a shove, pushing it off the beach before leaping aboard at the last instant. The boatman pushed the gearbox lever and the throttle, and with a puff of black smoke the little steam launch backed off the sand and swung out into deep water.

Captain Jones looked away from shore. He had another ship to care for, cargo to load and discharge, passages to make and schedules to keep. When he finally allowed himself to look back at the *Lady Rebecca*, she had all but disappeared in the early evening haze.

AUTHOR'S NOTES

*H**ell Around the Horn* is a work of fiction inspired by a particular voyage around Cape Horn by the windjammer *British Isles* in 1905. (I think that *British Isles* is a horrible name for a ship so, in the novel, I renamed her *Lady Rebecca*.) While all the characters in the novel are fictional, many were inspired by the real officers and crew aboard the *British Isles.* Captain James Pratt Barker, his wife Mary and their children sailed aboard the ship as did, Apprentice William Jones, Mate Rand, Second Mate Atkinson, the Welsh sailor G.H. Harhy, the sail-maker Pugsley and the carpenter Gronberg. The American sailor, Fred Smythe, is a composite of many of the young educated sailors who sailed before the mast in the latter days of sail. He was inspired most directly by Fred Harlow but was also borrowed in part from Richard Henry Dana, Herman Melville, Felix Riesenberg and Basil Lubbock, among others.

The novel itself was directly inspired by "*The Log of a Limejuicer: The Experiences Under Sail of James P. Barker, Master Mariner,*" by James Barker and Roland Barker; "*The Cape Horn Breed,*" by Captain William H. S. Jones and "*The War with Cape Horn,*" by Alan Villiers. Specific scenes were inspired by "*The Brassbounder,*" by David W. Bone and "*By Way of Cape Horn*" by Paul E. Stevenson.

THE LAST DAYS OF SAIL

At the turn of the century there were between four and five thousand large and medium-sized sailing ships circling the globe, still managing to pay their way. Most of these ships came to be known as "windjammers." They were very a different breed from the "clipper" ships of fifty years before. Whereas the clippers were built for speed and to carry high value cargoes, the windjammers were built to carry bulk cargoes as cheaply as possible. The windjammers were significantly larger ships of iron or steel and carried more cargo than the clippers, which were were usually built of wood. Though the windjammers were considerably larger, they carried smaller crews than the clippers. The windjammer can be looked upon as the most advanced development of the sailing ship and perhaps also, the most brutal.

The windjammers sailed on the last profitable trade routes for sailing ships, the long windy passages below Cape Horn and the Cape of Good Hope, where the fueling stations were too few and far between for steam ships. The windjammers carried wool, grain, coal, iron, nitrates, case oil and other bulk cargoes. These remaining sailing ships cost less to build and operate than the steamers and held on with a surprising tenacity. The last voyage of a cargo carrying windjammer was in 1957. Almost a dozen of these great old ships survive to this day, including the *Star of India*, now a museum ship in San Diego, built in 1863, a full two decades before the construction of the *British Isles*, the inspiration for the *Lady Rebecca*.

CAPE HORN WINTER OF 1905

Alan Villiers writes in his book, "*The War with Cape Horn*" that the winter of 1905 was particularly brutal for sailing ships bound west around Cape Horn. At any one time, four to five hundred ships were attempting to round the Horn. That year, between forty and fifty had to turn back and run to the Falklands, Montevideo or even as far as Rio de Janeiro for repairs. A number of these ship were too damaged to be worth repairing and were cut down and sold as coal and sand hulks. A dozen or so ships would give up the attempt at westing entirely and turn and run before the winds, easterly around the bottom of the world. Six or seven ships simply disappeared, sinking in the Cape Horn storms or being lost in the Antarctic ice. As brutal as the voyage of the *Lady Rebecca* was in the novel, she was one of the lucky ones. She survived and finally arrived in Chile.

THE VOYAGE BEHIND THE NOVEL

The six or seven ships that were lost that year left no record whatsoever. The ships that survived were only slightly better documented. Most would leave no more record of their passage than their wake on the sea itself. The voyage of the *British Isles* that inspired this novel was very different. Its story would be revealed in stages over a period of 65 years.

In the 1930s, Captain James P. Barker sat down with his son, Roland, who, in addition to being a sailor himself, would become a writer. Captain Barker told his son about his life on sailing ships and Roland turned it into a memoir, *"The Log of a Limejuicer: The Experiences Under Sail of James P. Barker, Master Mariner."* Much of the memoir was an account of the 1905 voyage of the *British Isles* around Cape Horn. Though Captain Barker would have a career in steamships and later serve as the captain of the *Tusitala*, the last US flag square-rigger, the memoir ends in 1905, on the coast of Chile, less than halfway through the voyage that continued through 1908. It was if, after the brutal months rounding Cape Horn described in the book, that anything more would seem anti-climactic. The New York Times review of the book raves, "In the *"Log of a Limejuicer*," Captain James P. Barker tells a great story of rounding the Horn...This single passage makes an astonishing tale without an exact counterpart in books of the sea."

Captain Barker would retire as the Marine Superintendent for Prudential Lines in January 1946. He died on August 9th of that year, survived by his wife Mary, his two daughters and three sons. In his career, Captain Barker rounded Cape Horn forty-one times.

That might have been the end of the story but in 1956, Captain William H. S. Jones wrote a book titled, *"The Cape Horn Breed."* Fifty one years before, he had sailed as a first voyage apprentice on the *British Isles*. Oddly, Captain Barker never mentioned an apprentice named Jones in his memoir. This may have been part of the motivation for Captain Jones to write the book, a half century after the ill-fated voyage. He wrote that his memoir was based on a diary that he kept in pencil in a small notebook, that he had retained for the intervening years. He said that the pencil markings on some of the pages had been rinsed away by saltwater, so that in some cases, he had to rely on his memory.

So, after the publication of the captain's recollection of the voyage, followed decades later by the apprentice's version, one might assume that the record was complete. But it was not the case.

In 1970, sixty-five years after the voyage, Alan Villiers, a square-rigger sailor, captain, shipowner, writer and documentarian, heard of a collection of ship's Articles and official logs stored in a large hanger at Hayes, Middlesex in Great Britain. The crates and crates of documents were about to be thrown away. Villiers examined the documents in the hangar and found what he described as a "treasure trove." There were hundreds and hundreds of logs from sailing ships and thousands from steamers. One of the logs that Villiers discovered was from the 1905 voyage of the *British Isles*.

Based on these newly discovered logs, Villers wrote, *"The War with Cape Horn,"* which focused on the particularly brutal winter of 1905. One of the logs that Villiers paid special attention to was that of the *British Isles*.

So why write a novel about a voyage that is so well documented? One reason is because the primary sources do not agree, one with the other. The remarkable thing about the three accounts of the voyage of the *British Isles* is how widely Captain Barker, Apprentice Jones and the official log disagree on key points. They did not for, example, even agree on how many had died during the voyage. The official log reported three deaths at sea, while Captain Barker reported four, and Apprentice Jones counted six. If we assume that the official log is accurate, then the two memoirs are, at least in part, each historical fiction. In the simplest terms, they are the stories that the story tellers wished to be told. Alan Villiers thought that both Captain Barker and Apprentice Jones may have revealed more about themselves than they had intended. (Villiers was not an admirer of Captain Barker.)

Beyond the differences detailed in three accounts, what I found particularly interesting as a writer, were the differences in perspective. The ship, as seen through the eyes of the captain and a first voyage apprentice, is a very different place. I decided to write a novel of the fictional *Lady Rebecca* as seen through the eyes of the captain and an apprentice but also, as seen by an American sailor before the mast and by the captain's long-suffering wife. In doing so, I hoped to capture a more complete picture of the remarkable individuals who sailed on a beautiful, if often dangerous ship, attempting to round the merciless Cape of Storms in the middle of the winter. I will leave it to the reader to judge whether or not I've succeeded.

ROGUE WAVE

The *British Isles,* and her fictional sister the *Lady Rebecca*, were struck by a rogue wave in 1905. Rogue waves are typically two to four times taller than the other waves on the sea and seem to appear from nowhere, often coming from a direction counter to that of the wind or current. They can be up to one hundred feet high and are usually far steeper than a normal wave. These waves can indeed be ship killers, sinking modern ships far larger than any windjammer.

Perhaps the most remarkable thing about rogue waves is that until quite recently, oceanographers and even many ship's captains claimed that they did not exist. The surviving captains of ships struck by rogue waves were dismissed as exaggerating, telling sea stories, or for seeking an excuse for their own failings in preparing their ship for a storm at sea.

Oceanographers had a good reason to dismiss the existence of rogue waves. They had a very functional mathematical model for waves and sea states that agreed quite closely with observations at sea. The model worked. There were no rogue waves predicted by the model, therefore there were no rogue waves.

Even sea captains could be skeptical. Alan Villiers who had sailed before the mast and as ship's captain of square-riggers around Cape Horn, comments in his book, *The War With Cape Horn*, "It is strange that the ship [the British Isles] was so much damaged from her brush with the Horn. She was in the area for ten weeks which is at least seven longer than enough, but she was strongly built to take that sort of punishment indefinitely."

What she was not built for, however, was to be struck by a rushing vertical wall of water the size of a ten story building.

From the standpoint of the scientific community, rogue waves only came into existence on January 1, 1995 on the Draupner drilling platform in the North Sea off Scotland. The platform was hit by an unusually high and steep wave. What was different this time, however, was that there was a downwards-pointing laser sensor installed on the drill rig, which accurately measured and documented the wave heights. In one night, the mythical wave was captured in a form that scientists could accept. We now understand that rogue waves do indeed exist and they look just like the wave described by Captain Barker that nearly sank his ship.

SUSANNAH

The *British Isles* did informally race the German windjammer *Susanna* from Wales to Chile. (The actual ship's name was spelled Susanna. Captain Barker, however, spelled it with an ending "h," which I have continued to do in the novel.) Despite the difficult passage, the *British Isles* (and *Lady Rebecca)* beat the German windjammer to port. In his memoir, Captain Barker thought that the captain of the German ship had given up in the attempt to round the horn to the west and had turned and run before the wind instead. He wrote, "the *Susannah* ran her easting down, rounded Australia, sailed over a vast expanse of storm racked Pacific Ocean, and finally arrived in port in Iquique after a passage of two hundred and seven days."

Given the length of the passage, the explanation is not implausible. Nevertheless, Captain Barker had it wrong. The captain on the actual *Susanna* had a faulty chronometer which indicated that he was father east than he actually was, so they kept sailing west, farther and farther into the Pacific Ocean until the captain finally turned north. He had sailed almost 500 miles farther to the west than he needed to, and therefore, when he turned east toward Chile, had to sail back an additional five hundred miles. The *Susanna* holds the unenviable record for the longest passage around Cape Horn in history. Despite the lengthy passage, however, the ship arrived in port without significant damage or any loss of life.

ONE DEGREE OF SEPARATION

Faulkner wrote, "The past is not dead. It isn't even past." The days of the windjammers seem a long way away. We will never again see ships that sail without engines or electricity, that are wholly out of touch with the world once their t'gallants sank below the horizon and that sail the vast oceans powered only by the wind and the brawn of sailors setting and trimming the sails. Nevertheless, the windjammers are not entirely gone. Close to a dozen of the original ships remain as museum ships around the world and several are still actively sailing. The *Padua*, one of the last Laeisz Flying P-line ships, is sailing as the *Kruzenshtern*, a Russian flag school ship, as is the sail training ship *Sedov*, originally the *Magdalene Vinnen II*. Add in the dozens of sail training ships of various ages and the few sailing cruise ships and there are still square sails on the vast oceans, despite the exaggerated rumors of their demise.

Beyond the ships themselves, I came across a more personal connection to Captain Barker recently. Once a month, a group of folks from around New York City who love the music of the sea get together to sing sea shanties. The get-together is informal but has the rather grand title of the "William Main Doerflinger Memorial Sea Shanty Session" at the Noble Maritime Museum in Building D at the Snug Harbor Cultural Center in Staten Island, New York. I attend whenever I can, which recently has been somewhat infrequently.

Snug Harbor was originally a grand and unique retirement home for indigent sailors, called Sailor's Snug Harbor, established through the generosity of Captain Robert Richard Randall, a wealthy ship's captain and merchant, in 1833. From the mid-1800s to the 1960s, old sailors lived in a row of five Greek Revival mansions on the New Brighton waterfront.

Starting in the 1930s, William Doerflinger, an archivist and collector of folk songs, began traveling to Sailor's Snug Harbor to record sea shanties sung by old sailing ship sailors from the very last days of sail. In 1951, Doerflinger published "*Shanty Men and Shanty Boys*" later republished as "*Songs of the Sailor and Lumberman*." The volume is considered to be one of the essential collections of work songs of the sea.

For those of us who gather to sing shanties at Snug Harbor, there is a special magic to the setting, because the space where we gather was where Bill Doerflinger set up his tape recorder to record the sea shanties sung by the old sailors.

What does any of this have to do with "*Hell Around the Horn*?" After the book was largely written, I learned that Bill Doerflinger also recruited retired ships' captains to sing for him at Snug Harbor. One of these retired captains was none other than Captain James Pratt Barker, ex-master of the windjammer *British Isles*. At Snug Harbor it is easy to imagine Captain Barker singing out in full voice, *Rise Me Up from Down Below,* or one of the other shanties that he sang for Doerflinger. And now, we latter day shanty singers sing the same old songs in same building where Captain Barker and all the rest sang, recalling their days on the mighty oceans beneath a cloud of canvas.

A THANK YOU TO THE READERS

Thank you for reading *Hell Around the Horn*. I thought that it was a story worth telling, about a time and a remarkable group of people who should not be wholly forgotten. I hope that you found that reading the book was worth your time.

I would love to hear your thoughts and feedback on *Hell Around the Horn*. Whether you loved or hated the book, or fell somewhere in between, your comments and perspectives are valuable and I would love to hear them. Please contact me through my website, *rickspilman.com.* I will respond to all emails and would love to hear from you.

Feel free to return to the on-line retailer where you bought the book and post a review. It need not be more than a line or two and it will be greatly appreciated.

Also, if you get the chance, please stop by the Old Salt Blog (*oldsaltblog.com*), a virtual port of call for those who love the sea.

Thanks again,

Rick Spilman

ABOUT THE AUTHOR

R ick Spilman has spent most of his life around the ships and the sea. Professionally, he has worked as a naval architect (ship designer) for several major shipping lines. An avid sailor, Rick has sailed as volunteer crew on the replica square-riggers "*HMS ROSE*" and "*HMS BOUNTY*," as well as sailing on modern and period vessels along the New England coast, the west coast of Florida, the Caribbean, the Great Lakes and the southwest coast of Ireland. He is also an avid kayaker.

Rick is the founder and host of the *Old Salt Blog*, (*oldsaltblog.com*) a virtual port of call for all those who love the sea. He has been published in the Huffington Post, gCaptain, Forbes online, and several canoeing and kayaking print magazines. He was also a nautical columnist on the Clarion science fiction blog and a Cooley Award Winner in short fiction at the University of Michigan. His video has appeared in the Wall Street Journal on-line and in National Geographic Traveler.

Rick lives with his wife and two sons on the west bank of the Hudson River.

To learn learn more go to *rickspilman.com*

SAIL PLAN

1. Flying jib
2. Outer jib
3. Inner jib
4. Foretopmast staysail
5. Fore Royal
6. Fore Upper Topgallant sail
7. Fore Lower Topgallant sail
8. Fore Upper Topsail
9. Fore Lower Topsail
10. Fore Course
11. Main Royal

12. Main Upper Topgallant sail
13. Main Lower Topgallant sail
14. Main Upper Topsail
15. Main Lower Topsail
16. Main Course
17. Main Topmast staysail
18. Mizzen Royal
19. Mizzen Topgallant sail
20. Mizzen Upper Topsail
21. Mizzen Lower Topsail
22. Mizzen Course

GLOSSARY

AB – Able seaman, able to hand, reef and steer.

Amidships – the middle section of the ship.

Anchor, catting – to secure the anchor to the cathead, typically for a short or coastal voyage. For longer voyages, the anchor would be hoisted onto the deck and lashed securely.

Apprentice – a young man who signs on for a four year training period, a ship's officer in training.

Armstrong Patent – slang, a ship with few winches or other mechanical labor-saving devices, where the strong arms of the crew were all that raises, lowers and trims the sails.

Articles – short for Articles of Agreement, a contract between the captain of a ship and a crew member regarding stipulations of a voyage, signed prior to and upon termination of a voyage.

Athwartships – perpendicular to the centerline of the ship, across the width of the ship.

Barometer – a device to measure the barometric pressure. A rising barometer suggests good weather whereas a falling barometer indicates increasing storms.

Barque – a sailing ship of three or more masts having the foremasts rigged square and the aftermast rigged fore-and-aft.

Beam – the breadth of a ship.

Before the mast – traditionally sailors lived forward of the main mast while officers berthed aft. Sailing before the mast was sailing as an able or ordinary seaman.

Best bib and tucker – slang, one's best clothes.

Binnacle – a stand or enclosure of wood or nonmagnetic metal for supporting and housing a compass.

Body and soul lashings – lashings of twine around the waist, pant legs and wrists to prevent the wind from blowing open or up a sailor's oilskins.

Bogie stove – also bogy and bogey, a small cabin stove.

Bolt-rope – a line sewn into the edges of a sail.

Bowsprit – a large spar projecting forward from the stem of a ship.

Brace, Braces – on a square-rigged ship, lines used to rotate the yards around the mast, to allow the ship to sail at different angles to the wind.

Brassbounder – a ship's apprentice, from the row or rows of brass buttons on an apprentice's dress jacket.

Bulwark – plating along the sides of a ship above her gunwale that provides some protection to the crew from being washed overboard by boarding seas.

Bunt – the middle part of the sail. When furling the sail, the last task is to "roll the bunt," which is hauling the furled bunt on the top of the yard and tying it with gaskets.

Buntlines – small lines used to haul up the bottom of the sail prior to furling. There are usually four to eight buntlines across the foot of the sail. When a sail is to be furled, the buntlines and the clewlines are hauled, gather up the sail. When the sail is supported by the buntlines and clewlines, the sail is said to be hanging in its gear.

Burgoo – a porridge of coarse oatmeal and water.

Bute Dock – a dock built in Cardiff, Wales by John Crichton-Stuart, 2nd Marquess of Bute opened in October 1839.

Capstan – a vertical windlass used for raising yards, anchors and any other heavy object aboard ship.

Cardiff, Wales – the capital and largest city in Wales and the tenth largest city in the United Kingdom. In the early twentieth century, Cardiff was the largest exporter of coal in the world.

Clew – the lower corners of a square sail or the lower aft corner of a fore and aft sail.

Clewlines – lines used to haul up the lower corners of a sail prior to furling. See also, buntlines.

Clipper ship – a very fast sailing ship of the mid 19th century that had three or more masts and a square rig. The clipper ship era began the 1830s and ended around 1870.

Close-hauled – when a ship is sailing as close to the wind as it can. A square-rigged ship could usually sail no closer than five to seven points to the wind.

Compass Points – the compass is divided into 32 points. Each point is 11.25 degrees.

Course – In navigation, the course is a direction that the ship is sailing, often also called a compass course. In sails, a course is the lowest square sail on a mast. The main course is often called the main sail and the fore course is often referred to as the fore sail.

Coxcombing – a variety of different styles of decorate knot work using hitches and whipping. French Whipping is a common style of coxcombing.

Cringle – an eye through which to pass a rope, a small hole anywhere a sail, rimmed with stranded cordage. Similar to a grommet.

Cro'jack – the mizzen course. See **Course**

Crosstrees – two horizontal struts at the upper ends of the topmasts used to anchor the shrouds from the topgallant mast.

Davits – frames used to store ships boats which can be quickly swung over the side to allow the boats to be lowered.

Deal planks – A softwood plank, often fir or pine.

Dogwatch – a work shift, between 1600 and 2000 (4pm and 8pm). This period is split into two, with the first dog watch from 1600 to 1800 (4pm to 6pm) and the second dog watch from 1800 to 2000 (6pm to 8pm). Each of these watches is half the length of a standard watch. Effect of the two half watches is to shift the watch schedule daily so that the sailors do not stand the same watch every day. See **Watches**.

Doldrums – region of the ocean near the equator, characterized by calms, light winds, or squalls.

Donkey boiler – A steam boiler on a ship deck used to supply steam to deck machinery.

Donkey's breakfast – a thin sailor's mattress typically filled with straw.

Downhaul – A line used to pull down a sail or yard

Fife rail – a rail at the base of a mast of a sailing vessel, fitted with pins for belaying running rigging. See **Pin rail.**

Figurehead – a carved wooden decoration, often of person, at the prow of a ship. While figureheads are often carvings of women, they can also be of men as well as animals or mythological creatures.

Flying jib – a sail outside the jib on an extension of the jibboom.

Fo'c'sle house, or fo'c'sle – the accommodation space for sailors. At one time in merchant ships, sailors were berthed in the raised forward part of the ship referred to as the fo'c'sle. Later when the accommodations were moved to a cabin on the main deck the deck house continued to be referred to as the fo'c'sle.

Footropes – a rope of cable secured below a yard to a provide a place for a sailor to stand while tending sail.

Fore-reaching – a form of heaving-to in which the ship continues to slowly sail forward on a close reach rather than losing ground and drifting backward.

Foremast – the forward-most mast.

Foresail – the fore course, the lowest square sail on the foremast.

Forestay – stay supporting the foremast.

Freeboard – the amount of ship's hull above the water, the distance from the waterline to the deck edge.

Freeing port – in a steel bulwark, a heavy hinged flap that allows water on deck to flow overboard.

French leave – slang, departing without permission, explanation or leave.

Furious Fifties – the name given to strong westerly winds found in the Southern Hemisphere, generally between the latitudes of 50 and 60 degrees.

Futtock shrouds – shrouds running from the outer edges of a top downwards and inwards to a point on the mast or lower shrouds, and carry the load of the shrouds that rise from the edge of the top. See **Shroud**.

Gammoning band – The lashing or iron band by which the bowsprit of a vessel is secured to the stem to opposite the lifting action of the forestays.

Gantline – a line rove through a block for hoisting rigging, spars, provisions or other items.

Gaskets – gaskets are lengths of rope or fabric used to hold a stowed sail in place, on yachts commonly called sail ties.

Gunwale – also gunnel, the upper deck edge of a ship or boat.

Half-deck – the cabin where the apprentices are lodged. The location of the half-deck can vary between ships, from the cabin to the tween deck to a separate cabin on deck. The half-deck refers not to a specific location but to its function as home to the apprentices.

Halyards – a line used to raise a sail or a yard. Originally from "haul yard."

Harriet Lane – slang for canned meat. Harriet Lane was a murder victim, who was chopped up by her killer around 1875. Merchant sailors came to call any canned meat, Harriet Lane.

Hatch – an opening in the deck of a ship. The main deck hatches are the main access for loading and discharging ship's cargo.

Hatch coaming – A raised frame around a hatch; it forms a support for the hatch cover.

Hatch cover – planks usually held together by metal strapping which form a rectangular panel. These were supported over a hatch by hatch beams. The hatch covers were then made watertight by stretching a tarpaulin across the hatch which was held tight by wedges.

Hatch wedges – wedges used to secure the hatch tarpaulin

Hawser – a thick cable or rope used in mooring or towing a ship.

Heave to, hove to – in extreme weather conditions, to heave to allows the ship to keep a controlled angle to the wind and seas by balancing effects the reduced sail and and a lashed helm, to wait out the storm. The ships drifts backwards slowly generally under control without the need for active sail-handling.

Jackstay – an iron rod, wooden bar, or wire rope along a yard to which the sails are fastened.

Jarvis Patent brace winch – a manual winch invented by Captain John Charles Barron Jarvis that drastically reduced the number of sailors required to brace the sails. The winch also improved crew safety as it moved the sailors toward centerline and away from the ship's rail, decreasing the chance of sailors being swept overboard or injured by boarding waves. Notwithstanding that the winches were very successful, they were never adopted on British or American ships.

Jib – a triangular staysail that sets ahead of the foremast

Jib-boom – a spar used to extend the length of a bowsprit on sailing ships.

Latitude – a measure of the north-south position on the Earth's surface. Lines of latitude, or parallels, run east–west as circles parallel to the equator. Latitude ranges from 0° at the Equator to 90° at the poles.

Lazarette – a below deck storage area in the stern of the ship

Leeward – the direction away from the wind.

Lee rail – The deck edge on the side of the ship away from the direction from which the wind is blowing. The **weather rail** is the on the other side of the ship.

Limey – slang for a British sailor or ship. Also called lime juicers. From the British policy of issuing lime or lemon juice to sailors to prevent scurvy on long passages.

Liverpool deck – on some of the later windjammers, an accommodations cabin/deck amidships which spanned the entire beam of the ship.

Liverpool pantiles – slang for hard bread said to resemble roofing tile in shape, consistency and flavor.

Local Apparent Noon – the moment when the sun is observed to be at its highest point in its travel across the sky. By measuring the altitude (the angular distance from the horizon) and noting the time difference between Local Apparent Noon and Greenwich time, a ship's officer can determine the ship's latitude and longitude. See **Sun Sight** and **Sextant**.

Longitude – a measurement of the east-west position on the Earth's surface, an angular measurement, usually expressed in degrees. Points with the same longitude lie in lines running from the North Pole to the South Pole. By convention, one of these, the Prime Meridian, which passes through the Royal Observatory, Greenwich, England, establishes the position of zero degrees longitude. The longitude of other places is measured as an angle east or west from the Prime Meridian, ranging from 0° at the Prime Meridian to +180° eastward and −180° westward.

Lying a-hull – similar to being hove to except that no effort is made to maintain control of the ship's hull in relation to the wind and sea. Sails are furled and the ship is allowed to drift, generally sideways to the seas.

Madame Cashee – a brothel keeper in Callao, Peru immortalized in a sea shanty.

Main mast – the largest mast on a sailing ship. The middle mast on a three masted ship.

Main sail – the main course, the lowest square sail set on the main mast.

Mainstay – stay supporting the main mast leading forward on the centerline of the ship.

Marline – a small, usually tarred, line of two strands twisted loosely left-handed that is used especially for seizing and as a covering for wire rope.

Marlinspike – A marlinspike is a polished iron or steel spike tapered to a rounded or flattened point, usually 6 to 12 inches long, used in ropework for unlaying rope for splicing, for untying knots, opening or closing shackles and a variety of related tasks.

Marlinspike sailor – a sailor who become proficient at knot tying, splicing, ropework, sewing, and use of a marlinspike.

Meridian or line of longitude – half of an imaginary great circle on the Earth's surface terminated by the North Pole and the South Pole, connecting points of equal longitude.

Mizzen – the aftermost mast and smallest mast, the third mast on a three masted ship.

Mooring lines – lines or hawsers used to hold the ship fast against a dock.

Official Log Book – the official record of the voyage, listing crew signing on and off. A record is also kept of discipline, injuries, births or deaths that occur on the vessel, as well musters and drills.

Ordinary, ordinary seaman – a less experienced sailor not rated Able. Not trusted for tasks such as steering without supervision.

Outhaul – a line used to haul or stretch a sail on a yard or boom.

Pannikin – a small metal pan or cup.

Peggy – a sailor assigned to menial tasks.

Pierhead jumpers – the last sailors brought aboard a ship before she sails, often purchased from boarding house masters or crimps.

Pin rail – a strong wooden rail or bar containing holes for pins to which the running rigging is belayed fastened on sailing vessels usually along the ship's rail.

Pisagua, Chile – a port on the Pacific Ocean which was a major nitrate exporter from the 1870s through the early part of the 20th century.

Point of sail – a sailing vessel's course in relation to the wind direction. When the wind is astern the ship is on a "run." When the the wind is coming across the side, the ship is on a "reach." When the wind is more from aft it is a "broad reach." When the wind is on the beam, it is a "beam reach" and when the wind is forward of the beam, it is a close reach. When a ship is sailing as course as close to the wind as possible it is "beating" or "going to weather."

Poop deck – the raised afterdeck. The helm is aft on the poop deck.

Port Stanley – a port in the Falkland Islands that is the last port of refuge before rounding Cape Horn to the West.

Preussen – a German steel-hulled five-masted ship-rigged windjammer built in 1902 for the F. Laeisz shipping company. Until 2000, the *Preussen* was the only 5 masted ship-rigged ship ever built. She had a reputation for speed. Captain Barker bragged that he had sailed past the *Preussen,* although records suggest that the tow ships never crossed paths.

Ratlines – small lines secured horizontally to the shrouds of a ship every 15 or 16 inches forming rungs, allowing sailors to climb aloft.

Reach – a point of sail in which the wind is blowing across the side of the ship. When the wind is more from aft it is a "broad reach." When the wind is on the beam, it is a "beam reach" and when the wind is forward of the beam, it is a close reach.

Reef – to reduce the size of a sail by tying in ropes or gaskets in cringles in the reef-bands which are parallel to the top of the sail.

Río de la Plata – the river of silver, the Spanish name for the River Plate, so named because of the gray color of the silt in the river/estuary.

River Plate – a large estuary between between Argentina and Uruguay formed by the confluence of the Uruguay River and the Paraná River.

Roaring Forties – the name given to strong westerly winds found in the Southern Hemisphere, generally between the latitudes of 40 and 50 degrees.

Robands – small plaited lines used to tie the square sails to the yards

Rogue wave – a large and spontaneous ocean surface wave that occurs well out to sea, and is a threat even to large ships. Rogue waves have been known to reach over 100 feet in height.

Rolling hitch – (or Magnus hitch) is a knot used to attach a rope to a rod, pole, or other rope.

Rolling the bunt – when furling a sail, rolling the middle section of the sail up on the yard to be secured with gaskets.

Royals, Royal sails – the traditionally, the highest sails on any mast. Some ships set skysails above royals.)

The sails in order from the lowest to the highest – course, topsail (usually upper and lower topsail), topgallant sail (often upper and lower t'gallant sails) and the royals. Some ships set skysails above royals.

Run – the point of sail in which the wind is directly behind the ship.

Running rigging – rigging used in the raising, lowering and trimming of sails and other gear aboard ship. Running rigging is intended to move, whereas standing rigging is not.

Sailor's palm – a tool of leather and metal which fits on a sailor's hand so that he can use his palm to push a heavy sewing needle through tough material such as rope, leather and canvas.

Salt horse – sailor slang for salted beef.

Scupper – opening in the side of a ship at deck level to allow water to run off.

Serving and parceling – to protect rigging again chafe, the wrapping of canvas (parceling) over the rigging followed by tightly wound marline (serving). The rigging is them usually tarred over.

Sextant – an instrument used to measure the angle between any two visible objects. When used to navigate at sea, the sextant is used primarily to determine the angle between a celestial object and the horizon.

Shanty – a sailor's working song used when handing sail, pumping or using the capstan.

Shantyman – a sailor who leads the singing of the shanty.

Sheet – a line used to control a sail, secured to the sail clew.

Ship-rigged – a vessel with at least three masts square-rigged on all masts.

Shroud – standing rigging supporting the mast from side to side.

Slop chest – store of clothing and personal goods carried on merchant ships for issue to the crew usually as a charge against their wages.

Sou'wester - a waterproof hat having a very broad rim behind, favored by seamen.

Spanker – a gaff rigged fore-and-aft sail set from and aft of the after most mast.

Square sail – a sail, usually four sided secured to a yard rigged square or perpendicular to the mast.

Standing rigging – the fixed rigging that supports the masts, yards and spars of a sailing ship. Standing rigging includes stays and shrouds and unlike running rigging is not intended to move.

Starboard – the right side of a ship, nautical term for the right.

Stays – standing rigging used to support the masts along the centerline of the ship. Each mast has backstays and forestays.

Staysail – a fore and aft sail set on a stay, either between the masts or between the bowspriat and the foremast

Sun sight – the most common sight taken in celestial navigation. A ship's officer with a sextant can determine the ship's latitude by measuring the sun's altitude (height above the horizon) at Local Apparent Noon. With an accurate chronometer, the officer can also determine latitude observing the time of Local Apparent Noon as compared to the time in Greenwich, England.

Square-rigged – A ship or a mast with sails set on yards rigged square, or perpendicular to the centerline of the ship.

Susannah, Susanna – a German four-masted ship that took 99 days to round Cape Horn on a passage of two hundred and seven days from Port Talbot to Iquique, Chile in 1905 - the longest rounding on record.

T'gallant fo'c'sle – the space beneath the raise deck on the bow of the ship. The space could be used for stores and gear or as an accommodations space for the crew.

T'gans'ls, t'gallant, top gallant sails – the sails set above the topsails. In many windjammers the t'gallant sails were split, like the topsails, into upper and lower t'gallant yards and sails to make sail handling easier.

Tiger Bay – an area around Butetown and the Cardiff Docks in Cardiff, Wales. Tiger Bay had a reputation for being a tough and dangerous area. Merchant seamen arrived in Cardiff from all over the world, staying only for as long as it took to discharge and reload their ships. Consequently the area became the Red-light district of

Cardiff. The name "Tiger Bay" became used in a number of port cities to refer to any rough and boisterous "sailor town."

Top – a platform on each mast at the upper end of the lower mast section whose main purpose is to anchor the shrouds of the topmast that extends above it. The top is larger and lower on the masts but performs the same function as the cross trees.

Top-hamper – slang for the sails, masts and rigging of a ship. Can also refer to only the light upper sails and rigging.

Topping lift – a line used to support the yards when the yard is lowered or the sail is furled. Depending on the rigging of the ship the lifts can also be used to adjust the angle of the yards when under sail.

Topsail – the sail above the course. A large and powerful sail, after 1850s most topsails were split into upper and lower topsails to make sail-handing easier. Windjammers tended to have upper and lower topsails.

Turk's head – an ornamental knot that resembles a small turban.

Vang – A line used to swing a boom or yard.

Watches – regular periods of work duty aboard a ship. The watches kept on sailing ships usually consisted of 5 four-hour periods and 2 two-hour periods. On many merchant ships the watches were divided into the captain's and the mate's watch or starboard and port watches. The captain did not stand a watch so the Second Mate stood the watch in his stead. By tradition, the captain's watch stood the first watch on the sailing of the ship from its home port, while the mate's atch took the first watch on sailing on the return voyage.

Weather rail – The deck edge on the side of the ship in the direction from which the wind is blowing. The lee rail is the on the other side of the ship.

Wet dock – A wet dock is a dock in which the water is impounded either by dock gates or by a lock, allowing ships to remain afloat at low tide in places with high tidal ranges. The level of water in the dock is maintained despite the raising and lowering of the tide. This makes transfer of cargo easier. It works like a lock which controls the water level and allows passage of ships.

Wharfinger – an owner or manager of a wharf.

Windward – the direction from which the wind is blowing.

Windbound – ship that is becalmed, incapable of moving due to lack of wind.

Windjammer – a large square rigged sailing ship common in the later portion of the 19th and early 20th century, often built of steel or iron, designed for maximum cargo capacity.

Worming – wrapping a thin line in a cable's strands before serving and parcelling.

Yard – a spar rigged horizontally, perpendicular or "square" to a ship's mast, used to set a square sail.

Yard Arm – the extreme outer end of the a yard.

24627240R00140

Made in the USA
Lexington, KY
31 July 2013